ELECTRIC GREEN MAMBAS

BRYAN CASSIDAY

Bryan Cassiday
Los Angeles
ISBN 9781737628217
Published in the United States of America
First Edition: November 22, 2021

ACCLAIM FOR BRYAN CASSIDAY

"A fast-paced detective novel, enhanced by exceptional characters and a striking ending."—*Kirkus Reviews*

"A potent shot of contemporary LA noir that will have readers hooked from page one."—*BestThrillers.com*

"A deftly crafted roller coaster of a ride for the reader, Bryan Cassiday's novel, *Bolt*, is a truly riveting read from cover to cover."—*Midwest Book Review*

"Fans of Dennis Lehane and James Ellroy will love *Force of Impact*."—*BestThrillers.com*

"This series is great. It keeps you expecting and delivers a lot of unexpected turns. I recommend this if you love post-apocalypse reading material."*****—Amazon reviewer

"*Sanctuary in Steel* made me feel like I did the first time I watched Romero. Fresh, exciting and engaging like any outbreak story should be."—Iain McKinnon, *Domain of the Dead*

"*Sanctuary in Steel* is way up there with the best of the zombie stories in terms of plotting and pacing, propelled by great characters and unique twists."—*Readers' Favorite*

"Cassiday blends thoughtful suspense and pulse-pounding terror to deliver a novel with both bite and creeping dread."—David Dunwoody, *Empire*

BOOKS BY BRYAN CASSIDAY

- Ice in the Blood
- Horde (Zombie Apocalypse: The Chad Halverson Series Book 6)
- Crime Blotter USA
- Murder LLC (Scott Brody Thriller 2)
- Bolt (Scott Brody Thriller 1)
- Riptide of Fear
- The Payout
- Force of Impact (Ethan Carr Thriller 3)
- Dying to Breathe (Ethan Carr Thriller 2)
- Countdown to Death (Ethan Carr Thriller 1)
- The Bus Stops Here—and Other Zombie Tales
- Two Moons Rising
- Alien Assault
- Comes a Chopper
- Zombie Apocalypse: The Chad Halverson Series Books 1–5
- Helter Skelter
- The Anaconda Complex
- The Kill Option
- Blood Moon: Thrillers and Tales of Terror
- Fete of Death

Chapter 1

Myles Wasson put up more of a fight than the killer had expected. Wasson was a frail guy, around five nine with thin, bony shoulders and lanky limbs. From the looks of him you wouldn't think the guy would put up much of a fight.

But fight he did, almost ruining the killer's plan to do the guy.

Wasson was a brainy guy, not a fighter. What was the guy doing putting up such a strong fight? wondered the killer. Wasson didn't want to die. It was that simple. Wasson may have been frail, but he had a strong will to live. The cliché was right: it wasn't the size of the dog in the fight, but the size of the fight in the dog. Wasson was going to do everything he could to stay alive one more day, one more hour . . .

The killer got a good grip on Wasson's scraggly neck and commenced to squeeze with both gloved hands.

"I'll give you ten . . . thousand dollars . . . if you . . . let me go," Wasson managed to say, in a ragged voice through the death grip constricting his throat, frantically trying to pry away the hands that were crushing his windpipe, his face flushing and sweating, a rictus slashing his lower face, baring his teeth.

"You have a lot more than that," came the reply with a snicker.

"How . . . how much do you want?"

"I want you dead. That's what I want."

"A hundred . . . a hundred thousand," gasped Wasson, his eyes bugging out of his head, looking like swollen concord grapes about to burst behind his wire-rim spectacles.

"You can't buy your life back."

"How much is he paying—"

The killer didn't think Wasson was going to finish his sentence. Wasson's voice had deteriorated to an emaciated squeal, like steam jetting out of a heated tea kettle starting to cool off.

“This isn’t about money.”

“It can buy . . . what-ever you w-ant,” said Wasson in a death rattle.

“What I want is you dead. What I *need* is you dead.”

It wouldn’t be long now, the killer decided, continuing to throttle Wasson, whose red face looked like it would explode any second. Instead, it turned blue from cyanosis, and the killer could feel what little strength Wasson had left ebbing away. Wasson’s hands that were trying to pry away the death grip around his throat held on gamely, but limply, then dropped to his sides, as his body became dead weight.

The killer laid Wasson supine on the parquet floor, continuing to squeeze the narrow windpipe, making sure Wasson was in his death throes. Motionless, Wasson put up no resistance, looking up at his attacker with the lifeless eyes of a doll peering through his glasses that sat askew on the bridge of his pinched wedgelike nose.

The killer began releasing Wasson’s throat by degrees, prepared to apply more pressure if Wasson showed signs of persistent life. No creature wanted to die, the killer knew. None gave up the urge to live without putting up a fight to the bitter end. Though frail in body, Wasson had a powerful intellect that would not give in easily.

Indeed, that was Wasson’s problem. The guy knew too much and couldn’t be allowed to live. He was one of them and knew all. Could destroy all. Could become another superkiller.

The thing was, the killer didn’t want Wasson to be dead quite yet. The killer needed Wasson’s blood to paint the walls. A dead guy didn’t bleed. The killer wanted Wasson to be on the verge of death so the guy couldn’t put up any more fight, but his blood would flow.

Wasson gulped a deep breath, his face starting to regain its natural color.

The killer spun Wasson over, produced a silenced pistol, and shot him three times in the back, none of the shots fatal. The killer needed a lot of blood for paint.

Wasson groaned.

The killer kicked Wasson in the head to knock him out. The killer wanted the guy alive a little longer, but not conscious. The only thing Wasson was good for now was bleeding out.

Without Wasson's blood the killer couldn't paint and put the finishing touches to his work.

Chapter 2

They were in a car wash in the Valley in her Porsche.

Brushes were whirling and flapping against the car. Soapy water sprayed the entire vehicle as it moved slowly through the wash. Like driving under a frothing cataract.

"Why did you want to meet here?" said the PI Scott Brody, riding shotgun.

Though he was over six feet and muscular, he had plenty of leg room in the compact 911 Carrera. Wearing jeans and an aloha shirt with hibiscus prints on it, he wasn't used to meeting clients in car washes, though he had met them just about everywhere else—once, even in a sewer. That particular client feared eavesdroppers hanging on his every word were about to spring out of the woodwork. He figured the only place they could be truly alone was in a sewer.

"I fear my condo is bugged," said Evelyn Martin. "I don't want anyone listening in."

With black shoulder-length hair and glittering cornflower blue eyes, her lissome figure shoehorned into jeans and a yellow T, she was all of five seven in her early thirties with an ice-smooth white complexion.

With the cloudburst of water spraying the car, it was hard for Brody to hear, even with the windows closed.

Brody nodded, considering the raucous waterfall pouring down the windshield. "A parabolic mic won't work here. That's for sure. Unless it's in the car."

He cut his eyes around the Porsche's interior.

"I had an audio specialist sweep my car a couple days ago," said Evelyn.

"Perfect," said Brody, terminating his inspection. "Why didn't you have your condo swept?"

"It would have cost too much," she said, making a moue.

"Why would someone bug your condo?"

"My brother's missing. I think he's been kidnaped or worse. I could be next."

"I see."

"I want to hire you to rescue him."

"First things first. What's his name?"

"Tyler Keogh."

"You suspect foul play?"

"I do. He's been gone over three days without contacting me. He told me he was flying to San Francisco. I called his hotel. He never got there. So where has he been for the last three days?"

"I don't understand who's bugging your condo."

"He said he had enemies. He thought someone was out to get him."

"That's all he told you?"

"He didn't elaborate."

"Why was he going to San Francisco?"

"For a Mensa convention. You know them?"

Brody nodded yes. "Brainiacs."

"Right. They have high IQs."

"Why was he meeting them?"

"He's one of them," she said, eyeballing him.

"He thought someone was spying on him because he's a member of Mensa?"

"He didn't explain. He just said someone was out to get him. That I should assume my condo is wired."

"Maybe he decided to cancel his trip without telling you."

"I haven't been able to contact him. He doesn't answer his cell."

"He could be trying to get away from it all, taking a vacation at a remote lake out of range of cell towers."

"He's not like that. He's very rational and orderly. He doesn't do things on the spur of the moment."

"People have been known to change as they age."

"He hasn't changed."

"What do you think happened to him?" said Brody.

She shook her head, compressing her full lips. "Nothing good."

The car wash rinsed the soapy fluid off the Porsche with a blast of fresh water.

"What's his job?" said Brody.

"He's an aeronautical engineer. He helped design the Boeing 737 Max."

"The passenger jet that was grounded?"

"Right. Is that important?"

"I dunno. It might have something to do with his disappearance."

"He never talked about it. He also teaches part-time at UCLA."

"Is he married?"

"No. He plays the field."

"How old is he?"

"Forty-three."

"Hmm. Maybe he's shacked up with one of his girlfriends and doesn't want to be disturbed. It could be that simple."

"I don't believe it. Why would he book a hotel room in San Francisco and fail to check in?"

"OK. You know my rates. Are you OK with them?"

"Fine."

"Did he say he had to do anything before he left for San Francisco?"

Frowning, she thought about it. "Oh, yeah. He said he had to see one of his friends before catching his flight."

"What friend?"

"One of his Mensa buddies. Myles Wasson."

"Any idea where he lives?"

"Tarzana. I don't know his street address."

"Did Keogh say why he had to see Wasson?"

"No."

"Have you asked Wasson about your brother?"

"I haven't been able to contact him. I left a message in his voicemail, but he hasn't answered."

The pounding of the car wash's thunderstorm relented. They emerged into the glaring afternoon sunlight.

“I’ll need a thousand dollars down,” said Brody, slipping on his aviator shades.

She scooped up her purse from the foot well, snapped it open, fished out her wallet, counted out ten blue-striped Ben Franklins, and handed them to him.

“I don’t want to hear from you until you have a solid lead,” she said, replacing her wallet, and snapping shut her purse.

“Will do.”

“Good-bye, Mr. Brody.”

Chapter 3

Brody found Myles Wasson's address on the Internet. It was easy enough. It wasn't like the guy was hiding, and it wasn't a common name.

Brody drove his Mini onto the 405 over the hill into the Valley. The lady's voice on his car's GPS told him which exit to take. She told him to turn right, turn left, turn right again, go five miles, etc., until he reached Wasson's Tudor-style house.

Wasson's street was in a preferential parking zone where you needed a permit sticker on your bumper or a tag hanging from your rearview mirror. Brody curbed his car a couple blocks away where two-hour free parking was allowed, got out, and walked back to Wasson's house.

A silver Mercedes SL roadster was parked in Wasson's driveway. The house, constructed mostly of brick, had a pitched roof and two front-facing gables with half-timbering consisting of stucco and thin cedar boards. Instead of red brick, the mahogany front door had white travertine marble framing it.

Brody strode up to the door and rang the doorbell.

No response.

He tried again. With the same result.

He had Wasson's phone number. He dredged his cell phone from his trouser pocket and punched in the guy's number. The call went to voicemail.

The house showed no signs of activity. He saw no movement through the windows.

He approached the bay window and squeezed past a rhododendron bush to peek through the glass. From his angle the sun was reflecting off the pane into his eyes, blinding him. He edged closer to the glass and peered through it without the glare of the sun's rays blocking his view.

He scoped out the capacious living room.

And saw a pair of shod feet sticking out from behind a sectional sofa, the feet lying motionless on the parquet floor.

He returned to the front door, bent over, withdrew a SIG P365 from his concealed leather ankle holster, and tried the doorknob, careful not to make any noise. To his surprise the doorknob gave. He twisted it all the way to the right, nudged open the door, and slipped into the foyer.

Peeking around the lobby wall he cast around for the feet he had seen from the window, holding his SIG near his shoulder. He spotted a toned blonde pushing thirty standing over a man's body that lay prostrate on the floor perforated with three bullet wounds in the back. A clear plastic bag enveloped the man's head.

"Don't move," said Brody, stepping into the living room, his piece trained on the blonde.

The blonde started at the sight of him. "It's not what you think."

He saw the Glock 17 in her hand.

"You're standing over a dead body riddled with slugs with a gun in your hand, and it's not what I think?" said Brody.

"He was already dead when I found him."

"Drop the piece."

"I know what you're thinking."

"What am I thinking?"

"That I shot him. You're mistaken."

"Drop the piece. Then talk."

Grudgingly, she dropped the Glock. She was wearing a sleeveless peach blouse that revealed her weightlifter's arms. It was a good bet she had muscled legs under her snug jeans. She could move fast when she wanted to, he suspected. He wasn't going to take any chances with her.

"Kick it over here," he said.

She complied. He felt better with the Glock out of her reach.

"Tell me why I shouldn't report you to the cops," he said.

"I found his body like this when I entered not ten minutes ago."

"Keep talking."

"The corpse shows signs of strangulation. Look at the ligature marks on his neck. And the plastic bag covering his head."

"I see three bullet holes in his blazer and in his back."

"He was strangled before he died. And the perp tried to suffocate him, too, with the bag."

"Why did you strangle and suffocate him when you have the Glock?" he said.

"*I* didn't strangle him. I found him like this."

"Then why shoot him?"

"Are you an idiot or what?"

"You expect me to believe—"

"I found him dead here and thought the perp might still be in the house. I took out my gun and was gonna inspect the house when you came in."

"A good example of overkill, don't you think? Strangulation, a plastic bag to smother him, and bullets in the back."

She shrugged. "The perp had a hard-on for Wasson."

Brody inspected the wounds, keeping his SIG trained on her. "The three bullets wounds weren't kill shots. Wasson survived them."

"How do you know? He could've died from loss of blood."

"If you look closely, you'll see the bullets in Wasson's body didn't hit an artery. He could have lived for some time after getting shot."

"Then that explains the plastic bag on his head. The perp used it to finish Wasson off."

"Why didn't he just put another bullet through him? Why use three different methods of murder?"

"He must've hated Wasson and wanted the guy to suffer. Filled him with lead and watched him writhe in pain."

"A crime of passion?"

"Could be. To kill him three ways I'd say a lot of hate was involved."

"Or . . ."

"Or what?"

"Or he wanted Wasson to bleed so he could use his blood as ink on the wall," said Brody, glancing at the graffiti scrawled on the wall with Wasson's blood still dribbling down it.

"Li Grande Zombi. Acid Is Groovy," she said, reading the graffiti out loud. "Do they still say 'groovy'? It's something out of the sixties."

"The perp shot Wasson for his blood, not to kill him. The longer Wasson lived and the more he bled, the more ink the killer would have."

"You're saying Wasson was used as an inkwell?" she said, pulling a face. "That's grisly and sick."

"No sicker than what the Manson Family did to Sharon Tate and her friends in Benedict Canyon. They butchered her and her pals and wrote on the wall with their victims' blood."

"You're saying a cult did this?"

"Looks that way."

"We're back in the sixties again. The perp is an old hippie?" she said, and snickered. "A flower child? He forgot to leave a peace symbol on the wall. And who's this Grande Zombi?"

Brody scrutinized the words *Li Grande Zombi*. The letter *i* in *Zombi* was a squiggly line with a dot on top of it. It looked like a snake, he decided.

"Zombies?" he said. "Are we talking voodoo?"

"That's a stretch."

"Why? Voodoo priests can supposedly raise the dead and turn them into zombies."

"You believe that nonsense?"

"*I* don't. But other people do. Wasson could be a sacrifice offered by a murderous cult that practices voodoo."

"Voodoo's down on the Bayou in Louisiana. We don't have it in California."

"We have everything in California. The nuttier it is, the more likely it's out here."

"A voodoo cult sacrificed Wasson," said Tess, her voice dripping with sarcasm. "Why Wasson of all people?"

"What's *your* explanation?"

She cockled her brow. "I still say it's a crime of passion."

Chapter 4

"Are we sure the stiff is Myles Wasson?" said Brody, unable to discern the victim's face.

"I haven't had time to turn the body over to look at his face," said Tess.

"You had time to see the ligature marks."

She threw him a penetrating look. "Are you still saying I did it? What's my motive?"

"What's your name, first?"

"What gives you the right to give me the third degree?"

"The piece in my hand."

"It's illegal for you to threaten me with a gun."

"I'm defending myself against a suspected murderer."

"Haven't you been listening? It wasn't me."

Circumspectly, Brody lowered his SIG. "What's your name?"

"Tess. Who wants to know?"

"Brody."

"Are you in the habit of breaking and entering?"

"The door was unlocked. I didn't break anything. Maybe that's because you broke the lock on the door when you entered."

"It was unlocked when I got here, too."

"Are you a friend of the victim?"

"I'm a private investigator on an assignment."

Amused, Brody cracked a half smile.

"What's so funny?" she asked.

"So am I. Ain't that a coincidence? Who are you working for?"

"Then you know I won't reveal my clients' names. So why are you even bothering to ask?"

"Say I believe you're a PI," said Brody, taking in the graffiti, "who do you think whacked this guy?"

"I don't like being called a liar."

"I didn't call you a liar."

"You insinuated it."

"You inferred it."

"Your intentions were clear."

Brody fetched a sigh. "Let's start over again."

"Looks like some kind of ritualistic killing," said Tess, eyeballing the bloody graffiti. "A voodoo cult by the looks of it. But looks can be deceiving. I have trouble buying voodoo in LA."

"Did Wasson belong to a voodoo cult?"

"No idea. We don't even know if this is Wasson."

Brody suspected the stiff might be Tyler Keogh. After all, Keogh had told Evelyn he was going to visit Wasson before flying to San Francisco. Keogh's premature death would explain his failure to check in at his hotel.

"Time for the big reveal," he said. "Let's make sure."

"I don't take orders from you."

"Please."

"You're one lazy PI."

Tess shook her head in disgust, withdrew a handkerchief from her lavender vinyl fanny pack, bent over, and, protecting her hand with the handkerchief, flipped the corpse's body onto its back.

"I shouldn't disturb the scene of a crime," she said. "The cops aren't gonna like it."

"Who's gonna tell them?"

Brody had checked out Keogh's photo on the Internet after Evelyn had hired him. The livid face of the corpse wasn't Keogh's.

"Your client?" said Brody, indicating the corpse.

"No."

"Myles Wasson."

"I know who it is. I came here to question him."

Who was she working for? wondered Brody. Would Evelyn possibly hire two PIs to do the same job? What would be the point? Playing them off against each other to see who gets the best results? Or was Tess working for another client on a different assignment?

Brody spotted a round black metal object with spokes lying near Wasson's head. He fished out his smart phone from his trouser pocket and photographed the object along with Wasson's corpse. While he was at it, he snapped a photo of the writing on the wall.

"So did I," said Brody.

"What is that?" she said, staring at the object Brody was photographing.

"Some sort of wheel," said Brody, shooting a closeup of the black object.

"I know what it looks like, but what is it?" she said, arms akimbo.

"Beats me."

"A wheel from a toy car?"

Brody zoomed in on the object. "It has jagged spokes. I never saw a car with jagged spokes on its wheels."

"The murderer might have dropped it."

"A member of a cult?"

"The question is, why would a cult want to kill a college History professor?"

"Why do cults do anything?"

"True. Let's go back to the Manson Family. They senselessly mauled Sharon Tate and her friends and painted the walls with their blood."

"They did it to trigger a race war, according to Vincent Bugliosi."

"Like I said, senseless to any well-adjusted human being." She gazed at the blood scrawled on the wall. "This place creeps me out." She sniffed the air. "I smell blood and death. My head is throbbing and my stomach is grumbling," she said, looking ill.

"I'm looking for Tyler Keogh. Do you know him?"

"Never heard of him. What's he got to do with Wasson?" she said, withdrew a pillbox from her fanny pack, tapped out two pills, and tossed them into her mouth.

She pulled a tiny half-full water bottle from her purse, took a swig, and swallowed her pills.

Brody gazed at her.

"Migraines," she said.

"My mother used to get those all the time."

"What's the answer?"

"The answer to what? Curing migraines?"

"To my question. What's Keogh got to do with Wasson?"

"They're friends. I thought Keogh might be here. This isn't looking good for him."

"You think he's dead, too?"

"He was supposed to check into a hotel three days ago. He never checked in. I thought Wasson might have intel on him. They were supposed to meet before Keogh was to leave town."

"One of us needs to notify the cops."

"You found the corpse first."

"My client doesn't want me to become involved."

"If I tell them, I'll have to tell them I found you standing over the dead body."

She gave him a look. "Not a good idea."

"But true."

"Leave both our names out of it. Phone the cops anonymously on a burner."

"I'm not convinced of your innocence."

"You're gonna tell them you think *I* shot Wasson?" she said, fuming.

Brody thought about it. "No."

"What do you want from me?"

"An alibi."

"I told you the truth. Actually, I don't have to tell you anything. You're not a cop."

Stooping, he picked up her Glock from the floor and sniffed the barrel.

"It's been fired recently," he said.

"No shit, Sherlock. I fired it."

Brody quirked an eyebrow.

"After I found the body," she went on, "I thought I saw someone in the hallway with a gun and took a shot at him in self-defense."

Brody scoped out the parquet floor. “I don’t see your brass anywhere.”

“I already picked it up.”

“I don’t see the shooter’s brass either.”

“He either collected them before he left or he used a revolver.”

“Or maybe you collected them before I got here.”

She cocked her head and gave him a sideways look. “Why would I do that?”

“I’m thinking out loud.”

“You got this ass-backwards. You should be assuming I’m innocent, not guilty.”

“You were standing over a dead body with a gun—”

“Fine, whatever.” She held out her hand, her jaw set. “I want my piece back.”

He handed her the Glock.

“I’m leaving,” she said, slipping the Glock into her purse.

She made a beeline for the front door.

He didn’t stop her. Like her, he didn’t want to get involved in Wasson’s murder. Telling the cops about her being here would involve him. For all he knew, she could be telling the truth about her innocence.

He needed to get out of here and call Evelyn.

Chapter 5

He heard buzzing and noticed flies corkscrewing around the corpse at his feet. Flies also flitted near the blood-scrawled wall. The odor of death and spilled blood was starting to get to him.

A window must be open in the house somewhere, he decided, watching the flies, who must have had an entrance point. Perhaps, the point of exit taken by the killer.

Knowing he needed to leave as soon as possible, Brody nevertheless stole through the house in search of the open window, gun in hand.

He found an open French window, a drawn curtain stirring beside it in the wind, in the master bedroom.

The killer could have left through the opening, but so what? Brody wondered. He had to get a move on.

He ducked through the front door, closed it behind him, wiped his fingerprints off the doorknob, and decamped. He strode down the driveway and onto the sidewalk at a business-like clip, trying not to draw attention to himself. He wondered where Tess had parked her car and whether she had already left.

He produced his cell, climbed into his car, and settled back in the driver's seat.

He called Evelyn. "We got a problem."

"Don't tell me you found him dead," she said, her voice trembling. "This is what I was dreading."

"I found a dead body, but not your brother's."

"What?" Confusion in her voice.

"Somebody murdered Myles Wasson."

Brody heard Evelyn's breath catch.

"You think this has something to do with Tyler?" she said.

"You said they were friends, and they were going to meet before Tyler left for Frisco."

"You think the killer did Tyler, too?"

Brody sighed. Optimism wasn't his strong point.

"It would explain why Keogh didn't make it to his hotel," he said.

"Why would someone want to kill Tyler and Wasson?"

"Do you know if either of them had anything to do with a cult?"

"What? Cult? Did I hear you right?"

Through his windshield Brody saw a rent-a-cop's patrol car cruising down the street. He looked down to avoid attracting the driver's inquisitive gaze.

"You heard me," he said into his cell.

"Tyler is an aeronautical engineer. He has a rational mind. I can't see him getting involved with the supernatural."

"It doesn't make much sense, does it? What about Wasson?"

"I didn't know him very well. I know he's a friend of Tyler's and they both belonged to Mensa. That's how they met."

"If Wasson belonged to Mensa, he must've been pretty bright. High IQ and all that. How could he be involved with a cult? Makes no sense. A cult is the last thing he would join."

"Are you sure a cult murdered him?"

"Li Grande Zombi and Acid Is Groovy were scrawled on the wall in Wasson's blood. There was a lot of blood."

"Jesus."

"Wasson was strangled, smothered, and shot in the back three times."

Evelyn gasped. "What? Why would anyone . . . ? Somebody must've really hated the guy."

"Or it was a ritual killing where a victim must be sacrificed in a certain fashion and drained of his blood."

"Could be a lone psycho. Like the Nightstalker Richard Ramirez or something."

"Could be. But I'm leaning toward a cult."

"Why?"

"Besides the blood on the wall, there was a talisman shaped like a miniature black wheel near the body."

"It doesn't sound anything like Tyler. I can't see him socializing with a cult that believes in the supernatural. Wasson's killing has nothing to do with him."

Brody shrugged.

He sighted the rent-a-cop's patrol car in the rearview mirror. It was coming to a halt. Maybe the guy was going to sit there and keep an eye on Brody's car. Brody decided he had overstayed his welcome.

"If you're right, your brother's life may not be in danger," said Brody. "But the fact remains he didn't check in to his hotel room three days ago. Which could indicate foul play—especially with one of his friends murdered."

"Like I said, Tyler didn't believe in the supernatural. He was an atheist who believed the secrets of the world could be unlocked through scientific research."

"The supernatural angle isn't tracking," said Brody, frowning. "Not with Mensa members involved."

"Did you tell the cops about the murder?"

"Not yet. There's another problem."

"What?"

"I found a PI at the scene of the crime."

Silence.

"How do you know he didn't kill Wasson?" said Evelyn.

"It's a she. And you're right, I don't know she's innocent. Her name's Tess. Do you know her?"

"You're the only PI I know."

"Maybe she's not a PI. Maybe she lied. Do you know anyone named Tess? A blonde gym rat in her late twenties?"

"I don't know her. You need to forget her and focus on finding Tyler."

"I need to get out of here. I'm being watched. Bye," he said, put down his cell, fired his Mini's ignition, and pulled away from the curb, glancing in the rearview mirror at the rent-a-cop's patrol car parked on the side of the street.

Chapter 6

Brody returned to his West LA apartment, which doubled as his office, and got on his laptop. He studied the photo he had taken of the black wheel at the murder scene and researched the symbol on the Internet.

The symbol came right up on his laptop's screen. Considered a mythical source of knowledge, it was known as a black sun used by Nazis, neo-Nazis, and various satanists. The jagged spokes in the wheel, or sun, were *sig* runes like the ones used by the Nazi SS (*Schutzstaffel*) in their infamous logo. The *sig* was one of eighteen Armanen runes introduced by the Austrian mystic Guido von List, who believed in a modern pagan religion known as Wotanism.

Brody wondered how Wasson was tied up with Nazis or satanists or voodoo. Was Keogh tied up with the same group? If Keogh hadn't been offed by the murderer already, Brody hoped he was lying low—just in case the murderer was out for him. Did Keogh know Wasson was dead?

And what about the Mensa connection between Keogh and Wasson? wondered Brody. Was that significant? Did Mensa have anything to do with the murderer's motive for taking out Wasson?

Brody decided to research Mensa on the Internet. A high IQ society with its headquarters in the United Kingdom, Mensa boasted members throughout the world. The American Mensa had the largest number of members with fifty-seven thousand.

He couldn't find anything mystical about the organization. It didn't sound like the Illuminati or the Freemasons. Membership was based strictly on a person's IQ as determined by a test—such as, the Stanford–Binet Intelligence Scales. If your score on the test was high enough, you could join the club. No connection to Armanem runes and satanism that he could see.

He found Wasson's name listed on the Los Angeles branch's board of directors. He wondered if he should check with other members on the board of directors to see if they could clue him in on a motive for Wasson's murder. A board member might even know what had happened to Keogh.

He followed his hunch, located the address of Mensa board director Heloise Delacroix, and drove to her residence, a Tuscan villa with flesh-painted stucco walls, a red-tiled flat roof, and a terra-cotta patio in Santa Monica.

In her fifties Delacroix had been a board director longer than Keogh. Whatever she did for a living paid well. All he knew of it was what he had seen at the Mensa website—that she was affiliated with Stanford University in some capacity, which wasn't explained. He guessed she might be involved with big tech.

He drove his Mini to her villa, found a two-hour street-parking space a block away from it, and curbed his car. He walked to her glittering marble-chip drive and crunched up it to the terra-cotta patio that fronted the marble steps to her stoop. He climbed the steps to her ornately carved, imposing wooden door.

He rang the doorbell.

No answer.

Figuring the bell might be out of order, he rapped on the door with his fist.

With the same result. No answer.

He stepped off the stoop and tried to peek through the front bay window, but the curtains were drawn shut.

He returned to the stoop and tried the front doorknob. Like the one at Wasson's house, Delacroix's door was open. Didn't anyone believe in locking their houses anymore? He debated entering the hallway.

He decided to check out the premises, nudged the door open farther, slipped into the hallway, and made for the living room.

"Ms. Delacroix?" he called out.

Silence.

He entered the living room.

The first floor had a beam and shiplap cathedral ceiling. The second story only reached halfway across the capacious living room and had a wooden staircase leading up to it, where the landing had a maroon-painted steel balustrade overlooking the living room.

Wound around the balustrade's rail was a rope that reached to the chandelier in the living room and hung down from the chandelier with a woman's neck in the noose. The woman's face was livid from loss of blood, which had drained from the knife wound in her chest down to the white marble floor.

More of her blood decorated the living room wall, where the murderer had scrawled Li Grande Zombi and, underneath it, Acid Is Groovy.

Heloise Delacroix wouldn't be answering any more doors.

Hearing the door creaking behind him, he started and wheeled around to confront the intruder, his body tense and ready to spring into action.

Tess was standing behind him. This time, she was the one holding a gun, its barrel trained on him.

He didn't relax at the sight of her. She could be the killer.

"I think you have some explaining to do," she said, glancing up at Delacroix's corpse hanging from the chandelier.

"I know as much as you do," said Brody. "I just got here. The question is, what are you doing here?"

She shook her head no. "The question is, why do I find dead bodies around you whenever you pay someone a visit?"

"And what's your answer?"

"I was following you. You're the one that led me here. You're the one with the answers."

"What gives you the right to follow me?" he said, annoyed.

"Because you know where all the dead bodies are."

"I came here to ask Delacroix some questions about Wasson. They were both on Mensa's Los Angeles board of directors."

"Why did you pick Delacroix instead of the other directors?"

"Does that make a difference?"

"I want to know why you picked her."

"I liked the sound of her name. Nothing esoteric to it."

"Don't you find it odd she was murdered, like Wasson?"

"I do. Not in the same fashion, but there are obvious similarities, such as the scrawls in blood on the wall, that indicate it was the same murderer. A cult, possibly."

Tess gazed at the blood on the floor under Delacroix's body hanging from the chandelier then lifted her gaze to Delacroix's suspended body.

"Another case of overkill," she said. "Knifed and hanged. What's the point?"

"The killer knifed her before hanging her," said Brody. "Hence the blood, which he used to write on the wall. If she had died by hanging, she wouldn't have bled out."

"Why go to the trouble of hanging a corpse by the neck?"

Brody thought about it. "To make the murder look grislier?"

"Why?"

"To invoke terror. Bloodthirsty cults like to invoke terror."

Tess frowned. "What the hell's the motive for these two murders?"

"I've been thinking about that. The killer might have it in for Mensa's local board of directors."

"A cult?" she said, not buying it. "Why would a cult go after Mensa members?"

"Since cultists are emotional types, maybe they feel threatened by brainy types. Like they're the enemy. Who knows anything when it comes to cults? They come in all shapes and sizes with different beliefs. Could you lower your gun now? We're on the same side."

"Are we?"

"Maybe not. But why shoot me?"

"How do I know you didn't kill Delacroix?"

"I got here only a few minutes before you did. Not enough time to butcher her, hang her from a chandelier, and write on the wall with her blood," said Brody, looking at Delacroix and grimacing.

"Maybe. But then again, maybe you're returning to the scene of your crime."

"For what reason?"

"To gloat?"

"Think about it. I'm a PI. Why would I kill Delacroix?"

"Maybe you moonlight as a serial killer."

"I don't have time for this. Put the piece away."

She didn't look satisfied with his answers, but she lowered her pistol. "I suggest you stay away from murder victims. It's giving you a bad rep."

Brody needed to call Evelyn and fill her in on Delacroix. It wasn't looking good for Keogh, who also was on the Mensa board of directors. He could be lying dead, even now, in a large pool of his own blood.

Chapter 7

"One of us should report this to the cops," said Tess.

"Did you report the last murder?" said Brody.

"I thought you did."

"Not yet."

"One of us should call them."

"I'm not stopping you."

"I'm not calling them while I'm here at the scene of the crime."

Brody nodded yes. "That would raise all kinds of questions neither one of us wants to answer."

"You think they would suspect us?"

"If they don't have any other suspects, why not?"

"I'll leave an anonymous tip for them."

"They may be on their way here, for all we know. Somebody else could have reported it."

"If neighbors report us leaving this house to the cops, the cops are gonna suspect us—especially if we don't report the murder."

"Point taken. I can't guarantee we can leave here without being spotted by neighbors. They might've seen us enter the premises, as well."

"What do we do?"

Brody started when Delacroix's suspended body dropped a foot and a half from the chandelier until the rope snubbed it. There must have been a kink in the rope, he decided.

"Jesus," said Tess, her eyes gaping, staring up at Delacroix. "Is she still alive?"

"I doubt it. Not with all her blood on the floor and wall."

Tess produced her cell phone. "Fuck it. I'm calling the cops. This thing's bigger than the both of us. They got the personnel and the technical equipment to do a thorough investigation here."

"Mind if I leave while you wait for them?"

"Damn right, I do. You're in this mess as much as me. You're even more involved. You're the one that led me here."

"I need to make a call," he said, drawing away from her out of earshot and plucking his cell from his trouser pocket.

"You better not leave," she said, raising her voice. "I'll pull my gun on you again if I have to."

Brody waved her off. "Nobody's going anywhere."

He lowered his voice and spoke into his cell to Evelyn. "I don't want to worry you, but I'm sure Keogh's life is at risk."

"And I'm not supposed to worry?" said Evelyn. "What happened?"

"We found—"

"*We*?"

"Another PI is here."

"Again?"

"The same one at Wasson's murder."

"Who else hired a PI?"

"She wouldn't say."

"Somebody else is trying to find Tyler?" Evelyn said, puzzled.

"She's involved in this investigation somehow. She might not be trying to find Keogh, but she's trying to find out something that has to do with these murders."

"What did you find?"

"I was trying to tell you. Another director on the Mensa board has been murdered."

Evelyn gasped. "And Tyler's on the same board. You think the killer already got to him?"

"Dunno. I haven't found any evidence to that effect."

"Did the same killer do the two murders?"

"Looks that way. Looks like the work of a cult."

"You need to find Tyler before they find him," said Evelyn, her voice tense.

"Do you have any idea where he might be?"

"I can tell you where he isn't—at his hotel in San Francisco. That's all I know."

"If he suspected he was in danger, do you know where he might hole up?"

"We're not close. He has his life, and I have mine. Our lives don't often intersect."

"If you happen to think of a possible hidey-hole, let me know."

"Don't put this on me. I hired *you* to find him. That's *your* job."

"Hmm. If you think of something, let me know. That's all I ask. You know him better than I do, even if you two aren't close. You're blood relatives."

"How did he ever get involved with a cult? This is so not like him."

"I'll keep you posted," he said, terminating the call.

Tess approached him. "Maybe we should pool our resources."

"I'd rather swallow broken glass."

"What's that supposed to mean?" she said, hackles raised.

"I don't work with a partner."

"A lone wolf, huh?"

He stared at her.

"Well?" she said.

"I don't get along with anybody. So I work alone."

"We might get somewhere faster on this case if we help each other, instead of playing tag at murder scenes. You know what they say, two heads are better than one."

"We have different clients, who have conflicting interests. We'll get in each other's way if we work together."

"That's not always the case. Anyway, we're getting in each other's way as it is."

She had a point, he decided.

"Did you call the cops?" he said.

"They'll be here any minute."

Brody eyeballed the front door and mulled over booking.

"I suggest you stay," said Tess, reading his mind. "Otherwise, they're gonna consider you a suspect. I told them you were here when I arrived."

He gave her a look.

Chapter 8

The LAPD barged into Delacroix's villa seven minutes later.

Brody didn't want to talk to them, but he saw no way out of it. They were bound to have questions for him.

A middle-aged LAPD homicide detective wearing black slacks and an off-the-rack shepherd's check blazer without a necktie entered the living room, briefly surveyed the murder scene, face impassive, and strode up to Brody and Tess. Sporting a skull cut, he had a port-wine stain that extended onto his scalp from his forehead like the finger of an island and could be seen through his cropped hair.

"Detective George Macready here," he said. "Who am I talking to?"

"Scott Brody."

"Tess Hardwick."

"Who reported the murder?"

"I did," said Tess.

Macready nodded. "This is how you found the premises when you arrived?"

"Yeah."

"Are you a friend of the victim?"

"I never met her. I'm a private detective working on a case."

"You think you can do a better job than the police?" he said, cocking an eyebrow.

"Maybe my client does. You'd have to ask my client."

"And what about you?" said Macready, turning to Brody. "Are you a friend of the deceased?"

"I've never seen her before," said Brody.

"Then, if you don't mind my asking, what are you doing in her house?"

"I'm also a private detective."

"Oh, that's cute. We have two PIs who think they're better at solving crimes than the LAPD, the finest police force in the nation."

"I didn't say that."

"You two working as a team?"

"I don't work on a team with anyone."

"Let me get this straight. You two strangers just happened to break into the victim's house at the same time and found her dead. Is that it?"

"We didn't break in. The door was open. I wanted to question Heloise Delacroix."

"About what?"

"I'm not at liberty to say."

"Does that mean you have something to do with her sudden and violent death?"

"It means, I'm conducting a confidential investigation."

"Give me one good reason I shouldn't charge you with Delacroix's murder?"

"How's I didn't do it?"

"Is that supposed to be funny?"

"Sometimes the truth *is* funny."

"I'm not laughing. Who do you work for?"

Brody was becoming irritated with the grilling. "My client's name is confidential."

"What's his first name?" Macready paused a beat. "I bet you thought cops didn't have a sense of humor."

"They don't."

His expression menacing, Macready advanced on Brody. "I don't like private dicks. You guys are all the same. You couldn't cut the mustard on the force. You get fired, set up a second-rate operation in a fleabag, and call yourselves *detectives*—and I use the word loosely."

"Will that be all?"

"How do I know you didn't murder Delacroix?"

"Because I said I didn't."

Macready snorted. "I'll let you go."

"Thanks. You mean, finding a murder victim isn't a crime?"

Macready scoffed. "You're a laugh riot. Even so, funny man, you're at the top of my list of suspects, along with your partner here."

“I’m not his partner,” said Tess. “I demand an apology.”

“I’m looking for a murderer and I find Laurel and Hardy. Don’t that beat all?”

“I’m still waiting,” she said, seething.

“Murder makes strange bedfellows.”

Tess threw a withering glance at Brody. “Not in *this* world.”

“Not your type?” said Macready.

“He’s not anybody’s type,” said Tess.

Macready cracked a grin and leered at Brody. “I see what you mean.”

“I have things to do,” said Brody.

“I’m not done with you, buddy—”

“Brody.”

“Don’t interrupt me. Did you touch anything while you were here?”

“No.”

“I better not find your fingerprints on that knife sticking in the victim’s chest,” said Macready, looking up at Delacroix’s corpse, “or you’re going to the holding tank.”

“You won’t.”

“What kind of sicko would do something like this?” said Macready, running his eyes along the rope that stretched from Delacroix’s neck to the chandelier to the balustrade rail. It didn’t take him long to pick up on the bloody scrawls on the wall. “Some kind of ritualistic killing, looks like.”

“That’s how I see it,” said Brody.

“Who’s this Grande Zombi?” said Macready, reading the bloody words painted on the wall.

“Something to do with voodoo?”

“Delacroix. Was she Cajun? Voodoo down on the bayou?”

“Sounds like a song by Credence.”

Macready gave him a look. “I’m getting tired of your wisecracks.”

“I don’t know anything about this woman other than she’s dead.”

"Why would anyone hire you as a private dick?" said Macready with disgust. "Get out of here. You're tainting the crime scene. And I'm sick of looking at your face."

"Your face doesn't impress me, either."

"You better get out of here before I change my mind and bust you."

Brody set out to leave.

"But don't leave town," said Macready. "You and your girlfriend are at the top of my list of suspects."

"I demand an apology," said Tess.

"Well you're not getting it. You two get out of here before I bust you for trespassing."

Brody was glad he hadn't notified the cops about Wasson's murder. Which would have put him at the scenes of two murders committed by the same perp.

He headed out the door with Tess.

Chapter 9

"Are we breaking up our partnership already?" said Tess on their way out of Delacroix's villa, as Brody strode across the terra-cotta patio away from her with his long, powerful legs.

She hurried to catch up to him.

"What partnership?" said Brody, rounding on her.

"I thought we agreed two heads are better than one."

"Not if they're headed in different directions."

"We're not headed in different directions. We both want to find out who killed Wasson and Delacroix."

"But for different reasons."

"The point is, we're trying to catch a killer. So why not join forces?"

"I told you, I don't get along with anyone. I work alone."

"I got news for you—you're not my idea of an ideal partner."

"Fine," said Brody, continuing to break away from her, striding down the marble-chip drive, his footfalls crunching loudly, as she hurried after him.

"Maybe I know something about these murders you don't," said Tess, coming to a halt.

Brody followed suit and slewed around to look at her. "Like what?"

"Why should I tell you, if you don't want to pool our resources?"

"My last partner tried to order me around. It ended badly."

"I don't like taking orders either."

"Good. Let's go our separate ways," he said, walking away.

"Let's do that," she said, and stalked away in the opposite direction.

Brody drove his Mini back to his apartment and got on his laptop to access the Internet and research Li Grande Zombi. He couldn't find much. He did, however, find a blog that said Li Grande Zombi was a temple snake worshiped in voodoo. That could explain the squiggly line in the *i* in *zombi* scrawled in blood on Wasson's wall that had caught his attention. The *i* could represent a snake. Which meant Li Grande Zombi wasn't one of the walking dead. But what did the snake creature have to do with Wasson and Delacroix, or Keogh, for that matter?

Brody dug his cell out of his trouser pocket and called Evelyn.

"Do you know anything about Li Grande Zombi?" he said.

"Zombi? Those things that shamble around and eat people in horror movies?"

"As near as I can figure, it's a snake worshiped by voodoo believers."

"Never heard of it."

"The reason I ask is, the words were scrawled in Delacroix's blood on her wall, the same as at Wasson's murder with *his* blood."

"I'm not into that voodoo crap. I think it's disgusting. Don't they turn corpses into zombies in Haiti and raise them from the dead?"

"Supposedly."

"I don't want anything to do with it."

"The problem is, I suspect they're after your brother."

"He wasn't mixed up with that mumbo jumbo."

"Maybe there are things about your brother you don't know."

"Excuse me. I don't see him turning corpses into zombies."

"I don't see *anyone* doing it in this day and age."

He was having trouble concentrating. This occult mumbo jumbo was making him think about his life. He was thinking about something Camus had said, that life was meaningless and therefore nothing mattered. If nothing mattered, why was he doing this job, which was getting sicker by the minute? He had read a lot of philosophers when he was younger and trying to find his way. They were all trying to find the meaning of life.

Schopenhauer said the will willed to will. Nietzsche considered Schopenhauer's explanation an absurd tautology and said the will willed power. And then Camus said the will willed nothing, because life was meaningless.

If life was meaningless, why spend your life thinking about it as a philosopher? wondered Brody.

He had stopped reading philosophy when he came to the conclusion he had to make a living or starve to death. None of what the philosophers were saying helped him pay his bills. If you wanted to make a living, you had to provide a service that somebody was willing to pay for. The more people that wanted your service, the better off you were in terms of paying your bills. Which didn't guarantee happiness, but you would be happier than if you lived in a cardboard box in an underpass. Been there, done that.

He told himself to stop thinking. He was digging himself into a dark hole from which there would be no escape if he continued to dig.

"Are you saying zombies killed Wasson and Delacroix?" said Evelyn.

Her voice freed him from his depressing thoughts.

"Zombies don't exist," he said. "A voodoo cult might have killed Wasson and Delacroix."

"Of course, zombies don't exist. I was getting ready to fire you if you claimed zombies were committing these murders."

"Some of these religious cults can be fanatical. They're capable of anything. We need to find Keogh before they do."

"What if these bloodthirsty maniacs have already found him?" she said, knowing full well he might be dead, her tone grim.

"I'm not giving up that easily. If he's out there, I'll find him."

Chapter 10

Brody drove to Keogh's house in Brentwood with the intent to break in and see if he could find any clues to Keogh's whereabouts.

He parked at a curbside parking meter four blocks from Keogh's house, inserted coins into the meter, and walked the four blocks to Keogh's Mission Revival house, which had a pitched red tiled roof, overhanging eaves, mint green stucco walls, and a chased arched mahogany door.

He didn't bother ringing the doorbell. He knew Keogh wasn't home. He did try the doorknob on the off chance the door might be open.

The doorknob gave.

It must be true nobody locked their houses anymore, he decided, nudging the heavy door open and striding into the foyer.

He entered the living room, which had exposed varnished wooden beams. Tensing, he heard movement in a neighboring room. He withdrew his SIG from his ankle holster and pussyfooted toward the source of the noise. He half expected to see Tess when he rounded the corner, since they seemed to be operating on the same wavelength.

Gun in hand, he slipped into the doorway and peeked into a cozy studio furnished with a cherrywood desk and a leather recliner.

A blonde in her twenties wearing Jimmy Choo clear stilettos with six-inch heels and a tangerine leather miniskirt that revealed her shapely white thighs was leaning over the desk poring over papers strewn on the desktop.

Catching sight of him out of the corner of her eye, she looked up, startled. Her blue eyes widened at the sight of his pistol.

"Who the hell are you?" she demanded, becoming angry and asserting herself.

"Watch your manners. I'm the guy with the piece."

"Piece? You piece of shit. That's what you are. You're a fucking crook, and you're giving *me* a lecture?"

He couldn't help but notice her impressive silicone-augmented bust, which she made little effort at concealing with her low-cut cerise tube top.

"The name's Brody. I'm a PI. You're the one ransacking Keogh's studio. You got nerve calling *me* a crook."

"I call 'em like a see 'em. You broke into Tyler's house with a gun. That spells c-r-o-o-k in my book."

"The door was open because you left it open. Now who are you?"

"It's none of your business, but I'm Val Holiday, and Tyler's my old man."

"He's your father?"

"Boy, are you square, or what? He's my main squeeze, moron. And he's an asshole. Where is he, anyway?"

"I was about to ask you the same question."

"That dickhead treats me like dirt."

"Sorry to hear that."

"I don't want your pity. Look at me for Christ's sake. Is this the body of a loser in the genetic lottery? I didn't get the nickname Val the Bod for nothing. Do I look like I need pity?"

"You—"

"You think Tyler's bad? If you think he's the worst, you don't know nothing."

"I never even met him. I'm sorry—"

"I told you, I don't want your crocodile tears."

"I—"

"I've been treated worse. I still got bruises from my first husband's fists. What a mofo that douchebag was. He even broke my jaw once. I had to have it wired together."

"What I'm trying to say is, I don't like guys that beat up women."

"Can the cheap sentiment, Brady."

"Brody."

"Whatever."

"What are you looking for?"

"He said we're gonna get married. I'm looking for the prenup he wants me to sign," she said, waving a paper in her hand, which she glanced at and tossed down on the desk in disgust. "This ain't it."

"I see. You came here to sign a prenup."

"Hell, no. Are all PIs lunkheads like you? I want to show it to my lawyer. I never sign anything without showing it to him first."

"Can you answer—"

"He's not stingy with his money, I'll say that for Tyler. He bought me these Jimmy Choos," she said, admiring her stilettos. "Except for this prenup he wants me to sign." She returned her attention to the papers lying haphazard on the desk. "California is a community property state. Which means his wife-to-be, yours truly, should get half of everything he owns—if we get a divorce. Perish the thought."

"I know what it means. I'm trying to find him—"

"You didn't let me finish. He wants to ace me out of my rightful share. He said the prenup cuts me down to a quarter of his jackpot. That son of a—"

"Where is he? That's what I want to know. Do you know where I can find—"

"He cops an attitude like he's god's gift to women."

"When was the last time you saw him—"

"Does he really think a woman with my looks would fall for a guy twice my age? What a joke. It's all about the cash, Brady."

"*Brody*."

"Will you stop cutting me off?"

"Where can I find him?" he said, getting fed up with listening to her.

"If I knew, I'd demand to know what he did with the prenup. My lawyer will tear that thing apart."

"Will you listen to me?"

She started weeping. "I've been treated badly by men all my life. They think I'm their sex toy, and they can throw me around whenever they feel like it."

"I understand—"

"No, you don't understand. You don't know half of what I've been through."

"I—"

"You think this is bad? You must've lived a sheltered life," she said, sobbing.

"I can't imagine what you've been through—"

"That's right. You can't. And can the pity. I don't want pity. I—"

Brody lost his temper. "Where the hell is he? That's what I want to know. He might be dead."

Taken aback by his outburst, she looked at him, nonplussed.

"Do you understand what I'm saying?" he said.

"Dead?"

"As in murdered."

"Who would murder Tyler?"

It sounded like Val might, Brody decided.

"That's what I want to know," he said.

"I can't believe it."

"What about voodoo?"

"Voodoo?" she said, scowling with bafflement.

"Do any of his friends practice voodoo?"

"Are you kidding? His friends, what few he has, are Mensa egghead types. You know, that brain tank. They don't go around beating bongos, sticking pins in dolls, and chanting 'Black Magic Woman.'"

"Somebody's whacking out Mensa egghead types. Keogh could be their next victim—if he isn't already."

"We have our differences now and then, but I don't want him dead. I had no idea."

"When was the last time you saw him?"

"Uh, last week, or was it the week before?" she said, cocking her head in thought. "That was when he told me about the prenup."

"That was the last time you saw him?"

"I tried calling him afterwards, but it kept going to voicemail," she said with concern.

"He never called you back?"

"He only calls me when he wants me to come over and have sex."

"He never tells you if he's leaving town?"

"Never. He doesn't tell me anything." Her tone changed to anger. "It would be just like the bum to go and die on me before we got married. The inconsiderate—"

"I've heard enough," said Brody, spun around on his heel, and prepared to leave.

"Wait a minute. Where do you get off—leaving? You're a PI. Find that prenup for me. It must be on this desk somewhere."

"I'm on assignment."

"What good are you?"

Brody beat it, weary of her overpowering personality. Evelyn wasn't paying him enough to continue talking to Val.

Maybe Keogh pulled a disappearing act to flee Val, he decided, his ears ringing from her griping, as he stepped out the front door.

Chapter 11

Brody decided to check out another member of the Los Angeles Mensa board of directors. Somebody had to know something about where Keogh had gone. Keogh couldn't just disappear into thin air.

Val was no help. She didn't seem to care about finding her boyfriend Keogh. All she cared about was finding their prenup so her lawyer could inspect it. No wonder Keogh had decided to draw up a prenup before marrying Val. It didn't look like their marriage had much of a future—if Keogh ever showed up to consummate the union.

If Keogh had skipped town to avoid Val, he might still be alive, instead of a sacrifice for the cult that was butchering Mensa members.

Standing near his Mini Brody withdrew his smartphone from his trouser pocket, tapped the Notes app, and consulted the list he had made of the LA Mensa board of directors. He selected Eugene Frantangello, who lived in Woodland Hills in the Valley.

First, he phoned Evelyn.

"I met up with Keogh's girlfriend at his house," he said.

"What was she doing there?" said Evelyn.

"Looking for a prenup, she said."

"That's strange. Tyler never told me he was getting married."

"Her name's Val Holiday."

"I don't know the name. He has several girlfriends, according to him. I didn't know he was getting ready to settle down."

"She may be the reason he skipped town."

"I don't understand."

"She sounded annoyed at him for hiring a lawyer to write a prenup."

"You're saying he skipped town?"

"I'm saying I can see why he would, after meeting Val."

"You don't think he was attacked by this cult?"

Brody chewed it over. "I'm still working on the case. I'm giving you possibilities. I don't want you to get your hopes up. He could be in danger because he belongs to Mensa."

"You're not cheering me up."

"On the other hand, he might've had second thoughts about marrying Val and vamoosed."

"Is she that awful?"

Brody cleared his throat. "Actually, she's quite a looker. But she's not afraid to express her opinions, no matter how negative. And she was pissed at Keogh on account of the prenup."

"Maybe I should have a talk with her."

"Good luck."

"Did you ask her if she knew where Tyler was?"

"I did. She said no."

"Do you think she's telling the truth?"

"She *seemed* to be on the level. I wouldn't swear to it. She was angry at the time, making it hard to get a good read on her."

"OK. I'll see what I can get out of her. She might not be as hostile toward me as she was toward you."

"It wasn't me that was ticking her off. It was Keogh. She was taking it out on me."

"What are you doing now?"

"I'm checking with another Mensa member to see if he can help me locate your brother."

"All right. I'll let you go."

She ended the call.

Brody pocketed his cell, slid into his Mini's driver's seat, programed his GPS with Frantangello's address, and drove onto the 405 over the hill into the Valley. The traffic was heavy, but not as bad as at rush hour.

The GPS woman told him which exit to take to reach Frantangello's house. He had to turn her voice up louder so he could hear her directions through the clamor of the onrush of traffic surrounding him.

Brody found the craftsman-style house, which had a single dormer, a pitched roof, large overhanging eaves, cedar shingled walls, and a wraparound porch supported by stone pillars.

He parked on the side of the street a block away, out of sight of the house, walked to the front stoop, climbed the wooden steps, and rang the doorbell.

Nobody answered.

Which got his heart pumping.

Every time nobody answered the door, he suspected danger. The same thing had happened with his previous visits to Mensa members' houses. If things went true to form, the front door would be unlocked.

It was locked.

A good sign?

Perhaps.

A murder victim might not be lying inside in a pool of blood.

Chapter 12

Making sure no one was watching him he used a lock pick gun to pick the lock. As it happened, the dead bolt wasn't locked, so he didn't have to sweat picking it, dead bolts being harder to pick than doorknob locks. He picked the doorknob lock with ease.

He cracked the door, giving himself enough room to enter the foyer, and shut the door behind him. The house was quiet.

However, the hardwood floor creaked as he walked through the foyer.

"Hello?" he called out. "Is anybody home?"

He was greeted by silence.

He made his way to the living room and froze in his tracks.

The drapes were drawn shut. But there was still enough light for him to see a bloody body lying supine on the ivory shag carpet.

Wearing an unbuttoned scarlet cardigan the motionless thirtysomething man was portly with an auburn beard. He wore wire-rim spectacles, which lay out of true on the bridge of his nose, one of the lenses cracked and one of the wire bows broken off. He had large teeth whose cavities had been filled with silver fillings. Brody could tell because the guy's mouth was wide open.

It was Frantangello. Brody recognized him from his picture on the Mensa board of directors page.

His torso had been severed in half underneath the rib cage with some sort of cutting utensil, possibly a machete. Inside the bloody rib cage, tangled among the lungs, a black and brown mottled snake was coiled near his cleft spinal column, which gleamed snow-white, almost blinding Brody.

If the scene wasn't jolting enough, beyond Frantangello's corpse lay segments of his degutted blood-streaked entrails, which had been arranged like sausages to spell the word *Zombi*.

As at the previous Mensa murder scenes, words were scrawled in blood on the wall. Li Grande Zombi. Acid Is Groovy. Blood trickled down the white stucco, worming its way to the baseboard.

The blood hadn't had time to coagulate. The murder could have been committed as few as a couple of hours ago.

Maybe he was catching up with the killer, decided Brody, not eager to meet the bloodthirsty maniac, but that was his job.

What was the point of the snake in the torso? Brody wondered. Was it supposed to represent Li Grande Zombi, the snake god? Why was the perp leaving behind such ghastly murder scenes? These weren't random murders perpetrated by a sociopath. The victims had one thing in common: they served on the board of directors on the LA branch of Mensa. Their murders had some abstruse meaning that Brody needed to decipher to discover the killer's identity.

If Brody could figure out the motive, maybe he could uncover who was behind the slayings. At the moment, the serpent coiled in Frantangello's rib cage showed no interest in him.

He wasn't a big fan of any creature without legs. He had no idea if the snake was venomous. He stayed away from it and didn't make any sudden moves to attract its attention.

The sight of the desecrated corpse was revolting. He had seen mutilated bodies before, but there was something singularly malevolent about Frantangello's death. Brody stared at Frantangello's face, whose gaping rictus was frozen in horror.

Maybe the perp had kept Frantangello alive long enough to force him to watch himself being severed in half. And the snake—it looked like a cobra—when did it get into Frantangello's rib cage? Could it have been inside Frantangello before he was hacked in half with a machete? Had the snake squirmed through Frantangello's mouth, down his throat into his lungs, and eaten through their lining into his rib cage? The thought sickened Brody. Had the perp forced Frantangello to swallow the snake before killing him? Wouldn't Frantangello have suffocated while consuming the snake?

Brody inspected the body more closely.

Frantangello's throat had a puncture wound beneath the Adam's apple. A tracheotomy? Had the killer performed a tracheotomy on Frantangello to prevent him from suffocating while swallowing the snake? As the snake slithered down Frantangello's throat, did it gnaw through his lungs, or did it chew through his intestines before it emerged inside his torso and wound around his lungs and spinal column?

Brody turned ashen at the thought. Was he letting his imagination get the better of him?

Lying on the carpet the better part of a foot away from Frantangello's arm, a cell phone commenced flashing.

Brody watched the flashing, crumpled, and began convulsing on the carpet.

In the recesses of his turbulent mind he heard a door burst open.

Chapter 13

Gun in hand, Tess stormed into Frantangello's house, expecting trouble. Wired, she entered the living room, holding her Glock with two hands, Weaver style, wheeling it back and forth in anticipation of an assault.

Revulsion overwhelmed her as she beheld the ghastly murder scene. A severed corpse with a snake coiled inside its ribs and, a few feet away from it, Brody convulsing on the floor, foaming at the mouth.

Cultists, she decided. Satanists? Voodoo worshipers? Was Brody possessed? Had they sicced some evil spirit on him? Was the evil spirt even now wreaking havoc on his body and soul?

She shook her head in disbelief. She didn't believe in any of that hocus-pocus. She wasn't religious. She hadn't been inside a church in decades. She had a BA degree in American History from Berkeley. She saw religion as a political force, nothing more.

But what was happening to Brody? she wondered, grimacing at him as he trembled on the floor and thrashed his limbs, his mouth frothing.

Demonic possession? she wondered. Could it possibly be happening to Brody? Was Li Grande Zombi putting a spell on Brody? The snake in Frantangello's rib cage. Was that the snake god?

Ridiculous, she thought.

As Brody writhed at her feet, Tess didn't know what to do. How could she help him? She holstered her Glock, seeing no use for it.

Hunkering down beside Brody she tried to stop him from flopping around. She thought he might hurt himself while lashing out his arms and legs during his paroxysm.

"What's wrong?" she said, trying to stabilize him by gripping his shoulders.

His contorted, sweaty face grimaced back at her, baring his teeth.

"What happened to you?" she said.

He snapped his teeth back at her.

"Calm down," she said, her blonde hair cascading down on his chest as she tried to hold him still.

She glanced warily at the snake that was beginning to writhe in Frantangello's rib cage.

All she needed was that thing to strike them. It seemed to be attracted by the frenzied activity of Brody's uncontrollable shaking.

She had to get Brody to stop convulsing.

What was she supposed to do? Get an exorcist? Brody was quaking worse than Linda Blair in the Friedkin movie. At least, he wasn't swiveling his head and vomiting green glop.

"Do you need medication?" she asked Brody, figuring he might have a disease.

Brody jackknifed upward. She couldn't keep him pinned down. He was too strong. He threw her back on her heels. She gathered all her energy and struggled against him. She managed to push his trembling shoulders down flat on the carpet. He looked like a zombie with his eyes bugging out of his head as he quivered on his back.

She thought about calling 911. But they were in the middle of a crime scene—one of the grisliest murder scenes she had ever witnessed. The cops would be summoned, and she would have to explain herself to them—once again. She could hear their questions now:

"And you just happen to be at another murder scene that resembles Delacroix's murder?"

She would shoot to the top of their list of prime suspects in the Mensa murders. If they didn't arrest her outright, they would hang a tail on her, increasing the difficulty of her investigation—which was making little headway as it was.

She nixed calling 911.

She would have to take care of Brody herself without the help of paramedics. It would help if she had some idea what was wrong with him. Could he be having a heart attack? Did heart attacks last this long? A panic attack?

She wasn't a doctor. How was she supposed to know? she wondered, frustrated and angry at herself.

Brody tried to sit up.

She shoved Brody's shoulders down onto the floor again.

He was calming down, his shivering subsiding. She felt his tensed shoulders relaxing under her hands, as she pressed down on him keeping his back flat on the carpet.

He muttered incoherently.

"What?" she said. "What happened?"

He spluttered gibberish.

"Did you see who did this?" she said. "Who is the perp?"

Brody blinked his eyes like he was coming to his senses.

"What?" he said.

"What happened to you?"

"What are you doing?" he said, feeling her pressing his shoulders down.

She eased up on him and pulled away. "You had an attack—like you were possessed."

His eyes looked out of focus. He blinked them again.

"You were flopping around on the floor like a fish out of water," she said. "Remember Linda Blair on her bed in *The Exorcist*? I thought you were gonna levitate like her any minute."

He rose to a sitting position. "I have epilepsy. I must've had a seizure."

"Maybe the shock of seeing the murder triggered it."

"I didn't see the murderer kill Frantangello."

"Then what triggered your seizure?"

"I don't remember."

"Must've been this scene from a slaughterhouse."

"I've seen murders scenes before without having a fit." Brody mulled it over. "Maybe it was a flashing cell phone. Flashing can trigger a seizure in me. I remember seeing something flashing just before I blacked out."

"These murders are becoming more and more sadistic," she said, taking in the bloodbath in the living room.

"Maybe the killer is starved for attention. He figures he can get it by jacking up the shock value of his crimes."

"Are we supposed to admire his depraved work?" she said, pulling a face.

"Maybe he's trying to scare us off."

"What's with that snake?" she said, transfixed by the creature slithering between Frantangello's ribs.

"I'd bet it has something to do with the writing on the wall. Li Grande Zombi."

"What kind of snake is that?"

"Might be a cobra, what with that cowl around its head."

"Wonderful. Then its poisonous."

She trained her Glock on the snake's head.

"Don't," he said. "The cops'll trace your bullet."

She holstered her Glock. "Then let's split."

Gingerly, Brody got up off the floor, wobbling as he stood up.

"Are you sure you're all right?" said Tess.

"I should be OK soon. We need to go." He stared at her.

"What?"

"What are you doing here?"

"I followed you. You get good leads."

Brody shook his head no. "To murders. Not to Keogh."

"Well, we're closing in on the psycho. This murder didn't happen too long ago. The blood hasn't coagulated."

"I don't want to be here when the cops come."

"You oughta read minds for a living."

They made for the door.

"You really thought I was possessed?" said Brody.

"I was getting ready to call Max von Sydow."

Chapter 14

The whole voodoo thing was nagging at Brody.

He couldn't get his head around why practitioners of voodoo would want Mensa members dead—if they were indeed the murderers. Why would they target people with high IQs? Did they feel intimidated by intellectuals? And, most importantly, was Keogh on their list of victims or victims-to-be?

He parted ways with Tess after they left Frantangello's house.

He got in his Mini.

It looked like Tess was going to continue following him, he decided, watching her stride to her white Mustang convertible in his rearview mirror. He hadn't noticed her tailing him. She must be good at her job.

It was no big deal if she followed him—except he preferred working alone. Why couldn't she find her own leads for her assignment? He was curious who she was working for. Her client's ID might have some bearing on Keogh's whereabouts, though he didn't know how at this time.

He accessed the Internet on his smartphone, searching for experts on voodoo. He made an appointment to see Professor Mali, who taught courses on voodoo at UCLA.

He took the 405 south to Westwood, where the bucolic UCLA campus nestled among gently rolling hills. He parked in a parking garage on campus.

It was a beautiful, palm- and eucalyptus-studded sprawling campus with an eclectic mélange of old and new buildings. He consulted a map posted on Bruin Walk to locate Mali's office in Royce Hall, made his way to Janss Steps, three flights of steps constructed of bricks, climbed them, and arrived at Royce Hall, an old Lombard Romanesque building with a loggia and stone columns. Quasimodo could be lurking in its bell tower. It was one of the four original buildings on the Westwood campus.

Redolent of sandalwood, Mali's office was on the third floor. A plump middle-aged African American woman, Mali sat behind her metal desk in a brightly colored, loose, flower-print dress. She wore her hair in a peroxide-blonde skull cut and had a shiny complexion. Ivory hoop earrings ornamented her ears. A vase of lilacs stood on her desktop among a clutter of books and papers.

Brody introduced himself as a private detective.

"I'm glad you could see me on such short notice," he said.

"No problem," she said, smiling, showing her teeth. "I'm always eager to discuss the mysteries of the dark arts. Please have a seat."

She had a trace of a southern drawl, noticed Brody.

Brody sat down in front of her desk.

"What do you know about Li Grande Zombi?" he said.

Mali's happy face clouded.

Brody felt a sudden chill in the air.

She did not respond.

At length, she said, "Where did you hear of this name?"

Brody debated how much he should tell her. As far as he knew, the Mensa murders hadn't been reported by the press yet. Nobody knew of them save for him, the cops, and a few others.

"I saw it scrawled on the wall of a crime scene," he said. "Does it have something to do with voodoo?"

"Practitioners of voodoo do not speak his name."

"He's some kind of snake god. Is that right?"

"What kind of crime scene was this?"

"A murder."

Mali nodded yes, face somber. "Somebody put a curse on the victim and invoked the name of Li Grande Zombi."

"Is that like when they stick pins in a doll to inflict pain on their victims?"

"I will not have you mock my religion. I am a mambo, as well as a professor of voodoo."

"No offense meant. I don't know much about it. What's a mambo?"

"A voodoo priestess. You need to be wary."

"Me?"

"You're dealing with sinister forces. A person invokes Li Grande Zombi to cast a spell on his enemy. You could become possessed by a demon."

Tess had thought the same thing when she saw his seizure, Brody decided with a frisson of unease.

"I'm not the victim," he said.

"How do you know?"

"The person who was murdered is the victim."

"You could be the next one murdered."

Brody started. "Me? I'm not like the other murder victims. There's nothing linking us."

"You're messing with things that shouldn't be messed with. One must never take the dark forces lightly."

"I never take murder lightly."

"You cannot be too careful when dealing with voodoo curses. I will give you a gris-gris to protect you."

"I'm not the one—"

She picked up on something in him.

"You don't sound certain of yourself. Did something happen to you that you want to tell me about?" she said, searching his face.

He debated whether to tell her. His epilepsy was none of her business, he figured.

"It was nothing," he said. "I had a seizure when I was at the cult's crime scene."

She nodded, her face glum. "The curse was meant for you. You have done something to rile the dark forces."

"I'm not the one that was murdered."

"And yet you were stricken with a seizure."

"It had nothing to do with the murder."

He didn't want to go into it with her. This wasn't about him. It was about the three murder victims.

"You can't be sure," she said. "Something you are involved in now could be riling the forces of darkness. You need protection."

"It's not necessary."

"By your own admission, you experienced a seizure. You could have died. Next time, you might indeed die—unless you have protection."

"I'm not worried about a voodoo curse."

"Do not scoff. Better to be safe than sorry."

She opened her desk drawer and withdrew a crow's dried out black foot with black feathers on its ankle. She handed him the gris-gris, which emitted a rank odor similar to garlic.

Not wishing to offend her he accepted it, though he didn't believe in the effectiveness of talismans at warding off curses. Hell, he didn't believe in curses. His seizure had nothing to do with a curse. It was an epileptic seizure. He fiddled with the crow's foot on the desktop.

"Keep that with you at all times," she said. "The juju will keep you safe from the black magic of your enemy."

"I'm not one of the killer's victims. He's targeting other people."

"You may be infected by the evil spell because you were at the murder scene."

"What would be the point?"

"Maybe you're getting too close to identifying the murderer."

"I'm not a believer in voodoo. Its curses can't affect me."

"Thinking like that will not protect you from a voodoo spell," she admonished him.

"I don't need protection."

"Nonbelievers always scoff until it's too late and the demon possesses them. They die horrible deaths."

Brody turned the conversation away from himself.

Chapter 15

"Could these murders be human sacrifices to Li Grande Zombi?" he said.

"Voodoo worshipers don't normally sacrifice humans. They tend to sacrifice chickens, dogs, cats, goats, and similar animals and drain their blood to appease the gods. Worshipers engage in ritualistic, orgiastic dances during these sacrifices."

"They never sacrifice humans?"

"I wouldn't say never. There are documented cases of human sacrifice, but they are rare."

"What would be the point of a person practicing a ritual that sacrifices humans to Li Grande Zombi?"

"To get the great one to help the supplicant to do something, or to protect them from evil."

Brody produced his cell phone, swiped through his photos on it, selected one, and showed it to Mali.

"Do you recognize that symbol?" he said.

Mali stared at it. "No."

"It's not voodoo?"

"I've never seen it before."

"It's a black sun. The talisman was found at the scene of one of the murders."

"I can't help you."

Brody stood up to leave. "Thanks."

"Take your gris-gris with you."

To be polite Brody scoffed up the creepy corvid charm from the desktop and pocketed it.

At Mali's office door Brody faced her, doorknob in hand, and said, "Do you know why a believer in voodoo would hate Mensa?"

"Mensa? No. In fact, I'm a member of Mensa."

Her answer caught him off guard.

"Does that surprise you?" she said.

"What surprises me is I'm meeting so many Mensa members—most of them dead."

"I hope that doesn't include me," she said, as if to herself.

"Do you know Tyler Keogh?"

Mali smiled. "I never go to any of the meetings. I'm a member in name only, I guess you'd say."

"Eugene Frantangello? Myles Wasson? Do you know either of them?"

Mali looked blank. "Should I know them?"

"They're on the Mensa board of directors."

"I pay my yearly dues. That's about it."

Brody made to leave.

"You need to be careful," said Mali. "You don't want to end up with live things in you."

"Live things in me?" said Brody, puzzled.

"It's a voodoo curse. Not really voodoo. More like hoodoo, which has its roots in voodoo."

"Frantangello's corpse had a live snake writhing inside his ribs."

Mali gasped, her eyes widening. "You're dealing with forces more powerful than any person. Take care, Mr. Private Detective."

"I carry a gun."

"A gun won't help you against a curse. The curse will poison your mind and your soul and then your body. Your only hope is the juju I gave you."

Brody left, unsettled by her words, though he didn't believe her.

He hadn't come here for a sermon. He had come for a clue as to Keogh's whereabouts. He still didn't see any connection between Keogh and voodoo. And the black sun. How did that fit in? Mali said it had nothing to do with voodoo. It had to do with Nazis, as far as he could determine. Nazis and voodoo? Did the Nazis practice voodoo? He doubted it.

As he reached the landing to the stairs, he withdrew Mali's juju from his trouser pocket and tossed it into a trash can. He had enough pocket litter. Besides, the crow's foot stank. He descended the steps at a brisk pace.

Chapter 16

Reaching his Mini in the parking structure, Brody felt his cell vibrate in his trouser pocket. He took the call.

"Have you found Tyler yet?" said Evelyn.

"All I'm finding is dead bodies," said Brody.

"Not a good sign," she said, voice faint.

"What if we're looking at this the wrong way?"

"What do you mean?"

"I'm wondering if Keogh knows the killer's after him and has gone into hiding."

"I never thought of that. I was under the impression something had happened to him."

"So was I. If he's hiding, it will make my job of finding him more difficult."

"But he doesn't know you're the one looking for him."

"True. Do you have any idea where he might try to hide? A place only you two know about or something like that?"

"I can't think of any. We don't hang around together much. We lead our separate lives."

"I believe this ritual killer is after him—if he hasn't already gotten to him."

"Are you trying to bum me out?"

"I'm not gonna sugarcoat this for you. Wherever he is—whether he's in hiding or not—your brother's in danger. I believe he's on the list of human sacrifices drawn up by the killer."

"I don't understand any of this," she said in a burst of irritation. "Human sacrifices in this day and age? It's insane. Nobody believes in that nonsense."

"Something else that doesn't make sense is the talisman of the black sun I found at Wasson's murder."

"Isn't that a voodoo symbol?"

"I talked to a voodoo expert at UCLA. She says the black sun has nothing to do with voodoo."

"I don't get it."

"The black sun is a Nazi symbol from what I found on the Internet."

"One clue leads to voodoo, the other to Nazis. How can that be?" said Evelyn, frustration in her voice.

"Maybe the killer belongs to some new voodoo sect that has Nazis in it."

"It sounds like you're going down a rabbit hole, and you're never coming back out."

"I don't believe in cults and curses. There's a human being behind these murders, and I'm gonna find him. It could even be more than one killer."

"How many killers are we talking about?"

"I haven't had time to study any of these crime scenes thoroughly. Because the cops could show up any minute and think I'm the killer, I had to amscray."

"What do you plan on doing next?"

"Go back to Keogh's house. What type of car does he drive?"

"Uh, a black Audi."

"I didn't see it in his driveway the last time I was there. I'll check his garage this time."

"What difference does it make?"

"I can check with the traffic department to see if they've found any abandoned Audis. If I find they've impounded his car, it'll suggest foul play."

"Don't waste time," she said, shortly.

"It's not a waste of time."

She hung up before he finished his sentence.

She didn't sound happy, he decided, pocketing his cell. But then, what did she have to be happy about? A trail of dead bodies was greeting him, but the scarcity of clues was leading to a dead end.

Chapter 17

Mirisch and Drago were sitting in their ten-year-old silver Ford Taurus parked on the side of the street, watching Keogh's house.

A rangy guy with a hatchet face and long wavy dirty blond hair that he brushed back over his head, pushing thirty, clad in jeans and a maroon T, Drago was riding shotgun, popping pistachio nuts into his mouth, and negligently flipping the husks out his open window.

"How can you stand being on a stakeout without ever eating anything?" he asked Mirisch.

In his midforties, his face stubbled, Mirisch was dressed in loose charcoal grey trousers and a white button down, open at the collar. Worry lines creased his forehead giving it the look of a folded accordion.

"Knock off the chatter and keep your eyes peeled on the house," he said.

"I'm bored out of my mind. We've been watching it for an hour. Nothing doing."

Mirisch cut a glance toward Drago. "How do you eat so much without putting on weight?"

"I work it off. I exercise in the gym."

"I do, too, but I still got love handles. There's more to it than just exercise."

"I don't worry about getting fat. That's the key. If you worry about it, you get fat."

"You're full of shit. You know that?"

Drago stifled a yawn and popped another pistachio nut into his mouth. "I'd fall asleep if I wasn't eating. I don't know how you keep your eyes open."

"Did you throw up before you got in here?"

Drago gave him a look.

"It's a polite way of saying you smell like shit," said Mirisch.

Drago hung his mouth open.

"We're on a job, Drago. What the hell?"

"You call this working? Sitting watching a house where nothing happens?"

"The SAC wants us to find Keogh. This is his house, the last place he's been sighted. Hence we wait here for him to show up."

"And what if he doesn't show up? How do we know he's gonna show up here?"

"Because it's his house. Where else does he have to go?"

"If he's on the run, he'll probably stay away from here."

"He *is* on the run. Which is why nobody can find him. But his showing up here is our best bet."

"In other words, we don't have a clue where he is. Do you ever get the feeling we're out of the loop?"

"He missed his flight to San Francisco and vanished. That's all we know."

"What's so hot about this guy, anyway? Why does the bureau want him? Does he have a rap sheet?"

"No sheet. The director told me Keogh is a national security threat."

Drago yawned and stretched. "Sounds like a spy."

"Ours not to reason why—"

"Spare me."

"Who's that?" said Mirisch, coming to attention, sitting up in the driver's seat.

Drago watched a tall muscular guy walk up the driveway to Keogh's white-painted clapboard garage.

"Snap a picture," said Mirisch.

Drago picked up the Nikon camera that sat on his seat between his legs. The Nikon had an 800mm telephoto lens attached to it. The Taurus's tinted glass windshield would obscure his photos. In order to snap pictures of the guy, Drago had to stick his head out his window and aim his camera over the car roof.

"One of Keogh's buddies?" said Drago, peering through his camera's viewfinder.

Brody strode up to the garage door and peeked through its windows.

"From what I've heard Keogh didn't have any buddies," said Mirisch. "One of these egghead types. Thinks he's smarter than everybody else. Who wants a guy like that for a buddy?"

"Then who is this guy? Maybe we should brace him."

"No. I want to know what he's up to," said Mirisch, his eyes trained on Brody.

The Taurus had tinted glass all around. Mirisch had his window powered up and nobody outside of the car could see him. Drago's window was down, but Brody was on the opposite side of the street and couldn't see into the Taurus's interior.

"It's getting hot in here," said Drago, finished snapping photos, and ducked his head back into the Taurus. "Turn on the AC."

"I don't want that guy to know we're here. He might hear the AC working. The thing makes a racket."

"He's too far away to hear it."

"We can't take that chance. I don't want to spook him."

"I'm sweating like a pig."

"You got your window open. What more do you want?"

"I want your wife."

Mirisch snickered. "That's not gonna happen."

"I don't get it. What does she see in you?"

"There's lots to see."

Drago smirked. "That's what I mean," he said, patting Mirisch's paunch.

Mirisch gave him a look.

"If she spent one night with me, she would never go back to you," said Drago. "Believe me."

"You got a mouth on you. Where do you get off talking to me like that? I'm your superior."

"Only on the job, supe. Nowhere else."

"You got another job offer or something?"

Drago inspected his camera. "I was wondering when you were gonna say that. And then you're gonna say—"

"Did Walmart offer you a job as greeter?"

A bored expression on his face, Drago mouthed the words as Mirisch said them.

"Look," said Mirisch. "He entered the house."

"We could bust him for B & E," said Drago, scoping the house.

"The door wasn't locked."

"It's his word against ours. I say bust him."

"We want Keogh, not this guy."

"So we just sit here, while he robs the house?"

"We wait."

"Whoever said all things come to those who wait was a liar."

"We wait."

Mirisch's cell phone chimed in his trouser pocket. He answered and listened to the caller.

"Got it," he said at last, and hung up.

"Who was that?" said Drago.

"The US Marshals Service."

"What do they want?"

"To talk to us in two hours."

"What about?"

"About Tyler Keogh."

"What about him?"

"They said there are things we need to know about him."

"Like what?"

"They'll tell us in two hours."

Chapter 18

Brody slipped into Keogh's lobby, shutting the unlocked front door behind him.

He had discovered Keogh's Audi was indeed missing, the garage empty. Now he needed to find out the car's tag number so he could check with the traffic department to find out if they had impounded said car.

He needed to find a copy of Keogh's car insurance policy in order to find the tag number.

He entered the office. Val wasn't here now. Either she had found the prenup or she had given up looking for it and had left. If she had still been here, maybe she could have helped him locate Keogh's insurance policy.

He would have to find it on his own.

Hearing a noise in another part of the house, he started. He had thought he was here alone. He approached the doorway and poked his head around the jamb.

"You again," said Val, strutting down the hall toward him. "Did you break in again?"

"This is an emergency," said Brody. "I think Keogh might have been kidnaped."

"What's that got to do with breaking into his house?"

"The front door was unlocked. Which means, I didn't break in."

Val snorted.

Brody searched her face. "You sound remarkably calm for someone whose future husband has vanished."

Val waved him off. "He'll show up. You know, like a bad penny. Why do *you* want him to show up? That's what I want to know. What's in it for you?"

"I suspect he's been kidnaped."

Val coughed a brief, scornful laugh. "For what reason?"

"A ransom."

"Who do they think they'll get it from?"

"Maybe you."

"Me?" she said in shock. "He doesn't let me go anywhere near his money. The only way I get any is if he gives me some. *And* he has the gall to tell me to sign a prenup. Do you believe the nerve of that tight wad?"

"Do you know where his car is?"

"With him, probably—wherever he is."

"Do you know his license tag number?"

"Actually, I do. He's got a vanity plate. *Of course*. A guy with a head as swollen as a hot-air balloon would have to have a vanity. It's easy to remember. He's got one of those vintage black and yellow California plates that spells out EGOMAN. Short for *egomaniac*."

"Ah, good. I'll see if the traffic department found his car and impounded it."

"Why would he abandon his car?"

"He would if he was kidnaped."

Val changed the subject. "I still haven't found that prenup. It's bugging the hell out of me. We're gonna get married, and he splits. That's the kind of guy he is. Egomaniac. All he thinks about is himself. And his money, of course."

Brody retreated into the living room and, hiding behind the curtain, peeked out the picture window. The Taurus with the tinted windows was still parked out there. Cars with tinted windows aroused his suspicions, especially ones with all of their windows tinted.

He pulled back from the window.

Was somebody watching Keogh's house, or was someone tailing him? Brody wondered. Neither option was welcome. It wasn't Tess. She had a white Mustang. It was someone else. He had parked out of sight of Keogh's house just in case someone was watching the house. He would use the back door and cut across the neighbors' yards to return to his Mini.

For now he returned to Val, who was yanking out books on the bookshelves in the study and flipping through them searching for the prenup, suspecting it might be sandwiched between the pages.

“Is that your Taurus outside?” he said.

“No. I took an Uber here. I didn’t feel like driving.”

She held a book by its front and back cover and shook it, hoping for the prenup to fall out from between the pages.

“How long has that car been out there?” he said.

“I have no idea. And I don’t care. I’m getting sick of looking for that bastard’s prenup. I have better things to do. I’m his dream girl. I’m a fifteen on a scale of ten. And this is how he treats me.”

She gave the book one last shake and thrust it back onto the shelf in a pet.

Brody exited through the back door, bypassed a wooden shed in the backyard, cut across neighbors’ lawns, and returned to the street, out of sight of the Taurus with blacked-out windows.

Who would be watching Keogh’s house? he wondered.

Chapter 19

Brody drove his Mini back to his apartment-cum-office.

He plumped in his leather recliner and felt like sleeping. The vibrating cell phone in his trouser pocket had other ideas.

"I have terrible news," said Evelyn, her voice fraught.

Brody jerked upright, clenching his cell with tense fingers. "What happened?"

"They kidnaped Olivia."

"Olivia?"

"My seven-year-old daughter."

"Who did?"

"They didn't tell me."

"What do they want?"

"They want me to stop looking for Tyler, or they'll"—she sobbed—"kill Olivia."

Brody felt a shot of adrenaline course through his system.

"How did they know you're looking for him?" he said.

"That's what I want to know. Did you tell anyone?"

"Absolutely not. I never reveal my clients' names to anyone."

"Somehow they found out. You'll have to call off your search for Tyler."

"Are you sure that's what you want?"

"I have no choice. I don't want them to harm Olivia."

"Are you sure they have her? They could be bluffing."

"I couldn't find her at school today when I went to pick her up. I haven't been able to locate her."

"Did they say anything about a ransom?"

"All they said was to stop looking for Tyler."

"Do they know I'm the one you hired to find him?"

"I have no idea."

"Did you tell them?"

"They didn't ask."

"How do they know you're looking for Tyler?"

"How should I know? Does it matter?"

"If they don't know I'm the one looking for him, I can continue my search while you tell them you called it off."

She paused. "Sounds risky. I don't want to do anything that will jeopardize Olivia's life."

"I understand. But if they don't know I'm looking for Keogh, why should they harm her?"

"Maybe they *do* know you're looking for him. How can we be sure?"

Brody thought about it. "I can be more surreptitious about my search now that I know someone is trying to guard Keogh's whereabouts."

"Somehow they know I'm looking for him."

"Did you report him missing to the cops?"

"No. Not yet. I don't trust the cops."

"Maybe the kidnapers are just guessing you're looking for them. How did they contact you?"

"By phone. They said they were using a burner, and told me not to bother trying to trace the call."

"Did you recognize the kidnaper's voice?"

"Honestly, it wasn't a good connection. There was a lot of noise on the line. It sounded like a male voice with a chainsaw going in the background."

"Do you have any idea who it is?"

"None." She wept. "Nothing like this has ever happened to me before."

"Did you agree to their terms?"

"Of course. What's my choice? My little girl's life is in danger."

"Have you called the cops about Olivia?"

"Not yet."

"Good. Don't."

"Why not?"

"They'll get in my way. They already suspect me of a murder. I won't be able to do anything with them breathing down my back."

Evelyn fetched a loud sigh. "The kidnaper said the same thing. Don't call the cops. Or they'll kill—"

Her voice broke.

"Do you have any idea why someone wouldn't want you to find Keogh?" said Brody.

"None. He must've been kidnaped. Maybe Olivia's kidnapers are the same ones that kidnaped him."

Brody frowned. "It doesn't make sense when there's no ransom involved."

"I told you, they want me to drop my search for Tyler."

"Where's the percentage in it for them? What's the point of a kidnaping without getting money in exchange? Have they demanded money for Tyler's release?"

"They didn't say they had him. I was speculating."

"Keogh's life may be hanging by a thread. We have to help him. We can't stop looking for him now."

"You're endangering Olivia's life by continuing your search for him," said Evelyn, at her wit's end.

"I'll do it on the sly. Nobody will know."

"How can you be sure?"

"I'm not gonna raise any dust. I'll be discreet."

"The safest option for Olivia is for you to stop your search for Tyler."

"It's not the safest option for Keogh."

Evelyn let out a frustrated cry of anguish. "I don't know what to do. Why are they doing this to me?"

"After I find Keogh, I'll track down Olivia's kidnapers and deal with them."

"How long is this gonna take? She must be going out of her mind with worry."

"I have no way of knowing."

"I hate to say this, but Olivia means more to me than Tyler. He's my brother, but we're not that close. Olivia is my baby."

"I'll find both of them. I don't want you to sacrifice one for the other. Let's plan on saving both. That's our goal."

"Why is this happening to me?"

In his mind's eye he could see her wringing her hands.

"Keogh's Audi is missing," he said. "It wasn't in his garage."

"Maybe he fled the country. He could've driven down the coast to Mexico."

"Why do you say that?"

"Because it's like he dropped off the face of the earth."

Maybe he's six feet under the earth, he thought, but didn't say, not wanting to compound her distress.

She hung up.

He could only hope her phone wasn't tapped. How sophisticated were the kidnapers she was dealing with? he wondered. How much did they know—especially about him? If they were watching his every move, he could be jeopardizing Olivia's life by continuing to look for Keogh.

Chapter 20

Brody felt snakes writhing inside him, infesting him. They were slithering through his body between his ribs, around his organs, down his arms and legs. He could see the snakes corkscrewing down his arm, looking like oversized veins spiraling under his skin.

His body riddled with snakes, he felt nauseated. It felt like one of them was trying to squirm out of his stomach up into his throat, where he would choke on the serpent if it managed to worm its way into his windpipe.

He thought of what Mali had said, "live things inside you," the hoodoo/voodoo curse that terrified her.

He looked in the bathroom mirror. His carotid was throbbing. Or was that another snake? The veins in his temples were pulsating. But why were they so large? They were snakes writhing under his skin, making for his brain. Were they already in his brain, burrowing holes in it, turning it into a rabbit warren? Would his worm-eaten brain shut down any minute because it was nothing but holes excavated by snakes?

He stared at his face, the snakes underneath his skin rippling his flesh. He was sure they were going to burst through his skin. And yet they didn't. They kept writhing just beneath his skin, wreaking havoc on his insides, eating him inside out.

He must be suffering from internal hemorrhaging, he decided, and doubled over with pain, almost knocking his head against the porcelain sink beneath the mirror. The tap started dripping as his head hung in the sink basin. *Drip drip drip*. The sound increased in loudness then petered out. The pain knifing through him subsided. He straightened up and peered into the mirror.

The snakes were still writhing under his forehead's skin. They slithered under his scalp, still beneath his skin's surface. He watched in fascinated horror as his hair rippled in concert with the undulations of the snakes.

Dear god. Was he going mad? *Live things inside you.*

His eyes itched. He moved closer to the mirror to see why they were bothering him. They looked bloodshot. The tiny veins in his eyes were a bright vermilion. And . . . they were squirming. Like tiny snakes. Were they breaking through his cornea? They hadn't reached his tear ducts. Maybe they were still trapped inside him, he decided. Were they trying to find their way out of his body? Trying to find an opening? Trying to find his tear ducts? Was that what they were doing while moving? Or were they feasting on his internal organs, destroying him from the inside out?

He felt tickling in the pupils of his eyes. He leaned closer to the mirror to inspect the black holes that were dilating. Was that a snake's head peeking out of his right pupil? Had the creature found an escape hatch and was about to shoot out of his eye?

He couldn't tell. There seemed to be movement in his pupil, but maybe it was a reflection of the fluorescent light over the mirror. With his forefinger he pulled open the lower lid of his eye to get a better look. The snake was still embedded in his pupil. It hadn't escaped.

Meanwhile, the tiny red capillary snakes continued to writhe in the whites of his eyes. He wanted to scratch his eyes. Pluck them out. It wasn't just the itching. It was the seeing. Gazing at the snakes in his eyes was driving him mad. *If thine eye offends thee, pluck it ou*t. He didn't know how much longer he could stand his mental and physical anguish.

He reached for his eyes, preparing to gouge them out. At the last moment, he stayed his hands and jerked them away from his face.

The snakes were eating him alive. He almost wished they would find a means of escape through his pupils so they would leave his body in peace. Or in pieces, was the more likely scenario what with the tissue damage they were inflicting on his internal organs as they writhed around them eating him alive.

He heard bongos pounding, deliberately building to a crescendo.

He braced his arms on the sink so he wouldn't collapse. Infested with snakes, his legs felt like rubber. He didn't know what was holding him up. The snakes were taking control of his body making him move in ways he didn't initiate. All he could feel were the snakes slithering through his body, like a wave of pain washing through him, no part of his body free from the throbbing agony.

The bongos crescendoed.

He thought his head would explode.

He screamed. He couldn't take it anymore.

The scream caught in his throat. Or was it a snake wriggling upward to emerge from his intestines?

He stared in horror at his grimacing face in the mirror.

Were electric green scales growing on his face, glinting in the light? Was he turning into a snake with coruscating green scales?

"No!"

He woke up shivering, his body bathed in cold sweat under the sheets, his eyes bugging out. He jackknifed up, threw his sheets off, and inspected his sweaty body.

He didn't see any scales. Nor did he see snakes whipping under his skin.

He wiped the sweat from his brow with relief.

Was the nightmare induced by a voodoo curse? he wondered, despite himself. Mali had warned him he might be cursed. He had dismissed the thought. He didn't believe in such nonsense.

Live things inside you.

Voodoo was nothing more than the power of suggestion, he decided. The power of suggestion had precipitated his nightmare. Mali had instilled the fear in his mind, where it had taken root, festered, and mushroomed into a horrifying hallucination.

Chapter 21

Brody scarfed down a bowl of Cheerios and a glass of orange juice. He nursed a cup of hot green tea then called the LAPD to find out if they had impounded Keogh's black Audi with the tags EGOMAN.

The officer he spoke to said no.

Brody hung up.

Keogh's car could be parked legally somewhere, or maybe he was still using it, which would suggest his life wasn't in danger. In any case, it hadn't been abandoned for several days in a metered parking slot or in a restricted parking zone on the side of a street.

It could also mean Keogh had used his Audi to flee to Mexico, as Evelyn had suggested.

Then again, Keogh's car could be parked in a long-term parking lot at LAX. You could park your car there indefinitely without anyone reporting it to the authorities.

He supposed he could search the LAX parking lots for the car, but even if he found it, it wouldn't prove anything. Keogh could have taken a flight to somewhere other than San Francisco, or his kidnapers could have left the car at LAX to avoid detection.

Brody needed another lead.

Which left Mensa's board of directors, the ones that were alive—if there were any. Why was the kidnaper killing them? Or was somebody else killing them?

He had to be careful about visiting any Mensa members and interrogating them about Keogh. If the kidnapers learned of his visit, they would kill Olivia. He wouldn't even tell Evelyn about it.

Brody got out his laptop and examined the list of the LA Mensa board of directors.

A knock on his front door startled him.

It wasn't a friendly knock. More like someone hammering the wood with all his might with the bottom of his fist. The door rattled in its jamb.

Brody sprang to his feet and flung the door open.

Detective Macready stood in the hallway in his unbuttoned shepherd's check blazer, his badge fastened to his belt. He rubbed his hand over his mouth, sizing Brody up.

"You look like shit," said Macready.

"I didn't sleep well."

"We found another Mensa murder," he said, his expression stony.

Was he talking about Wasson or Frantangello? wondered Brody.

"Why are you telling me?" said Brody.

"Because you were seen leaving the scene of the crime."

Brody realized there was an African American uniform standing five feet from Macready in the hall with a prominent bent nose, jug ears, and a no-nonsense face.

Brody broke into a sweat. He said nothing.

"Well?" said Macready.

"I don't know what you're talking about."

"Eugene Frantangello. Come up with an explanation fast."

Brody revolved answers in his mind. If Macready had witnesses that could put him at the crime scene, Brody couldn't pretend he wasn't there. On the other hand, Macready could be bluffing, speculating that Brody had been at Frantangello's because he had been at the crime scene at Delacroix's. It appeared the same perp had committed both murders.

Brody tried to get a read on Macready's face and got nowhere. Brody couldn't tell if the guy was bluffing.

"Oh, Frantangello," said Brody.

"'Oh, Frantangello,'" mocked Macready. "That's your answer?"

"Tess said she was gonna contact you about that. You mean, she didn't?"

"Tess?"

Brody tried to recall her last name. “Hardwick. We both found Frantangello’s corpse.”

Macready took a step toward Brody, crowding him.

“One of the neighbors told me she was suspicious of what was going on in Frantangello’s house,” said Macready. “She’s the one that told us she suspected foul play. Not your pal Tess.”

Brody shrugged. “Tess said she’d take care of it.”

“So she was there, too?”

“She was.”

“It’s a crime to know about a murder and not report it.”

“I told you, Tess said she’d take care—”

“You want me to run you in?”

“She said—”

“It’s your duty to report a murder.”

“I can’t help it if she didn’t get around to it yet.”

“Do you want to go to jail?”

“For not reporting a crime? You’d never make it stick. Even if you did, it would only be a misdemeanor.”

“Did you kill Frantangello?” said Macready, boring his beady eyes into Brody’s.

“He was already dead when I found him.”

“You just happened to be at the scene of another murder, huh?”

“I’m in the middle of an investigation. I must be onto something, since I’m uncovering dead bodies.”

“You expect me to believe this?”

“It’s the truth.”

“Time to come clean, Brody, or you’re going downtown.”

Brody figured Macready was right. Brody looked guilty. He had some explaining to do.

“I’m trying to find Tyler Keogh,” he said. “He’s on the Mensa board of directors, as were Delacroix and Frantangello. I thought they might know where Keogh is. End of story.”

“And you’re working for?”

“You know I can’t tell you that.”

Jutting out his jaw Macready jabbed his forefinger into Brody's chest. "Don't leave town. You're still my prime suspect in these satanic cult murders."

"I had nothing to do with them."

"Do you drop acid?"

"No."

"Do you worship Satan?"

"Only on Tuesdays."

"That's not funny."

Brody shrugged. "It was a silly question."

"Oh, yeah? I'll be the judge of that. Do you practice voodoo? Do you worship Li Grande Zombi?"

Brody could see Macready had done his research. "No."

"Who do you worship?"

"Not you."

Macready scowled at him.

"You better be leveling with me," he said, spun on his heel, and left with the uniform.

Brody closed his door.

Chapter 22

Two minutes later there was another knock on his door.

Expecting Macready, Brody whipped open the door, ready to give Macready a piece of his mind for harassing him.

Only, it wasn't Macready.

Val Holiday was standing in front of him in her Jimmy Choo icicle-like stilettos.

"Is this a bad time?" she said, noticing his baleful expression.

"I thought you were a cop." Brody relaxed. "What's on your mind?"

"You dropped one of your business cards in Tyler's studio," she said, showing him the card. "I want to hire you."

"I'm not available."

She glanced at his card. "Your card says you're an Internet PI."

"That's right."

"Well, I want to hire you. Are you discriminating against me because I'm a woman?"

"That has nothing to do with it."

"All right, then."

Brody was curious why she wanted his services. "What do you want me for?"

"Could we go into your office?" She looked around the hall. "This is confidential."

"Fine. Come in."

She strutted inside in her ass-grabbing tangerine leather miniskirt. He closed the door behind her.

"I'm listening," he said.

"I want to hire you to find Tyler. I can't find the creep's prenup so my lawyer can pore over it with a fine-tooth comb. I have to have a copy of that prenup."

She plunked down on his sofa and crossed her legs, her mini riding up her creamy thighs.

Yet someone else who wanted Keogh. Maybe she had info that could help him in his search for Keogh.

"Do you have any idea where he is?" said Brody.

"I haven't a clue."

"He upped and left without saying a word to you?"

"He told me his lawyer was finished working on the prenup. That was the last I heard from him."

"Did you know he was supposed to fly up to San Francisco, but never made it there?"

"No. Who told you that?"

"I have ways of finding things out."

"Good. Find him and let me know where he's hiding."

"Why do you think he's hiding?"

"Because he's hiding from me."

"Why do you say that?"

"He doesn't want my lawyer to scope the prenup. He knows my lawyer will rip it apart."

"I see."

"He was an arrogant dickhead to begin with. He got even worse after he inherited a million bucks from his father's estate. Then he became unbearable."

"Then why do you want to marry him?"

"We're in love, of course," she said, swinging her leg up and down.

"I wish I could help you—"

"He became even more arrogant after the experiment."

Brody pricked up his ear. "What experiment?"

"Some experiment at Stanford. They wanted him for a test subject because he belonged to Mensa."

"Do you have any idea what this experiment was about?"

"I think he said it was being run by the federal government," she said, scrunching up her forehead.

"This experiment changed his personality?"

"It—what's the word?—*enhanced* it. He decided he was everybody's superior and looked down his nose on everyone from Mt. Olympus with his head in the clouds like everyone but him was a moronic bottom feeder."

"When was this?"

"Not long ago. A couple of months." She scoped out the coffee table in front of the sofa she sat on. "Do you have any blow I could snort?"

"No."

She pouted. "What do you do for entertainment around here?"

Brody chewed it over. "Was Keogh supplying you with blow?"

"He has a pipeline—like everybody else in LA."

"He snorted blow with you?"

"Oh sure. All the time. Blow, Molly, you name it. They made us horny."

"How do you know it wasn't the drugs that were affecting his personality rather than the experiment?"

"We've been doing drugs for years. They didn't mess him up. It was that frigging experiment."

"Do you know who was running the experiment? Who was funding it?"

"He never told me."

"And he disappeared right after the experiment?"

"A couple months later, I'd say."

"Interesting, but I already have a client."

"Did you hear me? I'm offering you a job."

"What can I say?"

"What kind of a bum are you—turning down a job?"

Brody didn't like Val. There was no way he was going to work for her—no matter how appealing she looked in her skintight clothing, what there was of it, and stilettos.

She wanted to hire him to do the same job he was doing for Evelyn—find Keogh. He could have gotten double the pay for doing one assignment. But he didn't like the idea of working for Val. And there was a conflict of interest representing two different clients on the same assignment. Who would he report to first? He was better off rejecting her offer.

"I told you all of this for nothing?" she said, leaping to her feet from the sofa.

He didn't know how she could stand in her stilettos, let alone jump in them.

"I'll tell you what," he said. "If I see him, I'll tell you first thing."

"Thanks loads," she said, stalking in a huff to the door, her Jimmy Choos knifing his carpet. "I have a good mind to report you to the cops for breaking into Tyler's house."

"His door was open. You left it open."

"That damn bastard. Does he really think he can hide from me? I'll find him by myself. I need your help like a hole in the head."

She slammed the door behind her.

Chapter 23

Brody had to keep a low profile.

He might even have to go into hiding. As soon as Macready found out about Wasson's murder—if he hadn't done so already—he would come after Brody, especially if a witness could put Brody at the scene of the crime. Three similar ritualistic murders with Brody at all three crime scenes couldn't be ignored by any cop worth his salt. The guy might even be able to wangle an arrest warrant for Brody from a judge.

It was a good idea to stay away from Mensa members, decided Brody. They had a nasty habit of turning up dead when he sought them out. On the other hand, where else could he get clues about Keogh's disappearance?

He got on his laptop, awoke it from Sleep mode, and searched for the LA Mensa board of directors. When he located the list, his eyes fell on the name Lisa Chang.

He withdrew his cell from his trouser pocket, punched out her phone number, and waited for her to pick up.

Heart beating fast, he listened to the phone ring, fearing the worst—that she wouldn't answer because she lay dead in a pool of her blood, gutted like Frantangello.

"Hello," said a woman.

"I'd like to speak to Lisa Chang," he said.

"Speaking," came the reply.

She was still alive, Brody decided with relief.

"I'm Scott Brody, a private detective. I'm trying to locate Tyler Keogh. Could you help me with that?"

"Who?"

"Tyler Keogh. He's on the Mensa board of directors with you."

"Oh. I think I know who you're talking about. He rarely shows up at our meetings."

"When was the last time you saw him?"

"I can't remember. I barely know the man. I doubt I've said more than three words to him."

"Do you know where I can find him?"

"At his home, I guess."

"He's not there. Where else could he be?"

"I'm not the right one to ask. I don't know him. All I know is, he's on the board of directors. Why, may I ask?"

"He's missing. I'm trying to find him for my client."

"Does this have anything to do with Myles Wasson's murder? He was a member of our board, too."

"It might. Keogh's life could be at stake."

"Goodness. I'd like to help, but I don't see how."

"How did you know about Wasson's murder?"

The last he had heard, Wasson's murder hadn't been broadcast on the news yet. Did she know more than she was letting on about the murders? Brody wondered.

"I saw it on the TV news," said Chang.

Which meant Macready must know about it, decided Brody. The question was, was there a witness that could place Brody at the scene of the Wasson murder? If so, Macready would be paying Brody another visit—maybe with a warrant this time.

"You might want to keep your door locked," said Brody.

"Excuse me?"

"There's a serial killer on the loose."

There was a pause.

"This is the first I've heard of it," she said. "You can assume this on the basis of one killing?"

"I shouldn't be telling you this, but Heloise Delacroix was also murdered."

"Heloise?" said Chang, a catch in her voice. "I didn't know."

"The cops haven't released the information yet. Don't tell anyone else about it. It's confidential. I thought you should know and lock your doors."

"All right," she said, her voice barely audible.

"You should think about hiring private security for protection."

"Do you really think that's necessary?"

"Do you want to go on living?"

"Ohmigod. Should I call the police?"

"They don't have the manpower to provide you with protection—unless you've been threatened. Has anyone threatened you?"

"No."

"Forget the cops. You're better off hiring your own security."

"Why would anyone want to target Mensa board members? Few people have even heard of us. This makes no sense."

Brody felt the same way. "Do you know if Keogh was mixed up with any cults?"

"What kind of cults?"

"Satanic cults? Voodoo cults? Anything like that."

"It doesn't sound like him, though I didn't know him—like I said."

"What about Delacroix?"

"Heloise had nothing to do with cults, I can assure you."

"Wasson?"

"His life is a closed book to me. Heloise, I ate lunch with frequently. She never said a word about cults. What do cults have to do with this?"

Brody decided not to enlighten her. After all, there was an ongoing investigation into these murders. He would be better off not revealing anything. The cops would tell the media when they were good and ready. Chang could learn about it from the TV.

"Just asking," he said.

"Strange question. Cults? What next?"

"What about you? Are you into cults?"

Chang laughed. "I don't believe in the supernatural. What do you take me for?"

"What about a black sun?"

"Black sun? It sounds apocalyptic. What does it have to do with these murders you're talking about?"

"I'm not sure."

"I never heard of a black sun."

"If you hear from Keogh, could you give me a call?"

"If I hear from him, it would be a first."

"Thanks for your help. And remember your doors."

Brody rang off.

Another knock on the door startled him. Three visitors within in an hour. He normally didn't get that many in a month—unless business was booming, and it never was.

He answered the door, not knowing who to expect.

Wearing a navy blue uniform with spandex bicycle pants, horn-rimmed glasses astride the bridge of his nose, a twentysomething FedEx deliverer with powerful legs stood in the hall, a package in his hand.

"Scott Brody?" he said.

"Yeah."

The deliverer handed him a large envelope and left.

Brody withdrew into his room, shut the door, and inspected the package. The return address was a private mail box number. No name. He didn't like the idea of getting a package without the sender's name on it. Nevertheless, he wanted to know what was in the envelope.

He tore the envelope open and peeked inside, his pulse quickening a tad.

He shook the object out into his open hand.

It was a medallion of a black sun, similar to the one he had found at Wasson's murder. The other object that fluttered out was a white chicken feather stained with blood.

Whose blood? he wondered.

The cult was trying to scare him off, he decided. They must have discovered he was investigating the Mensa murders and wanted him gone. They were conducting a psyops campaign against him, mau-mauing him with their black magic charms.

Brody didn't believe in charms and magic. Voodoo feathers and the black sun amulet weren't going to scare him away.

Hitler's elite *Schutzstaffel* (protective echelon) could be considered a cult with their tattoos, SS runes, silver daggers, and their *Totenkopf* (death's head) badges, but he had never read anywhere that they practiced voodoo.

What had begun in April 1925 as Hitler's coterie of personal bodyguards the SS later burgeoned into a huge, all but omnipotent force considered above the law within Nazi Germany. Heinrich Himmler as its leader saw to it that nobody could touch them. They were, in effect, an army of supermen that ran the Third Reich, accountable to no one but the Reichsführer-SS Himmler and the Führer Adolf Hitler.

What did any of this have to do with Keogh, an aeronautical engineer who belonged to Mensa? Brody wondered. Could it be possible these killings had nothing to do with Keogh? But then what had happened to him?

Chapter 24

Brody left his apartment, carrying his laptop with him. His enemies, including Macready, knew where he lived and might try something. Macready might arrest him. His other enemies could try something worse.

It was time for Brody to keep a low profile.

He needed to talk to Evelyn, but Olivia's kidnapers might be staking out her residence. If they saw Brody enter it, they would carry out their threat to kill Olivia. He drove his Mini to a nearby Ralphs parking lot, whipped out his cell, and called Evelyn.

"Do you know anything about an experiment at Stanford that your brother took part in?" he said.

"What kind of experiment?"

"All I know is it was an experiment. His fiancée told me about it. She said it made him more arrogant."

"I don't know anything about any experiment. Why are you still looking for my brother? The kidnapers will kill Olivia if they find out what you're up to."

"I'm keeping a low profile. I'm doing interviews by phone."

"It's too dangerous. You're off the case."

Brody flinched. He didn't want her to drop him.

"I feel like I'm getting closer to the truth," he said. "All I need is a little more time."

"Call if off, or I'll have to take measures to protect my daughter. You have no idea what a living hell I'm going through."

"We need to find Keogh. Everything hinges on him."

"Absolutely not. You're off the case. You're fired. That's my final word."

"Do you have any idea what the experiment was about?"

"You need to stop bothering me."

"I know I'm getting closer to finding him—"

She hung up.

A bullet perforated his driver's-side window and sang past his face. He whipped his head around to identify who had fired the shot.

He didn't spot anyone with a piece. Maybe the shooter was hiding in the high-rise office complex across the street.

He was a sitting duck here.

He fired his ignition, reversed out of his parking space, sped to the nearest exit, and merged into traffic on the main thoroughfare. Somebody had upped the ante. The threats weren't just bloodstained charms delivered to his apartment door. They had become bullets with his name on them.

Was it a warning shot, or had it been meant to waste him? Brody wondered.

Who would want to kill him? The kidnapers? The serial killer? Were they one and the same?

He glanced in the rearview mirror. He didn't see a car chasing him. Had the assailant retreated? Was he in the high-rise drawing a bead on him even now with his silenced rifle?

Brody stopped at a traffic light.

A bullet tore through his back window and buried itself in the back of his passenger seat. Brody flinched and ducked. He had to get out of here. He pulled into the right lane, cutting off the car behind him. The irate driver slammed on his brakes to avoid an accident and leaned on his horn. Brody hung a right.

Consumed with road rage, the middle-aged driver with a shaved head and a face like a slab of rare roast beef roared up from behind Brody in his SUV, drew alongside him, and screamed obscenities at Brody. Brody drew his SIG from his ankle holster and brandished it at the furious driver, glowering at the guy.

The driver's eyes bugged out of his head at the sight of the weapon. He slowed and dropped back behind Brody.

Brody put on speed. He had to get out of the line of sight of the high-rise that housed the sniper. He hung another right, his tires shrieking in protest as they bounced off the curb when he cut the turn too tight, denting his hubcap and shaving rubber off the side of his tire. The tart stench of burnt rubber greeted his nostrils. He caught sight of his passenger's-side mirror burst into pieces as a bullet shattered it. He fishtailed out of the turn. He blew past the Prius in front of him.

He scanned the cityscape through his windshield. He didn't see any cops. He had to get out of the sniper's line of fire. He hung a left. Spotting an eighteen-wheeler in front of him, he passed it and tried to cut in front of it to block the sniper's line of sight. But there wasn't enough room between the semi's cab and the fluorescent lime Challenger in front of it.

Brody accelerated, tried to pass the Challenger, and cut in front of it. But the twentysomething driver of the Challenger sped up to prevent Brody from passing. Brody cursed. What was the idiot trying to do? The fool wanted to race him, like it was some game they were playing.

Brody needed the big rig directly behind him to act as a shield against the sniper's bullet. He slowed down, hoping to cut in behind the Challenger and in front of the semi. The Challenger slowed, too, blocking Brody's Mini. Brody cursed. The driver hung his mouth open. The big rig's driver blasted his air horn as the Challenger kept slowing down, forcing the trucker to hit his air brakes.

Change of plans. Brody sped up, trying to put as much distance as possible as soon as possible between him and the sniper's high-rise. He swung into the left lane to get away from the halfwit in the Challenger. He peered in the rearview mirror. The high-rise was fading into the background. He had no idea how powerful the sniper's rifle was. With any luck, he had pulled out of its range.

He decreased his speed, not wanting to attract the attention of a cop.

His apartment wasn't safe. He couldn't go back there, now that bullets were flying in his direction.

He heard a noise behind him. He whipped his head around.

A diamondback rattlesnake was coiled on his backseat shaking its rattle.

Brody's heart skipped a beat.

Chapter 25

Somebody must have tossed the snake in the back when his car was parked on the side of the street in front of his apartment, decided Brody. It could have been the same guy that sent him the bloodstained chicken feather. Brody got the message. Li Grande Zombi. The snake god.

Brody whipped his head forward to concentrate on his driving. He cut his eyes toward the rearview mirror. He couldn't tell if the rattler was getting ready to strike. He didn't know much about snakes, had little contact with them. Weren't diamondbacks supposed to shake their rattle just before they struck?

He slammed his brakes. He had almost run a light.

His head jerked forward. The rattler's head jerked forward.

Was the snake going to retaliate against the car's abrupt stop by striking him? Brody wondered, keeping his head down, waiting for the snake to launch itself at him.

Brody had to park the car and shoot the snake. He couldn't shoot the diamondback from his current position without exposing his hand to a snakebite. Sweat poured out of his armpits.

He couldn't concentrate. The snake could launch itself at him any minute.

The light turned green.

His face streaked with sweat, Brody raised his head and drove forward, searching for a place to park, careful not to make any sudden moves that would attract the attention of the snake.

Where was a parking lot when you wanted one? wondered Brody. He couldn't even find a place to park on the side of the street. He was driving too slow. Cars behind him started honking at him.

He couldn't keep his eyes on the snake and on the road at the same time. Was the snake slithering closer to him? His palms sweated on the steering wheel, making it slippery.

He saw the red bull's-eye of a Target department store looming up ahead.

The thirtyish brunette who had been honking behind him passed him and screamed obscenities out her window at him.

Brody pulled into the Target's parking lot, found an empty space in a near-deserted corner of the lot, and parked, careful not to make any sudden movements that would annoy the diamondback.

Now what? he wondered. If he shot the snake, the gunshot would attract the attention of Target shoppers. They would notify the cops. Macready would no doubt run him in for discharging a firearm in public.

Was there some way he could get the snake out of his car without getting bit? He didn't think so. He wasn't going to take the chance. He had to kill it. He had to shoot it.

Gingerly, he withdrew his SIG P365 from his ankle holster, trying to keep one eye on the diamondback all the while.

Gun in hand, he looked around the parking lot. No one was watching him. If he got out of the car someone would spot him. He would have to blow away the snake without getting out.

Twisting his body uncomfortably in his seat, turning backward in his bucket seat, he balanced himself awkwardly on his knees on the springy seat and trained his SIG on the snake's small triangular head that was raised and staring at him. The diamondback flicked its forked tongue and started rattling its tail.

Anticipating the diamondback's strike, Brody fired.

His slug beheaded the snake.

With any luck, any nearby bystanders would think they had heard a backfiring truck.

Brody composed himself in the driver's seat. He managed to turn around and sit down so he was facing the windshield. Holstering his SIG he surveyed the parking lot. A middle-aged redhaired woman and her daughter were looking with concern in his direction.

He needed to get out of there.

He fired the Mini's engine, put the car in gear, reversed out of his parking space, and made for the exit. The redhead and her daughter watched him for a while but saw nothing untoward and lost interest.

Brody exited the parking lot and pulled into traffic, a headless snake in his backseat.

He had to go to ground somewhere. But where?

He heard a hiss behind him. Taken aback, he looked in the rearview mirror, eyes intent. The diamondback's head was lying on the backseat hissing.

What the hell?

The damned thing was still alive, he decided, his armpits sweating. Could the head launch itself at him and bite him? Didn't it know it was dead? Was it some kind of voodoo snake that never died? The work of Li Grande Zombi? Ridiculous, he told himself.

Nevertheless, the snake's head was still alive.

The SUV behind him honked. Brody had to concentrate on his driving.

He had to throw the diamondback's head out of his car. But how could he? If he tried to toss it out, it would bite him.

The head was flapping its jaws and twisting around on the backseat, flicking its tongue, trying to propel itself somewhere. Was it trying to reattach itself to its body, or trying to move closer to him to bury its fangs in his flesh? Brody wondered. Did it still have venom in its fangs, even though it was supposed to be dead? He figured it did.

Maybe the best thing for him to do was leave the head alone. Sooner or later it had to die. He wished there was some way he could speed it along to its grave. How many times did he have to shoot it for it to die? He doubted using its jaws for legs would propel it to the front seat.

He relaxed—more or less.

What he needed now was a bolt hole. He would take care of the living dead snake when he reached his destination. If only he had a roadrunner, it would make short work of the diamondback. Roadrunners killed rattlers by pecking their heads to pieces. The snake head wouldn't be hissing after a roadrunner's beak got through turning its brain into a colander.

He glanced furtively in the rearview mirror again to make sure the snake head wasn't getting too close.

An unbidden thought flashed through his mind. Could Li Grande Zombi make a snake immortal, raise it from the dead like a zombie? Brody shook his head no. Why was he even thinking such an outlandish thought? Somebody was trying to gaslight him with all this voodoo/hoodoo mumbo jumbo, sending him bloodstained feathers and tossing a diamondback into his car, none of which was going to prevent him from finding Keogh.

As long as Brody lived long enough.

And the way things were going that wasn't a sure thing.

Chapter 26

Brody knew an old, retired PI who lived as a recluse in a bungalow on the fringe of the Mojave Desert. Brody decided he could lie low there. Nobody would look for him in the desert, and he could get rid of the rattlesnake on his backseat.

The hermit's name was Casper Brody.

He was Brody's father. Everyone who knew him—and there weren't many these days—called him Cap.

Some say he got the nickname "Cap" because he never passed up an opportunity to use his gun on criminals. He liked to "cap" them. Others say "Cap" was just a shortened form of "Casper." All Brody knew for sure was that people called his dad Cap. And some of them referred to him as a serial killer.

Brody took the 10 east toward Twenty-nine Palms.

Before he reached the small town he exited the freeway and took a winding dirt road in the desert to his dad's.

He turned onto a dirt driveway that led to a casita with a flat, red-tiled roof in the middle of nowhere. He parked the Mini. The Spanish-styled white-painted stucco casita had all its windows open. The curtains fluttered out the windows in the hot, dry desert wind.

He got out and stretched. His back was hurting from the two-hour drive. The sun beat down on him like a sledgehammer. Seconds after he exited the air-conditioned Mini, he broke into a sweat.

Sweating freely, he walked down the dirt path to the casita's door. He wasn't sweating only because of the heat. Meeting his father made him nervous. They hardly ever saw each other anymore. The old man preferred it that way, as far as Brody could tell.

A wiry seventysomething man with a white beard and thinning white hair stepped out the front door and, squinting through his wire-rimmed spectacles, trained a Mossberg 12-gauge shotgun on him.

Brody froze. "It's me, Dad."

"I'm looking right into the sun," said Cap, "and my eyes aren't what they used to be. Neither are my ears. Tell me your name."

"I'm your son Scott," yelled Brody.

Cap lowered the Mossberg. "Why didn't you say so? Come on in."

He retreated into the hot casita, Brody in tow.

"Why don't you turn on the AC?" said Brody, his face dripping sweat.

"AC? What's that?" said Cap with a laugh.

"You're kidding. You live in the middle of a desert with no AC?"

"I got ten fans on, plus a ceiling fan. Don't you feel them?"

"I feel hot air blowing on me," said Brody, wiping sweat from his brow with the back of his hand, listening to the living room's ceiling fan hum overhead.

"There's no power out here. My genny can't handle an AC. They suck energy like there's no tomorrow."

The living room looked like a pack rat's paradise, cluttered with junk that could have been salvaged from a city dump. A rusted, unplugged refrigerator that didn't work and a broken stove with its heating coils turned vertical stood in the middle of the living room.

"Do you at least have a cold beer?" said Brody.

"I thought you'd never ask. You think I'm a caveman or something?"

Cap returned from the kitchen with two chilled bottles of Corona and handed Brody one.

"What brings you out here?" said Cap. "I haven't seen you in a dog's age."

"I got a snake problem. You know how to dispose of a diamondback?"

"I do it all the time in these parts," said Cap, smiling. "I didn't know you had them in posh West LA."

"It's not in West LA. It's in my car."

"You brought a diamondback here in your car?" said Cap, puzzled.

"Somebody planted it there. Follow me. And bring your shotgun."

Brody led Cap to his Mini. Wondering what was up, Cap followed, Corona in one hand, Mossberg in the other, his wind- and sunburned face furrowed in curiosity.

"Take a look in the backseat," said Brody.

Cap peered through the passenger's-side window into the backseat, where the diamondback's body lay motionless in a loose coil.

"Looks like you already took care of it," said Cap. "It's decapitated."

"Except the head's still alive," said Brody, gazing through the window, trying to no avail to locate the head.

He opened the Mini's door.

The snake head tumbled out, hissing and snapping its jaws, and landed in the dirt.

"Have you ever seen anything like it?" said Brody. "It's not natural."

"I've killed a lot of rattlers in these parts," said Cap, aiming the Mossberg at the hissing head. "I seen diamondbacks that can live for days after being decapitated. And that thing's still poisonous. Step back. The venom in its fangs can kill you."

Brody stepped away from the twisting, biting snake head.

With his grimy suede leather boot Cap kicked the head away from the Mini, drew a bead on the head, and fired. The shotgun blast decimated the head.

"Snakes are like zombies," he said. "You gotta kill their brains or the things go on living."

"I was beginning to think it was cursed."

"Why would you think that?"

"It's a long story."

"You came all the way out here just for me to kill that snake?"

"I need a place where I can hole up for a while. Things are getting too hot in LA."

"Hot? You want hot, you came to the right place."

"You know what I mean."

Cap grunted. "Got cops on your ass? They hate PIs like you and me."

"And somebody else is trying to waste me."

"A tag team match, huh? Even worse," said Cap, and took a long pull on his cold beer.

Brody followed suit and smacked his lips. "Some psycho cult."

Cap nodded. "They're the worst. Remember Manson and his family of drug-addicted loonies?"

"That's why I thought the snake might be cursed. A satanic or voodoo cult is butchering and mutilating victims, scrawling messages in blood on the walls."

"Sick bastards."

Warily, Brody withdrew the diamondback's body out of the backseat and flung it into the desert.

"That thing can't harm you without its head," said Cap.

Brody closed his Mini's door.

He and Cap returned to the casita.

"I doubt you'll want to stay here long," said Cap. "You gotta drink water constantly or you're not gonna make it. You'll die of heat prostration."

"I was under the misconception you had AC."

"That shows how long it's been since you've been out here to visit."

"The last time I was here you didn't seem too happy about seeing me."

Cap heaved a sigh. "I got my reasons."

"Like what?"

Cap sat down on a sofa, laying the Mossberg beside him, and hung his head down. "It's hard to talk about."

Brody sat across from him in the cluttered room on a creaky wooden chair with unbalanced legs, which rocked when he sat on it. Brody stiffened his right leg to absorb his weight as the chair with its short front leg commenced to tip over.

“I’d like to know,” he said, and took a pull on his beer, the droning ceiling fan thrusting hot air down on him.

Chapter 27

"I never wanted you to follow in my steps and get in the PI racket," said Cap, gazing down at the scuffed hardwood floor.

"I chose my own profession, Dad. You didn't force me to do this job."

"I guess I'm not expressing myself very well. I know I taught you the ins and outs of the business, but that's because you were there when I came home and talked about my job at dinner."

"And that's how I got interested in your job."

"That's the thing," he said, raising his head to eye Brody. "That wasn't my intention. I was talking business to your mother Jennifer to unload stuff off my chest. I wasn't talking to you."

"Well, I listened, and I wanted to follow in your footsteps."

Cap shook his head. "But I didn't want you to."

"Why not?"

"It's a lousy business. You're on your own. Nobody to help you. You gotta do everything yourself. It's not like some other business where you got wingmen to help you. You got camaraderie. But not in the PI business. For each assignment you sink or swim on your own."

"What's so wrong with that?"

Cap clutched his forehead. "This business will kill you. It'll treat you like crap and pay out pin money. And it's a dirty business dealing with the scum of society. Plus, every time you're on the job you have to worry about getting shot. I didn't want you to go through what I had to. There are better ways to make a living."

"Like what?"

Cap ran his hand along the back of his neck. "I dunno. I never wanted to tell you what to do with your life. I wanted you to find your own way." He paused. "And not end up like me."

"What's so bad about ending up like you?"

"Look at me. I live alone in a dump," said Cap, gesturing to the living room with his arms. "A desert rat living all alone in a shack waiting to die. I wouldn't recommend it. You oughta get married and settle down, or this is your future."

"You look healthy to me," said Brody, taking in Cap's tanned, leathery face.

Cap stared at Brody. "Appearances can be deceiving."

"What's so awful about living like you?"

Cap made a sound like a fatalistic groan. "It must be in the genes. In your blood. You inherited it from me. I guess you couldn't turn out otherwise."

"We all have to find our own way in life. I never felt like you were pushing me into this line of work."

"I should've tried to push you out of it."

"What's got into you?"

Cap remained silent for a long moment.

"Son, I got the big C. I got one foot in the grave. It's only a matter of time."

"I didn't know. I—"

Cap held his hand up. "I don't want your pity. Spare me. I'm a tough SOB. I'm gonna fight it till I'm gone."

"I know you will."

"But the fact remains, I'm gonna be gone soon."

"Is that what your doctor says?"

"He says the cancer's meta-, uh, metastasized. I hate saying that word. I can't pronounce it. It won't be long."

"Doctors can be wrong."

"I can feel it eating away at my insides. It's my liver."

"You never know how long cancer will take," said Brody, limply, not knowing what to say.

"The point is, I don't want you to end up like me. I let my job take over my life. I didn't have any personal life. Your mother left me, and I don't blame her. Look at me now. I live alone in a shack in the desert. Nobody knows me and nobody's gonna care when I croak. You gotta ask yourself: Is this what you want?"

"I am what I am. I can't be somebody else."

Cap drooped his head. “You’re probably right. You couldn’t have turned out otherwise. My genes were passed down to you. They poisoned you. I didn’t—”

“Didn’t what?”

“Didn’t want you to be like me and get trapped in this miserable job dealing with losers and thugs. You’re gonna see the dark side of life for as long as you live, and never the bright side. Is that what you want?”

“I want—want,” said Brody, struggling to utter the words. “I want to be like you.” He felt his voice break. “I always wanted to be like you. You’re my dad.”

His throat tense, Brody found himself on the verge of tears. He fought them back. His family didn’t show their emotions. They were taught to hold them in check.

Tears welled in Cap’s eyes.

They both sat silent, staring at each other, at a loss for words.

Cap was the first to move. He slugged back his Corona and retreated into the kitchen.

“Don’t tell me I didn’t warn you,” he said, not looking back at Brody. “Genes. It’s in the genes,” he muttered, barely audible. “We’re both cursed.”

Chapter 28

Brody heard a commotion outside.

It sounded like a vehicle approaching.

He peered out the window and spotted a dilapidated brown Ford F-150 pickup tooling down the road toward Cap's bungalow, its tires churning up dust.

"You got guests," he told Cap.

Cap strode out of the kitchen, a fresh bottle of Corona in hand.

"I never get guests," he said, pulling up beside Brody and taking a look out the window. "Who in his right mind would come to this rattrap?"

"They're headed this way."

"I don't know that pickup," said Cap, scowling.

The pickup parked at the base of Cap's driveway and disgorged two men—one pushing thirty with black hair tied in a ponytail and the other, the driver, a head taller, older, with a lantern jaw and chestnut hair cut in a high fade. They both wore jeans and Ts. High Fade's black T said Jason Goes to Hell in red letters with a silk-screen image of Jason brandishing a machete underneath.

High Fade was armed with a Ruger 9 mil pistol that he lifted out of his shoulder rig with his left hand.

"You know them?" Cap asked Brody.

"No."

Cap was already lunging to the sofa. He secured his Mossberg and returned to the window, staying out of sight of the intruders.

Brody leaned down, whipped his SIG from his ankle holster, and straightened up.

Ponytail withdrew a Benelli 12-gauge M4 tactical shotgun from a rack on the passenger's-side door of the F-150.

"Are you in some kind of trouble?" Cap asked Brody.

"A sniper tried to whack me in LA."

"One of these goons?"

"I didn't get a look at him."

Ponytail and High Fade strode down the driveway to the bungalow.

Cap flung open the door, stalked outside, and trained his Mossberg on the two men. "Hold it, you two."

"We got no beef with you, old man," said High Fade.

"Then drop the artillery," said Cap, squinting in the glaring sun.

"We're looking for a big guy over six feet. We think that's his car parked in your driveway. Name of Brody."

SIG in hand, Brody stepped out and stood beside Cap.

"You sure you can hit anything with your bad eyesight," Brody whispered out of the side of his mouth to Cap.

"I don't need twenty-twenty vision to hit a target with this 12-gauge," said Cap, his glasses fogging thanks to the sweat on his face.

Ponytail swung his Benelli's barrel toward Brody and fired.

Brody returned fire, blowing the back of Ponytail's skull off, accompanied by bloody clumps of brain. Ponytail collapsed.

The Benelli's blast blew a hole in the bungalow's front stucco wall beside the doorjamb.

Cap eyed the damage then irately discharged his Mossberg at High Fade, who rolled to the ground at the same time, anticipating the shot and dodging it. High Fade continued to roll on the ground, keeping his Ruger trained on Brody and firing. The constant rolling motion threw off his aim, dizzying him.

Brody dove to the ground. He aimed his SIG at High Fade, who kept rolling, making for a difficult target. Not only that, High Fade's rolling was kicking up clouds of dust obscuring his exact position.

"Who are you?" cried Brody. "Who sent you?"

High Fade's only answer was another bullet sent whistling in Brody's direction.

Brody fired back into the dust cloud.

Cap fired his 12-gauge.

High Fade stopped rolling.

The dust settled around his motionless body, revealing his buckshot-shattered, unrecognizable face, smeared with blood and dirt.

Chapter 29

Brody got to his feet and approached the two goons, his SIG at the ready in case either was still alive. Crouching beside them he felt for pulses in their wrists and found none.

He searched High Fade's trouser pockets to find out who the goon was. His pockets were empty. He didn't even have a pocket comb, let alone house keys or a wallet with ID in it. The same with Ponytail.

"Who are they?" said Cap, coming up behind Brody.

Brody shook his head at a loss. "No ID. Neither one has a wallet."

"They're hit men. They're the only ones I know that travel without ID, except for a spy. You got a spy on your tail?"

"I don't know why spies would want to waste me."

"Then they're hit men."

"Not very good ones."

"They weren't expecting you to be armed. Somebody put out a contract on you."

"It would explain the sniper that tried to pop me in LA."

"Any idea who would take out a contract on you?"

"The only thing I can think of is, it must have to do with the case I'm working on."

"You're rattling somebody's cage. That's for sure."

"*They're* not gonna tell me who," said Brody, leering at the two corpses at his feet.

"You're bleeding," said Cap, eying Brody's left shoulder. "You better check in at a hospital."

"Just a flesh wound. A slug nicked me."

Cap returned to his bungalow and inspected the fist-sized hole left by the Benelli's blast in the front wall of his bungalow.

"Sorry about your house," said Brody, remarking the damage.

Cap sighed noisily. "You can never have too much ventilation when you live in the desert."

"Without an AC."

Cap crouched in front of the hole and peered into his living room.

"What are we gonna do with the stiffs?" said Brody.

"I'll take care of them. I'll bury them where even a coyote can't find them."

"They're *my* enemies. I'm the one that should take care of their—"

Cap waved dismissively. "No problem. I'll lose their pickup, too. You need to get outa here."

"Not before I help you dispose of the bodies."

Cap shook his head no. "That ain't gonna fly. When these turkeys don't report back to their leader, he's gonna send reinforcements out looking for them. You need to beat it."

"I'm not gonna leave you alone to fight them."

"It's not me they want. It's you. Nobody wants a piece of an old codger like me."

"Are you sure?"

"Nobody's gonna even know anybody bought a bullet here after I clean up."

"I'll have to find another hideout."

"You do that."

Brody turned to leave, but changed his mind. "Do you have any artillery here?"

A broad grin cut Cap's face exposing a gap where one of his two front teeth used to be. "Do I? And how. Let's step inside."

Cap showed Brody inside.

"Do you have any submachine pistols, like an HK or a B&T MP9?"

"I got an HK MP5," said Cap, walking to an armoire in his hallway. "That's some serious firepower."

"I may be dealing with an entire cult that wants me dead. Voodoo-worshiping SS Nazis, as far as I can tell."

"Voodoo-worshiping SS Nazis?"

"The SS was into the occult from what I've researched on the Internet. It was run like a secret cult by Himmler."

"I'll believe anything in LA. The land of fruits and nuts gets weirder by the minute."

"That's an educated guess. I don't really know what I'm dealing with. All I know is there's a sadistic serial killer running amok in LA."

Cap pulled an HK MP5 from the closet and cradled it in his arms. "How's this beauty?"

"Nice," said Brody, accepting the MP5.

"Your wish is my command. I also happen to have a B&T MP9," said Cap, withdrawing an MP9 from the closet.

"Magazines?"

"What good's a piece without magazines?"

Cap slid a pasteboard carton of thirty-round magazines along the floor out of the closet.

"I owe you," said Brody.

"I almost wish I was going with you," said Cap, eying his hardware with a smile on his chapped lips.

"I don't want you mixed up in this. You're retired. I should never have come here. I led them right to you."

Brody felt like kicking himself. He hadn't been thinking straight when he had come here. He hadn't suspected that anyone was tailing him. Ponytail and High Fade had been good at hanging a tail but lousy at executing a hit.

"Don't worry about it," said Cap. "I'm not gonna tell anyone about this. Nobody'll ever know, other than me and you. I suggest you get a move on it, while I dispose of the stiffs."

Cap made a beeline for the goons' pickup.

Brody noticed Cap had a slight limp to his gait. Maybe Cap's knees were bothering him, but he never let on, decided Brody. Cap was like that. Their whole family was like that, never confiding in each other, never admitting they were in pain, hiding their feelings like feelings were a sign of weakness and needed to be attacked like chum by a swarm of starving piranhas.

Brody helped Cap load the stiffs into the back of the pickup.

Brody opened the pickup's passenger's-side door, opened the glove compartment, and rooted through it, searching for ID. There wasn't anything helpful. No car registration. Only an ancient beat-up, foxed map that had been folded the wrong way too many times. Brody choked on the dust that flew off the map.

"Any ID?" said Cap.

"Nothing."

"I'll torch the pickup when I'm done dumping bodies so nobody can lift any prints off it."

Brody picked up the dead diamondback's body from the ground and tossed it into the back of the pickup with the corpses.

"Maybe those two goons were the ones who planted the snake in your car," said Cap.

"They can have it back."

Brody repaired to the casita, collected the two submachine pistols and their magazines from Cap's bungalow, and transported them to his Mini.

Chapter 30

Wearing a pink dress Olivia Martin sat in a small locked room, not much bigger than a closet, with her stuffed grey Eeyore donkey that had a detachable pink tail. Gloomy Eeyore was always losing his tail. Which was why he had a metal button for the top of his tail where you could snap it onto his backside.

Olivia nervously snapped the tail on and off Eeyore. She wanted to get out of here, but the door wouldn't open. She had brought Eeyore to school with her for show-and-tell. She was glad he was with her. Otherwise, she would be all alone locked in this prison.

The room was sparsely furnished. It didn't even have a window. A small square wooden table stood in the middle of the room with a plastic glass full of water standing on the tabletop.

The twentysomething man that had taken her here had put the glass there and said she could drink the water when she was thirsty.

Olivia didn't know if she would ever drink the water. She didn't like the man. She should never have gotten in his car with him. But he had said Mom had sent him to pick her up from school. Maybe he had put poison in the glass of water. She didn't believe anything he said anymore—not after he had locked her up.

Dressed in a suit, clean-shaven, he had seemed like a nice man at first. He even smelled of cologne. She trusted men in suits. They seemed official like somebody you could believe. She believed him about Mom's sending him to drive her home.

She had realized something was wrong when she didn't recognize the roads he was driving on. None of the roads looked familiar. She had become scared and told him he was going the wrong way. Her heart in her mouth, she had dug her clenched fingers into Eeyore's belly while she was riding in the man's car.

Engrossed in driving, the man had ignored her.

At least she had Eeyore with her. Eeyore was her best friend. Without him in the car, she thought she would have passed out in fear.

Her pulse raced as the stranger had continued to drive her in the wrong direction. She had no idea where he was taking her.

He had ended up locking her in this room.

The air felt hot and stuffy in here.

She hoped her mother was on her way to free her.

She was getting thirsty. Maybe she should drink the water. She didn't want to die of thirst.

She buttoned Eeyore's tail onto his backside.

She wished Eeyore could talk. She would ask him what to do.

Chapter 31

Evelyn sat at a table on the patio at Barney's Burgers patio at the Brentwood Country Mart, which had a bucolic ambiance with a maroon-painted barn-shaped building as its main attraction.

Nursing a Coke she sat across from a thirtyish, pudgy, schlubby man with dark stubble mantling his face and dark wavy hair trailing over his prominent ears. Dressed in jeans, an untucked grey polo, and a safari jacket, looking like a B-movie director, he chewed gum and eyed her with an expressionless countenance.

"I need you to do a job for me," she said.

He removed the gum from his mouth, stuck it under the tabletop, and sipped iced root beer through a plastic straw in a paper cup. He belched.

"Root beer coming up," he said, rubbing his stomach.

"I don't have all day."

"What is the nature of the job?" he said.

She paused. She didn't like spelling it out for him, especially when other patrons on the patio might overhear her.

"Your specialty," she said.

"How did you get my name?"

"I got it on the Dark Web along with your phone number. Bill Diaz."

"Then you know what I do?"

Evelyn hesitated.

"Right," she said, determined to go through with it.

"You want me to take someone out?"

Evelyn nodded yes. "Could you give me a resume first? I want to make sure you're the right man for the job."

"I done jobs for the Mexican drug cartels like Jalisco New Generation and Sinaloa. And also for Black Cube, and the CIA."

"Black Cube?"

"It's an Israeli private spy agency run by Mossad agents. The Cube works for law firms and billion-dollar companies that need their services."

"Law firms use people like you?" said Evelyn in surprise.

"Everybody with money does. Don't look so shocked. Having money is a dirty business. People will do anything to get it and keep it. You weren't born yesterday."

"How do you fit in with Black Cube?"

"They hire independent contractors like me when it suits them."

"Do you have proof of this?"

"Impossible. They'll deny they know anything about me. The CIA and Black Cube don't leave paper trails of hiring guys like me. Everything's off the books. It's the nature of the beast. You'll have to take my word for it."

What he was saying made sense, decided Evelyn.

She withdrew a photo out of her Michael Kors olive leather designer purse and slid it across the white metal tabletop to Diaz.

"This is the man that needs to be dealt with," she said.

Diaz eyed the photo. He searched her face.

"Are you sure you want this done?" he said.

"Positive. He is endangering my daughter's life. He must be taken care of."

Evelyn couldn't think of anything else she could do. She was down to the final option. Whatever it took to save Olivia.

"I don't come cheap," said Diaz.

"How much?"

"A hundred grand. I'm jeopardizing my life doing this for you."

Evelyn drummed a rapid tattoo on the tabletop. She saw no other way to save Olivia. The kidnapers had forced her hand. She had brought this on herself because she had felt compelled to find Tyler and had hired Brody, who refused to give up looking for him.

The idea of killing Brody terrified her, but the idea of Olivia's death at the hands of kidnapers terrified her even more. If she had to choose between saving the two, she would choose

Olivia. Brody's refusal to put the kibosh on his hunt for Tyler was like putting a loaded gun to Olivia's head. The only way Evelyn could think of to get Brody to stop was with Diaz's help.

"It must be done," she said, her face drawn.

"I need half up front. Cash."

"I thought you guys took Bitcoin."

"Not to put too fine a point on it, the value of Bitcoin fluctuates too much and not everybody takes it. No crypto. I want cash."

"I can get it."

"When you get it, call me, and we'll arrange a drop where I can pick it up," said Diaz, rising from his seat, root beer in hand. "Then I'll do the job."

He swigged root beer and belched.

"I'll arrange a meet with Brody and you can take care of him there," said Evelyn.

"No problem. He'll never bother you again."

Evelyn chewed her fingernail coated with lime polish. She wished there was another way. The thought of what she was about to have done terrified her.

Chapter 32

Brody decided he needed a different car if he wanted to fly under the radar. The two hit men he and Cap had killed knew what car he drove. The cops knew his car, too. His Mini also had bullet holes in it, which attracted attention.

He drove the Mini to LAX, parked it in the long-term parking lot, and rented a car at the airport with a credit card for a shell company he had created in his line of work to cover his trail.

He rented a black Toyota Camry, a popular car that nobody would pay attention to, drove back to the long-term parking lot, and, making sure no one was watching, unloaded Cap's ordinance from the Mini, and transferred it to the Camry's trunk.

His cell phone vibrated in his trouser pocket. He took the call.

"Have you stopped looking for Tyler, yet?" said Evelyn.

"I can't do that. Somebody tried to blow me away. And they'll try again."

"Then stop your search."

"I have to find out who's trying to waste me and stop them. Or next time they might succeed."

"The person who tried to shoot you might be working for Olivia's kidnapers. Leave him alone, or they'll take it out on Olivia."

"They're gonna come again for me. I can't let that happen. I have to find them and deal with them."

"Drop the case. I fired you. Go home, and stop wasting your time."

"I wouldn't call saving my life wasting my time."

"Is that all you care about? Yourself? What about poor Olivia? She's just a child."

He had no desire to put Olivia's life at risk.

"Whoever's behind these attacks on me kidnaped Olivia," he said. "I'm convinced of it. When I get my hands on the guy, he'll free Olivia."

"What if he refuses?"

"You know the movie *The Godfather*? I'll make him an offer he can't refuse."

"What if you don't catch him?"

"I'll get him. It's my job."

"It's not your job. I fired you."

"You should reconsider or Keogh could end up dead."

Evelyn paused a long moment.

Brody was getting ready to hang up when he heard her voice resume.

"We need to meet," she said.

"If you fired me, what's the point?"

She paused. "We need to talk before I make my final decision."

Her voice sounded strained.

"Are you OK?" he said. "Is somebody with you? Are you able to talk freely?"

"I'm fine. We must talk."

"Are you being coerced?"

"Not at all. We need to meet."

"I don't understand."

"I have information I need to tell you. I can't talk about it on the phone. Our phones may be compromised."

Brody was suspicious. First she told him he was fired, and now she wanted to give him information. It didn't make sense.

"What kind of information?" he said.

Another pause.

"The kidnapers told me they will kill Olivia in two hours, unless I can prove you've stopped your search for Tyler."

Brody couldn't let them murder Olivia. It would be on his conscience for the rest of his life if she died thanks to him.

"How can I help?"

"I found out where they're holding her," she said.

"I'm listening."

"Not over the phone."

She told him where and when to meet her. He agreed. He was on the verge of telling her he would be driving a different car, but decided it served no purpose for her to know.

They hung up.

He was still bothered by the tension in her voice, but then again why wouldn't she be tense? Kidnapers were threatening to murder her daughter.

Nevertheless, he got the impression she was talking to him against her will, which was why he had thought someone might be holding a gun to her head. He shook it off. If they had her daughter, why would they kidnap her, too? It would be pointless. Using her daughter as leverage was all they needed.

As soon as Evelyn told him where they were holding Olivia, Brody would save the girl.

He wondered if the same people had also kidnaped Keogh. If so, why hadn't they demanded a ransom yet? Or had they already killed Keogh? But then why kidnap his sister's daughter?

Finished loading his ironware and ammo into the Camry, he climbed into the driver's seat, fired the engine, and drove out of the parking lot. He had a lot on his mind.

Chapter 33

Brody drove to the address Evelyn had given him over the phone. She said she was going to meet him on Ocean Avenue across from the park perched on the bluffs that overlooked the ocean.

When he arrived at the address, he thought he must have heard the address over the phone incorrectly. It was a construction site surrounded by plywood hoarding. He decided he better check out the address to see if she was there.

He parked at a meter that skirted the east end of the park, got out of the Camry, and crossed the street to the construction site. He checked the address painted on the curb to make sure it was the same one Evelyn had given him. It was.

He didn't see her anywhere. Maybe she was waiting for him inside the construction site. He walked on the sidewalk along the hoarding seeking an entrance. He rounded the corner and found a door with a padlock on the latch. The padlock was open.

He didn't know why Evelyn would want to meet him at a construction site. Maybe she chose it for its privacy. Nobody would be able to overhear their conversation.

He opened the plywood door, which creaked on its hinges.

Half of the construction site had a ten-foot-deep hole excavated in it. Concrete reinforced with rebar lay on part of the bottom of the hole. A cement mixer stood at the rim. Ten feet away from the cement mixer was a pile of dirt with a yellow bulldozer parked behind it. Beyond the bulldozer lay a stack of rebar.

He saw no sign of Evelyn.

He consulted his wristwatch. Maybe she was late, he decided.

"Evelyn," he called out, surveying the area.

Sporting Oakley wraparound shades, a man in a safari jacket stepped out from behind the cement mixer and trained a silenced pistol on him. Brody leapt into the hole, as the gun fired.

The bullet missed its mark.

Brody landed on his feet in the unpaved dirt and rolled over, which irritated his shoulder that had been grazed by one of High Fade's bullets. Blood commenced seeping from his wound. Standing up he whipped out his SIG from his ankle holster and watched the top of the excavation pit for the shooter to show his face. He caught sight of the guy stalking along the rim of the pit, gun in hand, searching for him.

Brody fired at the guy.

Startled, the shooter pulled away from the pit's rim out of view.

Heart pounding, Brody kept his eyes peeled on the pit's rim waiting for the shooter to reappear. Twenty feet from where he had stood over the pit he reappeared and drew a bead on Brody. Brody fired before the guy got his shot off.

The shooter reeled backward, windmilling his arms.

Brody didn't know whether his bullet had hit home, or the shooter had lurched backward in surprise. Brody kept a wary eye on the rim of the pit, not knowing where the gunman would appear next. Adrenaline coursed through Brody's body. He had no cover on the bottom of the pit. The only way he could survive was by shooting at the gunman before the guy could squeeze off a shot at him. Gun in hand, Brody had to keep cutting his eyes around the pit's rim making sure the shooter didn't show his face and start firing.

Brody surveyed the hole's rim. He didn't see the shooter. Could he have killed the guy? Brody was doubtful. He hadn't taken a good aim at the guy. Concerned about being shot he had fired at the shooter as soon as he had spotted him on the hole's rim without taking steady aim.

If the guy was still up there, why wasn't he resuming his attack? wondered Brody.

He considered scaling the dirt stairway that led to the pit's lip. The problem was, he would be a sitting duck if he climbed out of the pit and the shooter was still alive waiting to blow him away.

Brody started when he heard a noise above him. An engine was firing. It was the bulldozer. He realized his peril. He looked up.

At that moment, a pile of dirt and loam poured down from the top of the pit onto him. He spat out the dirt that cascaded onto his face. He had to get out of here before the dirt buried him alive.

The dozer retreated from the hole to retrieve more dirt.

Brody scrabbled out of the mound of dirt enveloping him.

SIG in hand, he mounted the dirt steps two at a time, and came up firing at the dozer's cabin. The shooter hadn't expected him to stage a counterattack and wasn't holding his piece. Instead, his hands were occupied operating the shifter and the steering wheel. Brody squeezed off three rounds, his rapid ascension of the steps throwing off his aim. Even so, one of the slugs found its mark in the shooter's throat.

The shooter cried out in pain and clutched his throat that spouted bright vermilion arterial spray. His artery severed, he would bleed out in seconds, Brody knew. Brody reached the top of the pit and lowered his pistol.

A flurry of questions pestered him. Who was this guy? And where was Evelyn? Had the shooter taken her out before ambushing him? Had Olivia's kidnapers changed their minds and decided to off Evelyn?

Brody cut his eyes back and forth across the site. He didn't see Evelyn's corpse anywhere.

The bulldozer's racketing engine continued to idle.

Somebody might have heard the gunshots. Brody's SIG wasn't silenced like the assailant's. He better beat it. He wanted to check the shooter's ID, since he had no idea who the guy was. He didn't think there would be time. Cops could show any second. He wanted to be long gone when they did.

He holstered his SIG and brushed the dirt off his clothes, face, and hair with his hands. He didn't want to look a mess and arouse suspicion when he emerged from behind the hoarding.

Chapter 34

Eeyore in one hand, Olivia knocked on the door of her locked closet with the other.

Fiddling with her blonde pigtails she waited.

No response.

She resumed knocking. She wasn't going to stop till someone opened the door.

The door swung open at last.

"What do you want?" said the suit, scowling down at her. "Stop making so much noise."

"I have to go to the bathroom."

The suit acquiesced, but didn't look happy about it. "All right. Make it snappy."

He let Olivia out of the poky room.

"On the right at the end of the hall," he said, walking with her.

He had loosened his tie since she had last seen him, and his jacket hung open.

She entered the bathroom and shut the door behind her.

"Leave the door open," he said, flinging it open, all but striking Olivia.

"I can't go with you watching me," she said, cowering in fear.

"Whatever. Leave it ajar."

She left the door open an inch, nervous he would fling it open again and hit her.

"Get on with it," he said.

She searched the bathroom for a window. All she could find was a tiny rectangular window that she couldn't even fit her head through. The frosted glass pane was opened about an inch at its base to allow for ventilation.

She wondered if there was some way she could signal through the window for help.

She stepped on the porcelain bathtub's rim to reach the window, stuck her hand outside, and waved. She couldn't yell without the suit hearing her. Waving wouldn't do any good, she decided. If there was anyone out there, they would think she was just waving hello.

Fiddling with Eeyore in her hand, she came up with an idea. She detached his pink tail and waved it outside the window, hoping someone would see it and come to her aid.

"Get a move on it," said the suit, "or I'm dragging you out of there by your pigtails."

Trembling with fear Olivia wedged Eeyore's tail into the upper corner of the window between the sash and the jamb, leapt down from the bathtub's rim, used the toilet, and flushed it.

She was washing her hands, with Eeyore thrust under her arm, when the suit flung the door open, slamming it against the side of the toilet and startling her. The door quivered on its hinges.

"You're outa here," he said, snatching her wrist and dragging her into the hallway.

"Ow. You're hurting me," she said.

"Shut up."

He tossed her unceremoniously into her room and locked the door behind her.

She massaged her sore wrist where he had grabbed her. She hoped someone would catch sight of Eeyore's tail hanging from the window and rescue her. They would understand that Eeyore would never go anywhere without his tail unless he was in extreme danger, and they would investigate.

She breathed easier. She had hope now.

Chapter 35

Brody drove his rental away from the construction site, parked on the side of the road, produced his cell phone, and called Evelyn.

"Hello," she said.

"Are you OK?"

"What?" she said in surprise.

"It's me Brody. Are you OK?"

"Oh, uh—yeah."

"Why weren't you at the construction site?"

"Oh, uh—uh—I couldn't get my car to start. I think I need a new battery. It doesn't always work."

"Why didn't you call me?"

"I—I—uh, I was getting ready to just as you phoned me."

"It's lucky you weren't there. Your janky battery might've saved your life."

"What do you mean?"

"A shooter bushwhacked me. He would've iced you if you had been there with me."

"Ohmigod. How could this have happened?"

Brody chewed it over. "Your phone must be tapped. He heard you give me the address and went there to ambush us."

"That's horrible. I was afraid it might be tapped." She paused. "What happened to the ambusher?"

"I had to take care of him."

Evelyn sighed. "What did he say?"

"You don't understand."

"What?"

"He didn't have a chance to say anything. I had to take him out."

"Oh."

"It couldn't be helped. It was either him or me. I wanted to question him to see who sent him, but he was already dead."

"Good."

"Good?"

"Good that you killed him, instead of the other way around."

"My slug hit his carotid artery. He bled out fast."

"Is he working with the kidnapers, do you think?"

"Could be. If so, they're gonna be mad and take it out on Olivia."

"Oh no."

"Maybe it wasn't them. Maybe it was the cult that's murdering the Mensa members."

"Aren't they the same?"

"Probably. Otherwise, why don't the kidnapers want us to find Keogh? If they're the ones that whacked or kidnaped him, they wouldn't want me to find him."

"So they tried to kill you to prevent you from finding him."

"A pair of hit men tried to blow me away in the desert, too."

"This is terrible. It shows how desperate these thugs are."

"We can't let them intimidate us."

"The best thing for you to do is to call off your search for Tyler, like I told you before. And then the kidnapers will free Olivia."

"They're not gonna stop gunning for me till I'm dead. I can't go back to my apartment."

"Where are you staying?"

"I'll let you know when I know. What did you want to tell me at the construction site?"

Evelyn hung fire. "It's not safe to tell you over the phone."

"One other thing. Why did you pick a construction site for a meet?"

"Because nobody would be there."

"And nobody would see a shooting."

"What? I didn't want anyone to overhear us."

"Nothing. I was talking to myself."

"What are you going to do next?"

"I'm wondering if this experiment Keogh took part in has anything to do with his disappearance."

"You can't let Olivia die," she said, beside herself, as he was hanging up. "Stop looking for him," she screamed.

The kidnapers would lose their leverage if they killed Olivia, decided Brody. He didn't think they would kill her—yet. Still, he could be wrong. He was dealing with dope-addled maniacs who worshiped a snake god. They were capable of anything. He couldn't trust them to act rationally. They might indeed kill Olivia—and for no reason.

He didn't want a child's life depending on what he did. The thing was, Keogh's life might also hang in the balance. And his life wasn't being used as a bargaining chip, which gave no one a good reason to keep him alive.

For these reasons, Brody figured Keogh's life was in more imminent danger than Olivia's. On the other hand, it could be true Keogh was already dead. Brody decided he had to act on the assumption Keogh was still alive.

Brody would have to continue his search for Keogh without tipping off the kidnapers about it, who would kill Olivia if they found out. It would help if he knew who the kidnapers were.

An all-news station was broadcasting on the car radio, as he determined his next move.

" . . . is wanted as a suspect in the torture and murder of Eugene Frantangello," said the newscaster.

Brody had been too absorbed in thought to pick up on the suspect's name. So the cops had found Frantangello's body, he decided.

"If anyone has seen the suspect Scott Brody, notify the police immediately," said the newscaster. "He is considered armed and dangerous."

Brody stiffened in his seat.

He couldn't say he was surprised. He had expected as much from Detective Macready. A neighbor must have spotted Brody at Frantangello's house. Which meant Brody could be placed at all three Mensa murder scenes.

Being a wanted man made his job considerably more difficult.

Chapter 36

Brody drove to an Internet café on the Third Street Promenade and parked in a nearby public parking garage where the first hour and a half were free.

He ordered a coffee and a glazed donut at the café and used one of their computers to access the Mensa website's LA board of directors. He selected Xochitl Cordova's phone number, dug his cell out of his trouser pocket, punched out her number, and placed the call.

It went straight to voicemail.

He decided to visit her in person rather than leave a message, having no idea when she would return the call, and he was in a bit of a hurry, considering Olivia's and, possibly, Keogh's lives were at stake.

He had questions for her, specifically about the experiment Keogh had taken part in at Stanford. Brody couldn't find any information on the experiment Val had told him about. He also wanted to know if Cordova knew about Keogh's connection to voodoo and satanic cults.

He drove to Pacific Palisades and arrived at her ranch house, a single-story L-shaped affair with a slightly pitched brown-shingled roof and a large picture window. A row of ethereal jacaranda trees swayed in the wind in the front yard like lavender wraiths.

He couldn't find a parking space on the side of the street, which had preferential parking. He took a chance and parked behind Cordova's silver Lincoln Navigator SUV in her drive. It didn't look like she was getting ready to leave anytime soon.

He strode to her door and rang the bell.

Nobody answered.

He tried again several times with the same results.

He tried the doorknob. It was locked.

He was getting a bad feeling about the place. With the three other Mensa members' murders on his mind, he found his way to the back door and knocked twice.

"Hello?" he called. "Mrs. Cordova?"

Nothing.

He twisted the doorknob. It gave. Nudging open the door he entered the kitchen with an island in the middle of it. He thought he heard movement in the house. He wasn't sure where it was coming from.

He stole across the kitchen's black and white checked linoleum floor to the living room and heard another sound—a dripping sound, like drops of water from a leaky tap.

Inside the living room he saw it wasn't a tap dripping. It was a body hanging upside down from a rope attached to a light fixture and tied around its ankles with its throat slit, leaking what little blood remained in the corpse, aided by gravity's pull. A huge, widening carmine puddle had formed on the hardwood floor under the corpse's black hair, whose bloody tresses hung down to the floor like a curtain.

It was Xochitl Cordova's body. Her scarlet skirt was hanging upside down over her chest, exposing her undergarments.

He started as he heard movement, the same movement he had heard when he was entering the kitchen. He looked in the direction of the sound.

A black snake was slithering across open newspapers scattered on the floor in the corner of the living room. To the right of the snake he saw writing in blood scrawled on the white stucco wall. Li Grande Zombi. Acid Is Groovy.

Yet another murder perpetrated by the cult, decided Brody.

He didn't know if the snake was poisonous.

He whipped out his SIG from his ankle holster. He didn't want to fire at the snake because the gunshot would draw the attention of neighbors. As long as the snake stayed away from him, he wouldn't shoot it. He wasn't planning on hanging around. Macready could be on his way here even now.

He heard a floorboard creaking behind him. Gun in hand, he wheeled around.

Tess was standing there, her hand gripping a pistol, her eyes glued to the macabre spectacle of Cordova's corpse suspended from its ankles.

"You again," he said.

"What are you doing here?"

"I have questions for Cordova."

"What questions?"

"None of your business."

"You're gonna be like that, huh?"

"What are *you* doing here?"

"I came inside because I thought you might need help," she said.

Seeing no threat from an assailant, she lowered her gun.

"I don't need help," he said, lowering his SIG.

"You have a knack for finding the murder victims of the serial killer."

"Are you following me? How did you know I changed cars?" he said, puzzled.

"Actually, I had this place staked out. I was waiting for Cordova to return so I could question her. I wasn't able to reach her by phone. I didn't realize she was tied up."

Brody gave her a look. "What did you want to talk to her about?"

"Now it's my turn. None of your business."

"I thought you wanted to help me."

"My client's confidentiality comes first. You, of all people, should know that."

"How do I know you didn't kill her? You admit you were here before me."

"No motive. I never met her before. I'm a PI doing my job."

Brody eyed Cordova hanging from her feet. "What's this remind you of?"

"Uh, Mussolini after the partisans machine-gunned him to death?"

Brody hiked his eyebrows. It was something he hadn't thought of.

"I was thinking of the hanged-man tarot card," he said. "Tarot cards would fit in with voodoo and belief in the supernatural."

"And then there's that snake," said Tess, glancing at the snake that had calmed down and had stopped moving for the moment. "The snake god."

"And the writing on the wall. Li Grande Zombi." Brody paused. "Do you believe in voodoo?"

"No. Just facts. Hard facts. I don't believe in invoking any occult forces to help me because they never do. It's a waste of time."

"Do you think your client wanted Cordova dead?"

She stared at him. "I don't sit in judgment of my clients."

"In other words, you don't want to know."

"Knowing too much can get you killed."

"So can knowing too little."

Brody saw a white powder in Cordova's brunette hair. He approached the corpse, pinched a dab of the powder between his thumb and forefinger, and sniffed it.

"What is it?" said Tess.

"I don't know," said Brody, and wiped the powder off his fingers onto his trouser leg. "It has no smell."

"Maybe the killer is a cokehead. He snorts flake while he commits murder."

"It doesn't smell like flake. Flake has a metallic odor."

"Maybe the killer is a junkie. He snorts horse."

"It could be pure skag. Diluted skag has a vinegary odor."

"We're overlooking the obvious," said Tess, eyeballing the graffiti-streaked wall. "Maybe it's acid like the graffiti says."

Brody took in the murder scene and nodded. "This looks like something out of an acid head's nightmare, worthy of the Manson Family. And LSD is odorless," said Brody, rubbing his fingers that had touched the powder.

"Maybe they need to be hopped up on acid to commit these murders. Do you think there's more than one killer?"

"If it's a cult, there could be several killers."

"Wonderful."

"I can't stay here. The cops have a BOLO out on me as a suspect in these killings."

Brody strode to the back door. He would have liked to search the place to see if Cordova had any files on Keogh or any documents concerning him. But he couldn't afford getting caught here by the cops. He had to stay one step ahead of them.

"Do you have any idea who the perp is?" said Tess.

"None. I haven't encountered any cult members in my investigation."

Tess strode after him. "I can't afford to be found here either."

They both exited through the back door to avoid attracting the attention of nosy neighbors.

"I still say we should pool our forces so we can find the killer faster," said Tess.

"That's not gonna happen till you tell me who you're working for."

"You know I can't do that."

"Can't you make an exception?"

"Not when it violates my code. Clients' names are sacrosanct."

"Then toodle-oo. I'll be seeing you."

Brody dashed into the bushes. He didn't want her to follow him and find out what kind of car he was driving or she would start tailing him again.

Chapter 37

Brody drove his rental out of Cordova's neighborhood and pulled into a deserted alley so he could figure out his next move without being disturbed.

He wanted to know more about the experiment Keogh had been involved in. Val had said it had made Keogh more arrogant. She was the only one who knew about it, as far as he could determine. He wanted to question her further, but they had had a falling-out.

He dredged his cell phone out of his trouser pocket and called her.

"OK," he said.

"Who is this?" she said.

"Me. Brody."

"OK what?" she said, nettled.

"I accept your offer of employment to find Keogh."

"I don't get it," she said, suspiciously. "You said you already had a client. Is this some kind of scam?"

"My other client fired me. I can work for you."

"So I'm not good enough, huh? I have to take backseat to this other—whatever—client. Is that it? Maybe if you come crawling to me on your knees."

"You're not making this any easier."

"Well, I'm mad at you. Why should I hire you? You shouldn't have refused me the first time."

"Wait a minute. I couldn't help it if I had a prior job."

"You should've quit it and taken my offer when I gave you the chance. I'm somebody who counts. You don't pass up an opportunity to work for me. That's not how it works. Pass me over and you'll regret it."

Brody remembered why he didn't want to work for Val. She was impossible to get along with. He felt himself becoming angry. He told himself to calm down.

"In retrospect, you're probably right," he said, eating crow. "I want to work for you and find Keogh."

He didn't want to work for her. What he wanted was to ask her more questions about the experiment. He figured working for her would make her more cooperative.

"Hmm. I guess I could stand hiring you," she said, "though I'm not in the habit of giving second chances. I never ask twice. I rarely ask even once. You don't know how lucky you are I asked you the first time."

He was trying to be diplomatic, but with Val it was impossible. He felt too tired to argue with her. The adrenaline high from hiding from the cops, shooting it out with two hit men at his dad's followed by another shoot-out with the ambusher at the construction site was wearing him out. He needed to unwind.

"Great," he said, his voice faltering. "I need to ask you about that . . . that experiment Keogh was . . . in. I need . . . ," he tailed off.

He yawned. He felt exhausted. He hadn't eaten since breakfast.

His jaw hung open. He nodded off, dropping his cell into the foot well.

"I can't hear you," said Val. "You'll have to speak up."

Chapter 38

Li Grande Zombi. Brody saw the writing on the wall.

The blood in the scrawled words was swelling, filling the wall, turning the entire wall carmine then pouring into Cordova's living room filling it with blood. Sloshing around, it streamed in torrents it was gushing in so fast, like the blood in the movie *The Shining* gushing out of the opening elevator doors of the Overlook Hotel and flooding the lobby, crashing against the sides of the room in waves.

He had to get out of the house before he drowned. He slogged through the foot-high, rising blood to the front door, pants soaked, his drenched shoes squelching. He tried the doorknob with his blood-soaked hand.

The door wouldn't open.

He saw a black water moccasin slithering through the blood. It would kill him if it bit him. It could swim fast through the blood, much faster than he could walk. He wouldn't stand a chance if it decided to attack. There was another one sidewinding behind it. There could be a dozen more submerged in the blood, for all he knew. It didn't bear thinking about.

The pouring blood continued to flood the room, thundering like a cataract. Yet he had no idea where it was coming from. It had started with the blood dripping from the scrawls on the wall, but then it had flooded in unseen at an astounding rate, its ingress slowed only by the rising level of blood impeding it.

His arms and legs were vibrating.

Glancing down at his right arm he saw something bulging under his skin, like a vein, but it was slithering. A snake. A snake was inside him corkscrewing through his body trying to crawl out from underneath his skin. There was one in his left arm, too, he saw. And in his thighs. He felt his thighs throbbing. There were snakes writhing in his thighs coiling around his femurs, sending screeching pain knifing through his body.

His body was infested with snakes undulating through his internal organs, he realized in horror. He had to get the serpents out of him.

Teeming with snakes, his legs turned to rubber. He could barely trudge through the rising pool of blood. A Day-Glo green mamba swam past him, slithering through the blood. Brody froze to avoid being bitten. He could have sworn he saw the mamba wink at him. He recoiled in horror.

Snakes everywhere. Around him. Inside him.

What if the snakes were inside his brain? It felt like they were coiling through his brain, even now, gouging grooves in it, building a nest in it for them to lay their eggs and raise their offspring.

His ear itched. Was a snake trying to crawl out of his ear? He couldn't stand it. He had to put an end to the pain.

He withdrew his blood-steeped SIG from his ankle holster and, grimacing in pain, trained the muzzle on his temple. He had to make the pain stop. He had to kill the snakes squirming inside his brain. He looked in a mirror in the living room and saw his face. His forehead was pulsing with baby snakes throbbing beneath the skin. Or were those veins? They were too thick for veins. They had to be snakes. Pain racked his head. His aching brain would explode any second.

There was only one way to stop the pain. He had to shoot himself in the head.

His forefinger sought the SIG's steel trigger, tickled it, applied pressure.

Shivering, he grimaced in agony. The gun wobbled in his hand. He couldn't steady his grip. Snakes were trying to bore their way out of his eyeballs, forcing the corneas to palpitate. His eyes were going to burst from his head like jack-in-the-boxes.

His hand holding the gun trembled with pain. He didn't know if he would be able to squeeze the trigger. The snakes inside his arm were wresting control of it from him. They were preventing him from pulling the trigger. He couldn't move his forefinger.

Clenching his teeth he tried to squeeze the trigger and blow apart his pounding temple.

A deadly krait undulated out of his nostril, terrifying him. He coughed. A venomous cobra stuck its head out of his mouth and, flaring its cowl, hissing, twisted around to face him. The krait emerging from his nostril faced him. His nose plugged by the krait, Brody gagged on the cobra stuck in his throat suffocating him.

He had to pull the pistol's trigger. He had to put himself out of his insupportable misery.

A twenty-five-foot-long green anaconda was slithering through the rising pool of blood swimming toward him aiming to wrap his body with its coils and crush him to death.

He couldn't shoot all of the snakes. There were too many of them. He had to shoot himself. It was the only solution, the only escape from his interminable pain.

He heard chiming.

It was his cell phone. He wondered how it could ring while submerged in blood, for, indeed, the blood level had now reached his rib cage, drenching his trouser pockets and the better part of his shirt.

He fished the cell out of his pocket and took the call.

"Where are you?" said Evelyn. "I've been trying to reach you for the last half hour."

I'm in a room filling with blood.

"I'm—I'm—," he said into his blood-drenched cell phone.

"You're what? I can't hear. Where are you?"

Where was he? In a lake of blood? A swamp of blood? He blinked his eyes. What he was seeing couldn't be real. He felt like he had been doped. He must be hallucinating.

He shook his head and closed his eyes. Despite his pain, he focused his thoughts on slowing down his breathing, slowing down his jackhammering heartbeat. There was no pain, he told himself. No blood. No snakes. None of this was real. Relax.

He felt his hyperactive pulse subsiding.

He slowly opened his eyes.

He was sitting in his rental, his clothes bathed in sweat.

"I'm in a car," he said. "What happened?"

"The kidnapers phoned me. They said they were going to kill Olivia in one hour because you haven't called off your search for Tyler," said Evelyn, at her wit's end.

"Calm down. I'm lying low. How could they know I'm searching for Keogh?"

"Whatever you do, stay away from Tyler. You're fired for Christ's sake. Which part of *fired* don't you understand?"

"I can't get close to him because I have no idea where he is."

"Stay away from him," she said, her voice tight as if she was on the verge of shrieking, and terminated her call.

Brody called Val and arranged a meet.

He didn't know if he was in any condition to drive, but he had no time to waste. He didn't want Olivia's, nor Keogh's, blood on his hands.

He hoped his hallucinations were over with. He didn't want to start seeing things as he was driving, or he might crash.

Did that white powder he had touched on Cordova's hair have something to do with his hallucinations? he wondered. He inspected his fingertips that had touched the powder. He didn't see any residual powder on them. Maybe it was because his skin had absorbed it.

He felt his sweat-soaked clothes. With any luck he had sweated the drug out of his system, whatever it was.

It must have been that white powder in Cordova's hair. The only drug he could think of offhand that could be absorbed through the skin was Tango & Cash, aka fentanyl. The serial killer could be a user. What if it was LSD? Could LSD be absorbed through the skin?

He would think about it later.

He fired the rental's engine and screeched his tires out of the alley.

Chapter 39

Brody met Val at Big Dean's sports bar at the base of the Santa Monica Pier. Featuring pub grub under a forest green awning, the restaurant had a patio that faced the ocean.

He arrived first and waited for her at a round redwood table under a large yellow umbrella that sprouted out of its center on the patio under the throbbing sun, the waves crashing into the pier's weathered pilings. From the terrace, he could see the brown arcade that reminded him of an armory built on the pier.

When she strutted onto the patio in her stilettos, all male eyes in the joint swung toward her, checking out her curves, both natural and synthetically enhanced. The women frowned at her.

He waved at her.

"This better be important," she said, taking a seat beside him in a skintight peach miniskirt and a sheer lemon halter top that invited bedroom fantasies. Her mini hiked up her thighs.

He wasn't immune to her physical charms.

"Don't get any ideas," she said. "I'm engaged."

The twentyish waiter with tattoos on his wrists and wearing a turquoise earring shaped like a tear dropped by their table.

"I'll take a Stella," said Val.

"Guinness," said Brody.

The waiter nodded and retreated, not before peeking down Val's halter top.

"I'm taking your case," said Brody.

"You already told me that on the phone. I thought you wanted to meet me to tell me you had a lead on Tyler's whereabouts. And where do you get off hanging up on me?"

Brody hemmed and hawed, trying to remember his conversation with her in his rental when he had begun experiencing his hallucination from hell.

"I didn't hang up. We were cut off," he improvised.

"Oh yeah?"

He wasn't going to tell her about his drug trip.

"I need to know everything you know about that experiment Keogh participated in," he said.

"What's the big deal?"

"You said he was more arrogant after he finished it."

"He was."

The waiter returned with their beers, set them down, and approached another table.

"How could you tell?" asked Brody. "In what way?"

"The creep kept putting me down for being an idiot," said Val. "I let him have a piece of my mind. Nobody gets away with doing that to me."

"Did he become violent?"

Val became defensive. "I don't want to talk about it."

She took a pull on her Stella.

"What about drugs?" he said. "You told me you guys used dope. What kind of drugs did he do?"

"What's that got to do with anything?"

"Drugs can affect your personality if you abuse them."

"It's none of your business."

"He might have been kidnaped by dopers in a cult. I'm trying to find out how he's involved with them."

"What's wrong with drugs? I told you we did recreational drugs. Are you some kind of prude?"

"Maybe it was the drugs, not the experiment, that made him more arrogant."

"I don't believe it. We've used drugs for years, and he never got this full of himself. It was the experiment that changed him."

"Drugs have something to do with these serial killings. The killer drops acid and maybe other stuff."

"Tyler isn't a dealer, if you're insinuating these killings are retaliations for drug deals that went south."

"I'm not insinuating anything."

"Then let's move on. Or I'm outa here," she said, and took a swig of her Stella.

He changed the subject. "Nobody knows anything about this experiment but you."

"It's just an experiment. So what? What's it got to do with his disappearing?"

"I'm trying to find out. What did he say to you about it?"

"After the experiment, he kept bragging about how much smarter he was than everybody else. It was a bore listening to him."

"Drugs and booze can boost your self-confidence."

"Enough with the drugs and booze. It was different. It was like he was talking down to me like I was a snot-nosed little kid. And he did it all the time. Not just after having a drink." Scowling, Val shook her head. "That experiment did something to him."

"Did he tell you what the experiment was about?"

"No. Wait a minute." She rummaged in her purse. "I found this card he brought back from Stanford on his desktop. I was gonna call the number on it, but forgot about it."

She handed him a business card. It was for a company called DDW LLC in Menlo Park, California, with a phone number listed.

"Is this the business that performed the experiment?" he said.

"He mentioned something about DDW when he told me about the experiment. He never went into any details about it."

"Could I keep this? I want to call them."

"I don't see how they're gonna help you find Tyler."

"You said the experiment altered his personality. I want to know why he participated in it and what the results were."

"I can't help you," she said, shrugging. "You think they kidnaped him?"

"The experimenters?"

"Yeah," she said, swinging her leg out.

Brody hadn't given it a thought. He didn't see why the experimenters would kidnap Keogh—unless they feared he was going to reveal something they didn't want revealed. It sounded plausible.

Brody needed to talk to them and find out more about this experiment. Keogh's kidnaping might have nothing to do with the Mensa murders.

“I don’t know what’s going on,” he said. “I don’t have any other leads to work. He’s in danger.”

“What kind of danger?”

“All I know is he’s on the Mensa board of directors and they’re all being murdered by some psycho cult. Did the experiment have anything to do with cults?”

“After he returned from Stanford, he never told me anything about what happened there.”

Brody took a pull on his beer, thinking.

Consulting her wristwatch Val stood up. “I got an appointment at the beauty parlor. Tell me if you find anything.”

She swung out of the café, mauled by the male customers’ hungry eyes eating her up.

Chapter 40

Nursing his beer Brody used his VPN and a burner app on his cell phone to call DDW's number. He had never heard of them, and he didn't want them tracing his phone number.

"Hello," a man answered in a gravelly voice.

"Hello. I'm calling about an experiment you conducted recently at Stanford."

"What about it?"

"I want to know the purpose of it as well as the results."

"You're out of luck."

"What's that supposed to mean?"

"The government funds our experiments. They specified in our contract that we cannot reveal to the public any experiment we perform with their funding."

"You conducted these experiments in secret?"

"What did I just say?"

"The one I'm interested in involved Tyler Keogh. Do you know which experiment I'm talking about?"

There was a pause.

"We have an NDA with the government," the guy said. "We're not allowed to reveal any intel about our experiments."

"Why are they so hush-hush?"

"Why is this your business? Who are you?"

"I'm a private dick. William Smithers is the name. Who am I speaking to?"

"Darryl Conyers, public relations executive."

"You should be happy to inform me what your company is hoping to accomplish with your experiments. Aren't they for the betterment of mankind?"

"The government doesn't like people that ask too many questions. Get my drift, Smithers?"

"What's the government hiding?"

"You're asking too many questions."

"A person's life may depend on the info you give me about this experiment."

"If I violate the NDA, the government could cite the Espionage Act and throw me in jail."

"Are you saying you're working for the government?"

"I work for DDW."

"I don't get it. What are you doing in these experiments?" Brody made up something outrageous. "Creating lethal viruses to use in biological warfare?"

"That's ridiculous," said Conyers in an access of rage. "And the government could throw you in the joint for making false accusations. I have a good mind to report you to the Department of Defense."

"The DOD is running this?" Brody said in surprise.

"I didn't say that."

"Just level with me and tell me the nature of the experiment. If it's harmless, why are you so scared to reveal it?"

"It's not up to me. My hands are tied by the government. Believe it or not, I'm warning you off for your own good. They don't like people snooping around here. I'm telling you, these guys mean business. They don't monkey around."

"What if somebody's life is at stake?"

"You expect me to swallow that? I don't see how this information can save a person's life."

"A person involved in your experiment is missing, feared dead."

Silence on the line.

"What does that have to do with the experiment?" said Conyers. "I don't see the connection."

"I don't yet, either. That's why I need to know what the experiment was about—"

"If you keep pestering me, I'm gonna report you to the government."

"I'm trying to save someone's life."

"Be good to yourself. Save your own life."

Brody took umbrage. "Is that a threat?"

“I repeat, be good to yourself. Go home and say nothing about this to anyone.”

Conyers hung up.

Chapter 41

Olivia wondered why it was taking so long for Mommy to find her.

She felt like she had been locked in a closet and left to die. She didn't know how much more of this she could stand. Part of her felt hungry. Another part didn't want to eat ever again.

She wanted to go outside, breathe fresh air, and feel sunshine on her face. Why were they locking her up? Who was doing this to her?

She didn't understand any of it.

Hadn't Mommy seen Eeyore's tail hanging from the bathroom window yet? How could she miss it?

Olivia approached the door and tried to open it. It was locked.

"I want to leave," she said through the door.

Nobody answered.

Instead, she heard a train's shrill whistle outside. Was she near a railroad track? she wondered.

Were they going to let her die in here and ship her body away in a coffin on a train? she wondered. Was this how people died? Locked in a cramped room with no windows and shipped away to a cemetery on a train? It reminded her of the prayer she said every night. *And if I die before I wake* . . . Other than that, she had never thought of dying. She didn't want to think of dying. A cold chill ran down her spine.

She held Eeyore up to her face and looked him in the eyes.

"Don't worry, Eeyore," said Olivia. "Mommy'll find your tail and bring it back to you."

Mommy would see Eeyore's tail and get here soon, she decided. She had to be patient.

To pass the time she started singing "Row, Row, Row Your Boat."

"Shut up in there," said the suit in the hall.

Why did she ever enter that guy's car? she chided herself. Mommy had always told her to never trust a stranger. *Even if he's wearing a suit*, she should have added.

Olivia lowered her voice, but kept singing, "Life is but a dream."

Chapter 42

Fixing to leave Big Dean's, Brody took a call.

"Have you called off your search for Keogh?"

"Who is this?" said Brody, not recognizing the voice.

"I'm the guy that's got Olivia."

"Release her," said Brody, bolting to his feet.

"Not so fast. Did you call off your search?"

"Yeah," Brody lied.

"That's more like it."

"Then release Olivia."

"The problem is, how do I know you're not lying?"

"Give her to me and I won't tell the cops you're her kidnaper."

The stranger thought it over. "Do you promise you called off your search."

"I promise," Brody lied. "Where's Olivia?"

"She's with me."

"Give her back to me, and I won't report you to the cops."

There was a long pause.

"No cops," said the caller.

"So far so good."

"To be safe I should kill her so she can't ID me."

"No deal," said Brody, clenching his cell with tense fingers.

"She saw my face."

"That's on you, not me. Give her to me and flee the country. I don't care where you go. I won't stop you."

"I had to show her my face or she wouldn't have gotten in the car with me."

"Your problem, not mine."

"There's only one way you can keep her alive."

"Name it."

"Sweeten the pot."

"I don't understand."

"Give me a hundred grand for the girl."

Brody gnashed his teeth. “That wasn’t part of the deal. You can’t keep changing the deal.”

The caller laughed. “I can do what I want, the way I see it. Or don’t you want the girl back—alive?”

“You can’t keep changing the deal. How do I know you’re not gonna change it again?”

“You forget. I’m the one calling the shots. Agree, or she’s dead.”

Brody didn’t have any choice. He had to comply with the kidnaper’s demands—or to pretend to.

“It’s gonna take me time to come up with the cash,” he said.

“You don’t have time.” The caller became belligerent. “I don’t like this kid. I’m sick of her singing. She sings terrible. I’m gonna waste her now—”

“No, don’t. I’ll get the money. Where do we make the exchange?”

“That’s better. All Ben Franklins. Unmarked.”

In some respects it might work out better this way, decided Brody. The promise of cash gave the kidnaper extra incentive to keep Olivia alive. And it also meant the guy had to meet Brody in order to collect the dough. Otherwise, the guy could’ve dropped Olivia off alone anywhere and hightailed it—if he was planning on letting her live, which Brody doubted, since Olivia had seen the guy’s mug.

Brody got the impression the kidnaper was working for someone else, since the cash hadn’t been part of the original deal. Brody figured the guy had cooked up the idea of a ransom on his own when he came to the realization that he had a well and truly valuable commodity on his hands.

The guy who profited from calling off the search for Keogh wasn’t this guy, decided Brody. He was dealing with a flunky, who, on the spur of the moment, had decided to go into business for himself. The question was, who had hired the flunky kidnaper? Who wanted Keogh to stay missing?

Brody didn’t have to time to figure it. He had to save Olivia’s life.

The kidnaper told him to meet him at the Hobart rail yard in the city of Commerce.

"How do I know she's still alive?" blurted Brody before the kidnaper had a chance to hang up.

"Wait a minute."

Brody waited.

"Mommy?" said a girl's voice. "Did you see Eeyore's tail?"

"I'm working for your mom," said Brody. "I'm coming to get you."

"Where's Mommy—?"

"That's enough," said the kidnaper, grabbing his cell roughly from Olivia, eliciting a scream of surprise from her.

"She better not be hurt," said Brody through his teeth.

"Shut the fuck up and get the dough. I'm calling the shots, not you. You got forty minutes to get to the rail yard. Or I'll put the hurt on her like you wouldn't believe. You won't even recognize her when I'm done with her."

"Hurt her and you're dead."

"You got thirty-nine minutes."

The kidnaper hung up.

Chapter 43

Brody had to leave now or he wouldn't get there in time. Even if he did leave now, he might not make it depending on the traffic volume on the 10.

Brody paid his bill at Big Dean's and stopped at a grocery store to buy a box of Kleenex. He would use the grocery paper bag containing the Kleenex to bamboozle the kidnaper into thinking it was the cash.

Brody hurried to his rental in the parking garage, tossed the bag into the passenger seat, fired the engine, and set out for the freeway to Commerce.

Brody wondered why the kidnaper wanted to meet at a railway station. Was he going to ride a train to escape after the handoff?

Stuck on the freeway, Brody eyeballed his wristwatch. He was running late. An accident up ahead had brought traffic to a crawl. Once he got past the accident he should be able to make up time.

He drove past an SUV overturned in the slow lane, hemmed in by squad cars with their light bars flashing red and blue. Hissing red flares set on the tarmac warned commuters to stay away.

Driving slowly, Brody faced away from the highway patrol cops in their butternut uniforms inspecting the accident so they couldn't ID him, pull him over, and bust him for murder.

Traffic picked up speed as soon as he got past the bottleneck precipitated by the accident.

He was going to be late to the rail yard by five minutes or so. He hoped the kidnaper would wait. Or would the guy think he got double-crossed and split? Apprehensive, Brody felt his palms break into a sweat on the steering wheel.

He exited the freeway and managed to find the Hobart Yard. Cloaked with yellowish brown smog, it was crowded with trains—some of them moving, some stationary. He parked on the side of the road.

Taking in the rail yard he heaved a sigh. It was a big place. He scoped the trains and intersecting tracks. The yard reeked of diesel exhaust. He didn't see anyone.

He honked his horn a couple times.

No reaction.

Bag in hand, he climbed out of the rental.

He hoped the kidnaper hadn't killed Olivia yet. It was just a matter of time. The guy had to kill her or she would ID him to the cops. The guy would never take that chance. They would put him away for ten years or more. If it was a third strike against him, he would get at least twenty-five years behind bars.

Keeping his eyes peeled for the kidnaper, Brody crunched across the ballast on the nearest railroad track. He didn't see anybody around. He heard a train chugging in the distance, vibrating the ground.

The guy could be pointing a gun at him even now, decided Brody, his heartbeat racing.

He ducked behind a red caboose parked on a track, surveying the yard.

He withdrew his SIG from his ankle holster and concealed it behind the paper bag he was gripping. He heard a whistle and saw a train approaching the rail yard. At the same time he picked up on movement behind a parked railroad car on the other side of three train tracks that ran parallel to each other in front of him.

He saw a suit minus a tie emerge from the back of the car, walking with a little girl, gripping her tiny hand in his mitt. Hugging a stuffed donkey she tried to pull away from him in futility. His other hand clutched a pistol.

He recognized Olivia from the photo Evelyn had e-mailed him.

"I thought you weren't gonna show up," said the suit, his face flushed.

Maybe the guy had been drinking to build up his courage, decided Brody. A point in Brody's favor.

"Traffic," said Brody.

"Where's the dough?"

Partially hidden by the caboose, Brody held out the paper bag that contained the Kleenex box.

The suit indicated the train barreling toward them.

"Just before that train arrives, throw the money across the track to me," he said.

"Let the girl go first."

Brody saw the guy's ploy. The train would screen the suit and give him cover while he inspected the contents in the bag. Brody couldn't let that happen. If he let the train come between them, the kidnaper would shoot Olivia in rage after finding out Brody had duped him with a box of Kleenex instead of cash.

"Let the girl cross the tracks to me first," said Brody.

"No dice."

It was getting harder to hear because of the onrushing chuffing train.

"Let her come over here," said Brody.

"Come out from behind that caboose and toss the money here. I don't got all day. The choo-choo's almost here," said the kidnaper, mocking Olivia's voice with a twisted grin.

Brody figured the guy might blow him away once he got the opportunity of a clear shot. Brody would have to take him out first. If Brody missed, the kidnaper would waste Olivia, after which the guy might return fire or bug out to save his skin.

Brody needed a kill shot. Anything less would end in failure, with Olivia murdered.

"How do I know you won't take a shot at me?" said Brody.

"I want the money before that train gets here. Or she gets it."

Brody didn't have much choice. He walked out from behind the caboose, clutching the paper bag in his left hand, concealing his SIG in his right.

"Let Olivia come to me," he said, approaching the track that the train was barreling down.

The suit shook his head no. "Toss the loot first. Do it now."

Brody figured the guy wouldn't shoot him before getting the cash. The guy wanted the train to screen his escape. He would blow Brody away after Brody flung the bag to him.

Brody would have to take the shot now. Concerned he might hit Olivia, he felt his pulse quicken. He couldn't afford to miss. He would get one shot. It had to be a kill shot. The train barreled toward them. Brody couldn't put it off any longer.

He dropped the bag, trained his SIG on the suit's head, and fired, as the train stormed toward them.

Olivia screamed.

The train's engineer tooted his horn.

Brody's vision was blocked by the train that roared between him and the suit. Box cars screamed past him. He couldn't be sure it was a kill shot. He couldn't even tell if he had hit the guy. There was no way Brody could check until the entire train passed by.

The engineer continued blasting the train's horn. Maybe he had seen the three of them near the track and was warning them to stay away, decided Brody.

The train blew past him. He thought it would never end. How many cars did it have? he wondered, seeing no end in sight. The kidnaper could be shooting Olivia even now.

He strained his ears trying to hear the crack of a gunshot on the other side of the train.

Crouching, he tried to peer under the train's bottom to see if he could spot Olivia. The train's spinning wheels speeding past him kept obstructing his view. He thought he could fit underneath the train if it slowed down, but it was going way too fast. If he ran under the speeding train, it would run him over.

There was nothing for it. He had to wait.

At last the caboose flew by.

Olivia was lying on the ground on her stomach, her stuffed donkey in her arms, next to the suit's motionless face-down body.

Sweating with apprehension, Brody pelted over the crossties to Olivia.

"Are you OK?" he said, his eyes locked on her with concern as he reached her.

She wasn't moving, he realized, his heartbeat ramping up. Had the kidnaper lived long enough after Brody had shot him to kill her? Was the kidnaper still alive?

He tipped over the kidnaper's body with his foot, revealing a face with a bloody bullet hole in the forehead.

Olivia lifted her head and looked up at him with worried eyes. "Where's Mommy? Why didn't she bring Eeyore's tail?"

A surging wave of relief swept over Brody, his eyes moist.

"I'm working for your mother," he said. "She sent me to get you."

The worry didn't leave Olivia's eyes.

"That's the same thing that man said when he picked me up at school and locked me in a closet," she said, glancing in fear at the suit.

"We need to get out of here, Olivia."

He helped her to her feet. She brushed dirt off her dress, her knees, and Eeyore.

He had to make sure the kidnaper was dead. Training his SIG on him, he felt for a pulse in the suit's neck. Nothing.

"Where's Mommy?" said Olivia.

"I'll take you to her. She wants to see you, Olivia. Let's go."

He reached out for her little hand. Reluctant at first, unable to overcome her distrust, she kept her hand to herself. At length, trusting his soft eyes that gazed down at her, she overcame her fear and extended her hand to him, and he held it.

Brody walked across the railroad track with her toward his rental.

"Eeyore was scared," she said. "He thought we were gonna die."

Chapter 44

Brody delivered Olivia to Evelyn at her condo.

Opening her door, overjoyed to see her, Evelyn scooped Olivia up in her arms and hugged her, her eyes glistening with tears.

"Mommy, did you find Eeyore's tail?" said Olivia.

"No, dear," said Evelyn, not knowing what Olivia was talking about. "We'll find it later."

Brody left them alone and returned to his rental. Parked in front of Evelyn's house, he dug out his cell phone and called another Mensa member on the board of directors. The phone rang three times. Brody hoped he wasn't too late, that the guy hadn't already been murdered. Brody prepared to hang up.

"Hello," said Lou Arano, a short, middle-aged guy with a receding hairline, according to his photo on the Mensa board of directors website. His petulant voice made him sound like he was perpetually pissed off at the world and everyone in it.

"You're alive."

"Of course, I'm alive. Who is this?"

"Scott Brody. I'm a PI."

"Is this a sick joke? Are you threatening me with your 'You're alive' routine?"

"I don't know if you know, but a lot of Mensa board members have been murdered."

Arano paused. His voice was lower when he spoke. "I heard Wasson and Delacroix were killed."

"Eugene Frantangello, too."

"Gene?" said Arano, taken aback. "I had no idea. How do you know all this?"

"It has to do with the case I'm working on. I'm looking for Tyler Keogh. Do you know where I could find him?"

"Keogh? That prick. I hope he's rotting in hell."

"Huh?" said Brody, surprised at the vitriol in Arano's voice.

"The guy's an arrogant twerp. He thinks he knows everything and wants everybody to kiss his royal ass."

"You two weren't on good terms?"

"I doubt that schmuck's on good terms with anyone. He's a world-class shite."

"Do you know where I could find him?"

"No. And I don't care. If we're lucky, maybe his car crashed off a cliff and he drowned in the ocean."

Arano's hatred gave him a motive to murder Keogh, decided Brody—if Keogh indeed was dead.

"Did you know Keogh was missing?" said Brody.

"I don't give a rat's ass."

"You didn't know?"

"How could I know? I go out of my way to avoid the lout. If I know he's going to be at a board meeting, I stay at home. I don't know how anyone can stand being in the same room with him. His swollen head takes up the entire room."

"Are you saying the board members wanted him dead?"

"I'm not saying that. You're twisting my words. I'm saying nobody on the board liked him."

"Do you know anything about an experiment he was involved in at Stanford?"

"This is the first I've heard of it. Not that that's strange. He was a closed book when he was around me, except when he was blowing his own horn telling us how smart he was."

"You'd like to see him dead?"

"I'd like nothing better than never to see him again. I wouldn't mind seeing his girlfriend, though. Now she is something. What she sees in that walking talking turd is beyond me."

"Do you know if he's into voodoo or satanic cults?"

"I can't say that it surprises me. He's a drug addict, too."

"Are you sure he's an addict?"

"He must be high on drugs. It's the only explanation for his gargantuan ego."

"Who do you think is committing these murders?"

"I have no idea."

"Aren't you worried? You may be next on their hit list?"

"I never worry. You can't control what happens to you. You can only control how you react to it."

"I suggest you hire a bodyguard."

"Are you making a death threat against me?" said Arano, smoldering.

"I'm offering you advice. Somebody is killing the Mensa board of directors. You're on the board. Therefore you're in danger."

"I don't live in fear. If *you* want to live in fear, be my guest. It's a free country—so they tell me."

"I'm not the one on the Mensa board of directors. You are."

"If you find Keogh, tell him I told him to go fuck himself."

"I'm trying to find out who would kidnap him."

"I'm tired of your yapping. If you don't mind, *I* have a life," said Arano, and slammed his handset down in its cradle.

Arano had just moved himself to the top of Brody's list of suspects in Keogh's disappearance.

Chapter 45

Evelyn flung the front door open and dashed out of her condo building toward Brody's parked car.

"Did you hear the news?" she said, her face beaming.

Brody looked puzzled.

"The police say they found Tyler," she said.

"Is he OK?"

"He was driving on the Coast Highway in Malibu, and a cop pulled him over for failing to signal. When the cop saw who he was, he remembered the BOLO out for him."

"Good news. I was thinking he might be dead."

She furrowed her brow with concern. "There's only one problem."

"What?"

"The driver's license he was carrying wasn't his. It belonged to someone else. And he claimed he wasn't Tyler."

"It must not be him."

"The cops are pretty sure it is. They want me to go to the station to ID him."

"I'd offer to take you there, but I'm a murder suspect and they'll throw me in jail if they see me."

"If it's a case of mistaken identity, I'll still need your services. Now that Olivia's safe, I don't have to worry about her kidnapers, and you can keep looking for Tyler."

"OK."

Evelyn returned to her condo, eager to go to the police station.

Brody was surprised the cops had found Keogh. He suspected Keogh had been murdered by the cult that did in the other board members.

He still had a raft of unanswered questions. If Keogh indeed had been found, why had he been staying away from his house? Was he worried the cult would waste him? Who was the murderer? Did Keogh know who the murderer was? Was he hiding out from the murderer and using an alias?

Since Brody was working for Val now, he called her.

"The cops say they found Keogh," he said.

"Where?"

"Driving in Malibu."

"Good. I need to talk to him. Where is he?"

"At the station."

"What station?"

"The LAPD station downtown. They say there's a problem."

"I don't understand."

"He was driving around with somebody else's driver's license."

Val paused a beat. "What? Why would he do that? They must've pulled over the wrong guy. Those idiots."

"His sister's going to the station to ID him."

"I need to know where he put that prenup."

"Don't get your hopes up too high. It might not be him."

Brody wished he could be a fly on the wall in the interrogation room at the police station when they questioned Keogh, if it was him.

"Are you at the police station?" said Val.

"I can't go there. They'll bust me. They think I murdered Wasson, Delacroix, and Frantangello."

"It sounds like the mercenary law firm I hired to read the prenup."

"His sister Evelyn is gonna ID him."

Brody watched Evelyn drive her SUV out of the condo's underground parking garage.

"Keep looking for Tyler," said Val. "The cops must have busted the wrong guy. Why don't they just take his fingerprints? Why do they need his sister to ID him?"

"They always want a relative to ID someone."

"Did they bust him?"

"For what? Unless they're charging him for failing to signal a turn. Nobody goes to jail for that."

"Do you think he's on the killer's hit list?"

"At the top—unless . . ."

"Unless what?"

"He's already dead, and the cops picked up the wrong guy."

"When can I talk to him?"

"Any time. You can go to the station now and ID him. It's up to you—"

She terminated the call.

Chapter 46

At LAPD headquarters at the Civic Center in downtown LA on 100 West 1st St., Detective Macready was standing in the interrogation room with the man identified as Keogh who the cops had brought in from Malibu. Keogh was sitting at a rectangular desk in a windowless room.

Forty-three, with long dark brown hair that fell over his ears, he was wearing a pair of polarized Ray-Ban Wayfarers. His chiseled lips curled up at the corners like they were sneering. Looking like an aging punk rocker he was wearing a black AC/DC T with blue jeans and dirty grey sneakers.

"Let me ask you once again," said Macready, wearing a brown blazer without a tie, his arms akimbo. "What is your name?"

"Sam Hodges. Can't you read the name on my driver's license?"

"Could you remove the sunglasses?"

"Sure. Why not?"

Hodges removed his shades, revealing jaded blue eyes.

"You're the spitting image of the missing person Tyler Keogh," said Macready.

"Never heard of him."

At that moment Evelyn opened the door and entered the room, wearing black slacks and a lime blouse.

"Tyler," she said, smiling and approaching him. "Thank goodness you're all right."

"Who are you?" he said.

"Your sister," said Evelyn, dumbfounded.

"I don't have a sister."

"What are you talking about?" She turned to Macready. "Is he drunk or on drugs?"

"The arresting officer gave him a breathalyzer test," said Macready. "He passed. He's not drunk."

"Don't you recognize me, Tyler?" said Evelyn.

"I never saw you before."

"You believe he's your brother Tyler Keogh?" said Macready.

"Of course, it's him," said Evelyn.

Pulling a face Macready ran his hand through his cropped hair. "I don't get it."

"Can't you take his fingerprints and clear this up?" said Evelyn.

"We already ran them. They're not in our database. Didn't he ever have his fingerprints taken?"

"I have no idea. Doesn't the DMV take them when you apply for a driver's license?"

"Ordinarily. However, people have the right to refuse. It's not likely but possible that he never had his fingerprints taken. In which case they wouldn't be in the database."

"What are you saying?"

"If they're not in the database, they're useless for purposes of identification."

"What about a retinal scan? Don't they use those these days?"

"You bet they do. And we tried that."

"And?"

"No match. There's no record of Keogh's retinal scans in the database. He never had his retinas scanned. That's quite common, actually. Most people haven't had their retinas scanned."

"What about facial recognition software?"

"We used it. It says he's Keogh."

"There you go."

"However, facial recognition software's accuracy isn't 100 percent. It's more like in the low 90s."

"That's good enough for me," said Evelyn.

"It's not good enough for legal purposes. Not only does he have a driver's license in Hodges's name, he has a Social Security card in his name."

"Maybe they're fake."

"I have someone working on that now."

Evelyn's cell phone chimed in her Salvatore Farragamo purse.

"Excuse me," she said, retreated into a corner of the room, and took the call.

"Is it him?" said Brody on the line.

"It *is* him, but he's denying it."

"Say again."

"I know it's him, but he claims he's someone called Sam Hodges."

"What about his fingerprints?"

"The cops did them. Tyler's fingerprints aren't in the database."

Brody thought about it. "What about his dental work?"

"What about it?"

"It can be used to ID someone. Everybody's dental work is unique."

"I'll ask."

Evelyn turned to Macready. "Did you check with Tyler's dentist for his dental records?"

Macready cleared his throat. "Why, no. Not yet. Who are you talking to?"

"His dental work will ID him."

"I have things to do," interrupted Hodges, bounding to his feet.

"Sit down, sir," said Macready. "We're not done yet."

"Am I under arrest?"

"You were cited for failing to signal when you made a turn in your vehicle."

"I have to go to jail for that?" said Hodges in exasperation.

"Not at all. Be patient. This woman claims you're her brother, who's on our missing persons list."

"She's mistaken."

"Who's your dentist?"

"Dentist," said Hodges, flabbergasted. "How should I know? I haven't been to a dentist in years. I can't even remember the last time I went."

"Do you know who his dentist is?" Macready asked Evelyn.

The door swung open.

Clad in café au lait stretch pants and a glossy lilac tube top, Val strutted into the room on her stilettos.

Cops with big eyes in the hallway peered into the room after her.

Chapter 47

"There you are," Val told Hodges. "Where's our prenup?"

"Who the hell are you?" said Hodges.

Val jacked her eyebrows. "*Who am I*? I'm your fiancée. Are you blotto?"

Hodges shook his head in bewilderment.

"Where's the prenup?" said Val. "I want my lawyers to tear it apart and rewrite it."

"I've never seen this woman before," Hodges told Macready.

"You're not gonna weasel out of our marriage this easy," said Val.

"This is insane," said Hodges.

"What happened?" Brody asked Evelyn over her cell phone.

"Val's here."

"Ask her who Keogh's dentist is. She might know."

"Val, who is Tyler's dentist?" said Evelyn.

Val gave her a look. "What's his dentist got to do with anything?"

"We can ID Tyler with his dental work."

Val mulled it over. "Let's see—uh. Hmm. Dr. Gold. No. Goldman. Irving Goldman in Century City."

"I'll call him," said Macready, holding up his forefinger.

He produced his cell, called the front desk, and asked the receptionist to put him through to Irving Goldman, DDS.

"This is a total waste of time," said Hodges, flinging up his hands, his patience wearing thin.

"That line's no longer in use," the receptionist told Macready over the phone.

Puzzled, Macready terminated the call.

"What happened?" said Val.

"The line's no longer in operation," said Macready. "Wait a minute," he said, his eyes lighting up. "Irving Goldman. That name rings a bell. Wasn't there a fire last week in Century City that killed a Dr. Goldman?" Macready snapped his fingers. "We have that case in Robbery-Homicide because his insurance company suspects arson. The suspicious fire is under investigation."

"What about his dental records?" said Evelyn.

"His office was burned to the ground. Everything in it destroyed."

"Can I go now?" said Hodges.

"You're going with me to find that prenup," said Val.

Hodges slapped his forehead. "This is like a really bad episode of *The Twilight Zone*. Somebody hum that theme song. I don't know you, lady, and I'm not going anywhere with you. I'd be busted for soliciting a hooker."

"Why, you," said Val, preparing to smash her purse into Hodges's face.

Macready snatched her purse and prevented her from taking a swing at Hodges.

"Everybody, settle down," said Macready. "We need to clear the air."

"Yes, teacher," said Hodges.

Macready gave him a look.

"I demand an apology," said Val, lowering her purse.

"Let's go over what we have here before we get too excited," said Macready, letting go of Val's purse.

A swarthy squat uniform pushing forty with a shaved head opened the door, entered the room, and sought out Macready, a driver's license and a Social Security card in his hand.

"His driver's license checks out, Lieutenant, and so does his Social Security card," he said, handing the license and the card to Macready and leaving.

Macready tossed the two IDs onto the tabletop in front of Hodges.

"His IDs check out," Macready told the room. "He must be Hodges, not Keogh."

"That's impossible," said Val. "I know Tyler when I see him. That's him."

"Then how come he's got a driver's license that says he's Sam Hodges? He just happens to look like Keogh."

"He must've had one of his Mensa friends print up a fake driver's license. Those guys are clever that way."

"It's the real McCoy. A genuine California driver's license in Hodges's name with his photo ID on it."

"All that proves is he has multiple driver's licenses, one in his real name, and one in this fake Hodges's name."

"And multiple Social Security cards?"

"Why not?"

"He says he's Hodges. I have to take his word for it, since it's backed up with two legitimate IDs."

"He's Tyler. He's doing this so he doesn't have to show me the prenup."

Macready shook his head. He surveyed the crowded room.

"Now that I have all of you together, which one of you creeps killed Myles Wasson?" he said.

"I resent your accusation," said Evelyn.

"Time to lawyer up," said Val.

"I'm outa here," said Hodges, and stalked out the door.

"Don't try to run away from me," said Val, pursuing him in her clacking heels.

"Aren't you gonna stop him?" Evelyn asked Macready.

"On what charge?" said Macready.

"Using false ID. Pretending to be someone he's not."

"We have no proof of that. Everything checks out. His license, Social, credit cards—they're all in Sam Hodges's name."

"I don't understand," said Evelyn, shutting her eyes in consternation.

"Ask yourself this: why would your brother pretend to be someone else?" Macready shrugged. "He has no motive that I can see. Or can you come up with one?"

Evelyn shook her head in befuddlement. "He must have his reasons. I have no idea what they are." She paused, a thought coming to her. "Maybe he's afraid he's the next Mensa member on the hit list and he's pretending to be someone else to avoid getting killed."

Macready torqued his mouth. “Possible. But does he really think that would work? Everybody who knows him thinks it’s him.”

“That’s why he printed up all that fake ID. To convince the serial killer he’s not Tyler.”

Macready fetched a loud sigh. “I don’t care if Hodges is Tyler. What I care about is catching the serial killer. Hodges, or whatever his name is, is your problem.”

“What about arson? Tyler must’ve burned down his dentist’s office so Goldman’s X-rays couldn’t ID him.”

“That’s a serious accusation. Goldman died in the fire. That’s murder. Where’s your proof?”

“It’s the only explanation that makes sense.”

“Get the evidence and I’ll throw the book at him.” Macready looked around the room, searching faces. “In the meantime, does anybody know where Scott Brody is? I have a warrant for his arrest for murder.”

Nobody answered.

Chapter 48

Driving down the Coast Highway Tess picked up on an unmarked black Chevy Suburban SUV with flashing blue fog lights and a flashing blue light on its dashboard coming up behind her. As it passed her, she noticed it had tinted windows.

She slowed down and pulled to the right of the road to let the guy pass her. Instead of passing her he halted in front of her car. She pulled over to the sandy shoulder and stopped.

She didn't know what was going on.

Two guys in black suits stepped out of the sedan and approached her.

Wearing reflective aviators the rangy blond one with a hatchet face, the driver, pulled open his suit so she could see he had a holstered sidearm on his hip and an FBI badge clipped on his leather belt.

Like that wasn't deliberate, she thought. *Feds. Not cops.*

Drago approached her. Mirisch followed him.

"Special Agent Drago of the FBI," said the rangy guy.

Tess looked up at him through her open window. "What's this about?"

"Where's Brody?"

"Who's Brody?"

"Scott Brody. He's a private investigator, like you. We saw both of you at Wasson's house. Where is he?"

"How should I know?"

"You're Tess Hardwick."

"Uh-huh."

"We want to talk with Brody."

"I don't work with him. I have my own agency."

"Tell us where Brody is," said Drago, adjusting his sunglasses.

A powder blue Lamborghini blew past them, crackling sand under its fat high-performance tires, drowning out Drago's voice.

"I dunno," said Tess.

"It's better for you if you give us straight answers," said Mirisch, standing to the side of Drago, his lined, middle-aged face grim. "To lie to an FBI agent is a felony. You could serve up to five years in jail."

Tess felt her heartbeat accelerating. She knew what he said was true. As bad as the fed with the mirror aviators was, Jack Webb with his world-weary face was worse.

"I'm doing the best I can," said Tess.

"Where's Brody?" said Mirisch, staring at her.

"I have no idea."

Weary of her evasive answers, Drago said, "Then find him and tell him to stop investigating the Wasson murder—all of the Mensa murders, for that matter. Understand?"

"And that goes for you, too," said Mirisch.

"Why?" said Tess.

"It has to do with national security," said Mirisch. "You have no jurisdiction in a national security matter. Consider yourself warned. Be advised this is your first and only warning."

"Let me get this straight. You want us to let a serial murderer run free, continuing to slaughter people?"

"Let us handle it. It's our job. We don't need help."

"I don't know where this Brody guy is."

"Find him and tell him."

Drago withdrew his business card from his jacket's breast pocket and handed it to her.

"Call us when you find out where he is," he said.

Drago and Mirisch retreated to their sedan.

Tess waited for them to leave. Their sedan out of sight, she fished out her cell phone from her purse that sat on the passenger seat and called Brody.

"Talk," said Brody.

"Feebs are looking for you," said Tess.

"What for? Do they want to bust me for Wasson's murder?"

"They want you to stay away from the Mensa murders. They didn't say anything about busting you."

"Don't they know the LAPD has a warrant out for my arrest?"

"They didn't say."

"How did they know I was on the case?"

"They saw you with me at Wasson's."

"Were they staking out Wasson's?"

"I dunno."

"What's the problem? I'm just doing my job. Why are they warning me off?"

"National security, they said."

"Wasson's murder?"

"That's what they said."

"I don't see the connection between Mensa and national security."

"You know feebs. They never tell anybody anything about what they're doing."

"I can't stay away. Keogh's life may be in danger. He could be the next one murdered. And then there's the little matter of my being a murder suspect. The only way I can clear my name is by finding the real murderer."

"How can you protect Keogh if you can't find him?"

"Haven't you heard?"

"Heard what?"

"The cops cited him for failing to signal his turn. They took him downtown."

"They found him?" said Tess in surprise. "So what's the problem?"

"He says he's not Keogh."

"Where are you?"

Brody hung up.

Tess felt her head pounding, a killer headache on the horizon rising like the sun burning holes in her grey matter.

If Brody had told her where he was, would she have called the feds and ratted him out? she wondered. She wasn't sure she wanted to know the answer. She had more questions.

Why would Keogh deny he was Keogh? And how could the serial killings be tied to national security? This case was becoming too complicated. Too many unanswerable questions made her head ache. Bottom line—it wasn't any of her business.

She plucked a Naratriptan pill out of a pillbox in her purse, popped the pill into her mouth, and dry-swallowed it. This job wasn't getting any easier. She didn't like dealing with the feds and avoided them at all costs. The problem with feds was they had too much power. They could come up with laws you never even heard of and toss you in the joint for years if they took a dislike to you.

They hadn't pulled her over out of friendship. She had to watch her back. Their warning was meant for her, as well as for Brody.

Chapter 49

Brody didn't want to give Tess too much information. He didn't know who she was working for, nor the nature of her case—other than it involved the Mensa murders. Every time there was another murder he found her at the crime scene. What were the chances? He couldn't rule her out as the serial killer.

Brody didn't know who *he* was working for either. Evelyn had hired him first, then fired him. She had rehired him after he had freed Olivia. In the meantime he had accepted Val as his client after Evelyn had fired him. Technically he was working for both of them, which created a conflict of interest.

He preferred working for Evelyn. She was easier to get along with. On the other hand, a hit man had tried to waste him at their last scheduled meet.

Brody needed to arrange another meet with her. With any luck a hit man wouldn't be waiting to ambush him this time. He still didn't know how the mechanic knew he would be at the construction site to meet Evelyn. Evelyn had said her phone was tapped. However, she had offered him no evidence of it.

His cell phone in his hand, his shoes and socks off, he was sitting on the beach, watching the two-foot dirty surf crash, gulls bawling and wheeling overhead. He should have brought a bath towel to sit on. The hot sand was burning his butt.

He doubted the cops would be looking for him here, which was why he had chosen the beach to think and plot his next move. The seashore relaxed him. He could think clearer being out in the open and breathing the fresh air blowing in from the sea.

He called Evelyn. They decided to meet at La Piazza restaurant at the Grove, a shopping center east of Beverly Hills.

Brody traipsed through the sand to his rental parked in the beach lot, put on his socks and shoes he was carrying, and climbed into the driver's seat. He reversed the rental out of its space, pulled onto the Coast Highway, hung a left onto the California Incline, drove up to the top of the bluffs, then turned right onto Ocean Avenue, where he hung a left onto Wilshire Boulevard, and drove east toward the Grove.

Whoever had hired the first hit man might have hired a second.

However, Brody doubted a hit man would ambush him at a restaurant in a busy mall like the Grove.

Brody didn't let his guard down, though. He was packing his SIG P365 in his ankle holster.

He didn't see any sign of Evelyn at La Piazza. He selected a table, ordered a Perrier, and told the waiter he was waiting for someone. The waiter left two menus at the table.

Brody spotted her ten minutes later. Wearing dark slacks, a cream button-down blouse, and a pair of butterfly gradient sunglasses, she spotted him and sat at his table.

They ordered margherita pizzas.

"Did anyone hang a tail on you?" he asked, scoping the concourse, trying to pick up on anyone suspicious looking their way.

"I didn't see anyone," she answered. "Why would anyone follow me?"

"A hit man was waiting for us at our last meet."

Fidgeting, she drank a glass of water. "Don't remind me. I'm lucky I had car trouble that time. Whew. What a break."

"I'm not trying to upset you, but have you figured out who would hire a hit man to ambush you?"

"No," she said, shifting uncomfortably in her seat. "Maybe—uh—it had something to do with Olivia's kidnapers."

"All right. We need to discuss Keogh. Why is he denying it's him?"

"I don't know what's going on."

"Are you sure it's him?"

She nodded yes. "Unless he has a twin I don't know about. And that's impossible. How could my parents have hid a twin from me?"

"Could he have amnesia?"

"I suppose. But why would he think he was someone else?"

Brody nodded. “And why would he be carrying around someone else’s authentic ID?” He paused in thought. “Maybe he’s afraid the guy that murdered Wasson and the others is after him.”

“That could be. But why pretend he’s someone else to me? He knows he can’t fool *me*. I’m his sister. What’s the point?”

“Maybe he really is Sam Hodges.”

“I don’t believe it.”

“Where do we go from here?” said Brody, leaning back in his chair.

“I want you to find out why Tyler’s pretending to be someone else. There’s something fishy going on, and I want to know what it is.”

“It might have something to do with that experiment he was involved in at Stanford. Nobody knows anything about it, which makes me suspicious.”

“I can’t help you. He never told me about it.”

“I’m suspecting a cover-up. The government was involved. It would explain why the FBI gave me a warning to stay away from Keogh.”

“The FBI? I don’t see how they could be involved.”

“Did you talk to Keogh after you left the police station?”

“I haven’t been able to find him. He’s disappeared again. I need you to find him. Maybe he was afraid of talking to the cops, but he’ll talk to me in private.”

“If it really is him, his life’s in danger. The Mensa serial killer hasn’t been caught yet, and there’s no reason to think he’s gonna stop killing.”

Evelyn slumped in her chair. “We’re right back where we started. Tyler’s still missing. If only the cops hadn’t let him go.”

“They had no reason to hold him.”

“But now his life’s in danger.”

“At least you know he’s still alive.”

“He was still alive at the police station, anyway.”

“I hear ya.” Brody mulled it over. “My advice is to look into this Stanford experiment he was involved in.”

“Why?”

"Keogh's problems seemed to start after it, and why is everyone involved in it so close-mouthed about it?"

Evelyn shrugged, took a bite of her pizza, and swallowed it. "Maybe it was harmless."

"Have you ever heard of the Department of Defense being involved in anything harmless?"

"How do you expect to find anything about this experiment?"

"The best way would be to talk to Keogh and get it straight from the horse's mouth. But if he's gone to ground, finding him could be tough. And he might have signed an NDA when he agreed to the experiment, which would gag him."

"Plus he's pretending he's not Tyler."

Brody snarfed his pizza wedge. "The best bet is for me to go up to Stanford, snoop around, and rattle some cages. Somebody involved in the experiment might be willing to open up about it."

Polishing off his pizza he wiped his hands with his napkin.

"If I find Tyler while you're gone, I'll ask him about the experiment," said Evelyn.

"I'll have to drive up there. The cops might be checking the flight passenger manifests searching for my name."

Chapter 50

It was a six-hour drive all the way up the 5 to Silicon Valley.

Brody made several stops along the way to take a break, get out and stretch, and grab a burger and a Coke.

Miles of freeway unraveled before him mesmerizing him like lost memories speeding by, impossible to apprehend.

He got the impression someone was tailing him. He checked his rearview mirror fitfully, but couldn't confirm. He kept seeing a black sedan. But it could have been a different black sedan each time he spotted it. He couldn't even tell what model it was.

Why would anyone want to follow him to Stanford? he wondered. Maybe he was getting paranoid. Maybe that fentanyl powder or whatever it was he had absorbed through his skin on Cordova's corpse was still acting on him.

At last he arrived at the Stanford Wu Tsai Neurosciences Institute building, where they had conducted the experiment, as far as he could determine. Conyers, the Stanford PR flack he had talked to on the phone, had conceded Keogh had taken part in an experiment—but that was as far as Conyers would go.

Most of the university had mission-style architecture with flesh-colored stucco buildings and orange tiled roofs.

However, the brand-new Neurosciences Institute, which had opened two years ago, was different, designed in a modern style. With a burnt sienna roof, it was a steel and glass rectangular building with an elliptical courtyard like a racetrack at its center where you could run yourself ragged for hours and end up going nowhere. Maybe that was the point. The more you found out, the less you knew. Academia.

By the time Brody got there, it was getting dark. He doubted any of the staff would be working at this late hour.

He found a motel, booked a room, grabbed a bite to eat at a nearby Burger King, returned to his room, took two Tylenol PM blue tablets to relax his tense body, and went to bed.

The next day after a quick breakfast of orange juice, coffee, and flapjacks, he parked his rental in the Neurosciences Institute multilevel parking garage, stretched his still-aching legs, yawned, and walked into the institute's lobby. He rambled around, found the directory, and located the name of the guy he had talked to on the phone about the experiment before he had left his hotel—Wo Fong, some kind of PR flack for the institute.

Brody took the elevator to the third floor, strode to Fong's office, knocked briefly, and entered.

"Hello?" said a Hispanic brunette secretary from behind her desk, her brown eyes wide, surprised to see him enter.

"I'd like to speak to Wo Fong."

"Do you have an appointment?"

"I spoke on the phone to him."

"You need to make an appointment."

His eyes locked on Fong's office, Brody strode past the secretary's desk and flung open Fong's door.

"Hey," cried the secretary. "You can't go in there."

Brody entered the room and shut the door behind him.

Dressed casually, sporting a goatee, a plump middle-aged Chinese guy wearing black plastic-framed spectacles looked up from his desk, perturbed.

"Who do you think you are?" he said, reaching for the handset on his desktop phone. "I'm calling security."

"I don't think anything. I *know* who I am. I'm Scott Brody, PI."

"Get you and your sick joke out of here."

Brody stalked to the window that overlooked the elliptical concourse below.

"Is this your idea of a Colosseum?" he said, gazing below. "Do you run chariot races down there and watch from the comfort of your office munching popcorn?"

"Have you lost your mind?" said Fong, aghast. "This is one of the leading universities in the country."

Brody stepped in front of Fong's desk. "We talked on the phone about the experiment Tyler Keogh took part in. The one funded by DDW LLC. Darryl Conyers gave me your name."

Fong relaxed somewhat, releasing his grip on the handset.

"We run a lot of experiments, and we get our funding from different organizations," he said.

For the first time, Brody realized there was another man in the room sitting on a black Naugahyde sofa with its back set against the side of the wall opposite the desk. About thirty, with a small nose and beady eyes, he was flipping briskly through a science magazine he had selected from a crooked pile of a dozen lumped on the coffee table in front of him. He had continued flipping through the magazine with darning-needle fingers despite Brody's impetuous entrance.

"This is important," said Brody. "It may have something to do with a string of murders that have been committed in LA."

"Nonsense," said Fong. "How could one of our experiments have anything to do with murders over three hundred miles from here?"

"That's what I'm trying to find out. What kind of experiment did you perform on Keogh."

"Like I told you over the phone, that information is classified. We do not discuss our experiments with anyone."

"Why not? What are you trying to hide?"

"Nothing. We perform sensitive experiments to benefit mankind."

"If they benefit mankind, why are you keeping them secret? Does that make any kind of sense?"

"Our experiments are highly sensitive."

"You're repeating yourself and begging the question."

"You need to leave," said Fong, pointing to the door behind Brody.

"I need to know what's going down. Your experiment on Keogh might have caused him to lose his memory. How does that benefit mankind?"

"Ridiculous," said Fong, dumbfounded. "He wasn't injured in any way. In fact, just the opposite. He was improved—" Fong caught himself.

"Improved? What do you mean *improved*? Improved how?"

Fit to be tied, Fong shot to his feet. "I don't need to explain myself to you. You have no right to barge in here and pelt me with questions."

"Did you do something to his mind? Is that what your neuroscience experiments are about?"

"Do you want me to call security?"

"I want you to come clean. What are you trying to hide?"

"Ask DDW. They're the ones that funded the experiment."

"I'm asking you. What are you hiding? Did you wipe Keogh's memory with your frigging experiment?"

"Everything in the experiment improved him. He's the best he can be."

"With amnesia? He can't even remember his own name. You call that being his best?"

"All of our experiments are beneficial to the human race."

"According to who?"

"According to science."

Brody reached over the desk and grabbed Fong by his collar. "You bastards. What did you do to him?"

"That's it," said Fong, his face red, shaking free from Brody's grasp. "I've had it with you."

Fong snatched up the handset and called security.

It wasn't long before two burly rent-a-cops stormed into the office and snagged Brody by his arms.

"Let go of me," said Brody, struggling to free himself.

One of the guards rammed his fist into Brody's solar plexus, doubling him over.

"Get that maniac out of here," said Fong.

The two armed guards manhandled Brody out of the office.

Chapter 51

The campus security guards frog-marched Brody through the lobby and out the plate-glass door. Outside, they shoved him down the concrete steps. Brody stumbled down the steps and collapsed on the landing, barking his knees and scraping the heel of his right hand.

The two guards glowered at him, daring him to try to reenter the building. The musclebound guy crossed his arms. The shorter one held his arms akimbo and jutted his face out at Brody with an angry scowl.

Brody felt like kicking their teeth in. But he knew the cops would come and bust him for trespassing and assault. He picked himself up and made for the concrete parking garage where he had parked his rental.

He heard footsteps running after him.

His adrenaline kicked in.

Preparing for an assault he wheeled around to face his attackers, figuring they were the rent-a-cops that had roughed him up in the institute. Ready to lash out, he was surprised to find the thirtyish guy he had seen in Fong's office paging through a magazine dashing up to him breathlessly, his mouth hanging open.

"I can help you," he said, coming to a halt in front of Brody. "But we can't be seen together."

"Help me with what?"

"I heard you in Fong's office."

"Do you know what they did to Keogh?"

The man turned and looked behind him, seeing if anyone was watching him.

"We can't talk here," he said.

"Why not?"

"They don't like anyone asking questions about any of our experiments." The guy knelt down and pretended to tie his sneaker. "Don't look at me. Pretend we aren't talking."

"I don't get it."

"We don't want them to know we're talking to each other."

Brody turned away from the guy, took out his cell phone, raised it to his face, and pretended to be talking to a caller.

"What's going on?" he said.

"Meet me in section 3D in the parking garage in a half hour. I'm going back to the institute now so they won't get suspicious."

"They? Who are they?"

"They have men everywhere in the institute eavesdropping on everyone. If they hear me say the wrong thing . . . ," the guy trailed off, as he commenced tying his other shoelace.

"All right. I'll meet you there. What's your name?"

"Vincent Joule."

Joule stood up and returned to the institute, ignoring Brody.

Brody glanced back in the direction of the institute and noted that the two rent-a-cops that had given him the bum's rush had retreated into the lobby out of sight. He resumed heading to the parking garage.

Brody checked his wristwatch. He had time to kill before a half hour was up. He returned to his rental in the parking garage and sat in the driver's seat, pondering.

Wo Fong's experiment had ostensibly helped Keogh, according to Fong. Yet Keogh's brains were scrambled, decided Brody. The guy had amnesia. Did Fong and his DOD cohorts consider amnesia beneficial? Brody didn't see how they could—unless Keogh had taken part in an experiment so awful, he was better off forgetting everything about it.

Maybe they had brainwashed Keogh. To what end? wondered Brody. Or had the experiment gone haywire? Was that why they were covering it up? Because it was a failure with dire consequences for Keogh?

Brody produced his cell phone and called Evelyn.

"I may be onto something," he said.

"Did you find Tyler?"

"I'm at Stanford trying to determine what experiments they conducted on him here."

"And?"

“I’m gonna meet someone, a whistle-blower who has agreed to fill me in. Nobody else will talk to me. The Neurosciences Institute’s PR flack blew me off and eighty-sixed me from his office.”

“Tell me what you find out. Then get back here and find Tyler.”

She hung up.

Brody called Val.

“I think I’m onto something,” he said.

“Did you find the shitheel? I’m convinced he’s got a shack job on Sunset. Some slut he met on one of those sugar baby apps. He’s boob hungry, you know. He’s pretending he’s someone else so he can play around with a tramp who struts around with her hot pants wedged halfway up her crack, her tramp-stamped ass hanging out. Find out her name and where she lives. I’ll take care of that dirty little gold digger.”

Brody rolled his eyes. “I’m investigating an experiment he was involved in at Stanford. I found a whistle-blower who’s willing to spill the beans about it.”

“Whistle-blower? What the hell did they do to Tyler?”

“I’m gonna find out in about fifteen minutes. The government’s involved.”

“Why didn’t he tell me about this?”

“I doubt he told anyone. Government projects are always hush-hush. Dollars to doughnuts he had to sign an NDA.”

“That’s what he wants me to sign in his prenup, if I can ever find it. My lawyer says no to signing NDAs.”

“I don’t know anything about that.”

“Get back here and find him. I’m not paying you to go to college.”

Brody pulled the cell away from his ear to put some distance between him and her shrill voice.

“Did you hear me?” she went on. “I want you to find him and drag his ass back to me. I’ll straighten him out. I don’t care what those mad scientists did to his brain. Even if they fried it into guacamole, he’s not backing out of our marriage. If he’s gonna try to use this experiment as an excuse to call off our marriage, he's got another think coming. That bird's not gonna fly. No way, buddy boy, is what I got to say to him about trying to pull a fast one. Hello? Are you there?"

"I have to meet the whistle-blower now."

"I told you, I don't give a flying fig about your Deep Throat. Whoever this clown is. Forget him, come back here, and find Tyler's prenup. It's *my* money you're spending up there. A fool and his money are soon parted. Am I getting through to you? Hello? Hello?"

Brody terminated the call. He would deal with Val later. He didn't want to be late to his meet with Joule.

Chapter 52

Brody climbed out of his rental and headed for section 3D, which was on the third level of the garage. He took the stairs, listening to his footfalls echo in the stairwell.

Joule wouldn't be taking such precautions as arranging clandestine meetings if he didn't think there would be danger, decided Brody. He was tempted to withdraw his SIG from his ankle holster as he arrived at the third-floor landing. But he didn't want anyone to see him holding a piece. They might notify security.

Brody pulled open the fire door and walked onto the third floor. He looked around for Joule, but didn't see him. Maybe Joule was late.

Brody wandered among the parked cars.

A young couple got out of a used SUV, locked its doors, hugged each other, and made a beeline for the elevator, ignoring him.

Brody kept moseying around.

He gazed out of the concrete parking structure at the Neurosciences Institute across the way casting around for Joule to no avail. Brody was becoming concerned something might have happened to Joule. Maybe someone had heard that Joule was going to spill his guts about the experiment. That someone could have put Joule out of commission one way or another.

Brody turned around and scanned the parking garage in search of Joule.

Not seeing him, Brody walked up the ramp to try the next level.

He thought he spotted smoke pluming from behind a concrete column twenty-odd feet away. He stole toward the column to get a better look. If somebody was behind it, he wanted to make the first sighting. It might be a security guard, for all Brody knew.

Brody peered around the column.

Joule was leaning against the other side of the column smoking a cigarette.

"You startled me," he said, eyes wide. "I didn't think you were ever going to get here."

"This is 4D, not 3D," said Brody. "You said meet at 3D. It's lucky I decided to search for you."

"I gave you the wrong level on purpose, in case anyone was eavesdropping on us or could read my lips. I'm glad you finally figured it out. You have no idea how dangerous it is for me to talk to you."

"I haven't figured anything out."

Tendrils of smoke unraveling from the cigarette wedged between his fingers, Joule scoped out the garage.

"I don't see anyone around," he said. "We can talk."

"What's the big secret?"

"Whenever the government's involved, there's always a lid on what gets out to the public, especially when the Department of Defense, the CIA, or the NSA is involved."

"The CIA? They're in on Keogh's experiment?"

"Not that I know of. But they have been involved in others here. I believe DDW LLC is a shell company for the Department of Defense."

"And DDW funded the experiment on Keogh, according to Conyers. He didn't admit working for the DOD, though. I asked him."

"Well, he wouldn't, would he?" said Joule with a half-smile. "It's not public knowledge. There's no written record of it anywhere. The government doesn't want to get blamed if something goes wrong, so they use a shell company to front for them. Plausible deniability."

"It's a dangerous experiment?" said Brody, pricking up his ears.

"This particular surgery has never been done before."

"Keogh was a guinea pig?"

"He volunteered, but he had to sign an NDA, of course."

"What kind of surgery are we talking about?"

"Let me preface this with a little background information. The amount of controversial experiments the government was, and is, involved in is mind-blowing. Have you heard of the Tuskegee Syphilis Experiment?"

"Vaguely. Did they do that here at Stanford?"

"No, but it was conducted by the government—the Centers for Disease Control and Prevention and the United States Public Health Service, to be exact. They conducted a study of syphilis in black males. The experimenters claimed they were treating the ones who had syphilis, but in reality they weren't. They were letting the disease progress so they could study the different stages it went through to kill a man. A lot of the test subjects died of syphilis."

"Were they treating Keogh for syphilis here? I heard he's a notorious skirt-chaser."

Joule shook his head no. "That's just one example of government experiments. What about the CIA's Project MKUltra?"

"I heard of that. They were testing LSD."

Brody thought of the graffiti scrawled on the wall of the serial killings. Acid Is Groovy.

"They ran the tests on people who didn't know they had consumed the drug to see how it affected them," said Joule. "They wanted to know if acid could be used to get test subjects to confess under interrogation. One CIA agent who had been dosed without his knowledge jumped out a window while he was tripping and killed himself. There are those that claim the guy was pushed to his death in an attempt at a cover-up."

"You're making these tests sound ominous."

"They are. This shit happens. And—"

"There's more?"

"You betcha. Remember Project Artichoke?"

"No."

"Back in the fifties the CIA wanted to be able to get people to do their bidding against their will. They used morphine and hypnosis, among other things, to erase their minds and control them."

"Erase their minds? Is that what happened here to Keogh? He has total amnesia. He can't remember a thing."

"You're getting ahead of the story. There was also the CIA's Project Midnight Climax where the CIA hired hookers to lure unsuspecting test subjects into a room equipped with a one-way mirror that CIA agents used to observe them."

"Sounds like voyeurs trying to get their rocks off."

"You're missing the point. It's all about control. The CIA wanted ways to control the test subjects. The agency used hookers to do it in Midnight Climax."

"I don't see what this has to do with Keogh."

Joule took a deep draft on his cigarette and blew out a cone of smoke. "It's all leading up to that. I'm giving you background material so you understand what's going down."

"I don't need all this background info. Let's cut to the chase."

"Wait a second. One more experiment. Dr. Leo Stanley. Does that name ring any bells?"

"Never heard of him."

"He was a doctor at San Quentin who experimented on inmates. He transplanted testicles from dead inmates into living ones. He also transplanted testicles from goats and boars into living inmates."

"Jesus. What did they do to him?"

"Applauded him. He died of old age when he was ninety."

"Don't tell me they transplanted Keogh's testicles."

"No. You know Stanford's in the heart of Silicon Valley, right?"

"Yeah. So?"

"Listen to this. They implanted a microchip in Keogh's brain to increase his IQ. If certain knowledge isn't in his memory, the microchip can access it via the Internet and transmit it to Keogh's intellect."

Brody couldn't believe it. "A microchip in his brain?"

Joule nodded yes. "At the Wu Tsai Neurosciences Institute."

"Why? I thought he had a high IQ to begin with."

"Exactly. That's why they selected him. They wanted to make him even smarter."

"He agreed to be a test subject?"

"Keogh is ambitious and arrogant. He wants to be the smartest person in the world. The government did a prolonged study of him to make sure he was their best candidate. They found out everything about him. His finances, the women he was shacked up with, his egotism, everything."

"It's fantastic," said Brody, incredulous. "Did Keogh know they were investigating him? Didn't it bother him?"

"You'd have to ask him."

"He won't even admit he's Keogh, let alone the government experimented on him."

"I don't think he cared the government was investigating him." Joule smiled. "Well, who wouldn't want to be the smartest person?"

"But at what price?"

"That's the thing. We don't know, do we, until we do the experiment. The experiment had never been done before Keogh's."

"Now he has no memory. How could he possibly be the smartest man in the world without a memory?"

"How do you know he isn't pretending to have lost his memory? All I know is, a lot of people want him."

"For what?"

"To work for them. That's why the government is trying to keep the experiment under wraps. They want Keogh all for themselves. They don't want foreign governments finding out."

Brody tried to wrap his head around it. "Does the government know he's living in Malibu?"

"That I don't know. I don't work for the government. I work for the university." Joule leaned closer to him, so close Brody could smell Joule's deodorant. "In fact, I shouldn't be telling you any of this. They only let you see what they want you to see—"

Joule's head snapped to the side, a bullet embedded in his temple. He crumpled to the concrete floor, dropping his burning cigarette.

Wide-eyed, Brody cast around for the source of the bullet. He didn't see a shooter. It could have been a sniper at the Neurosciences Institute building. He darted around the column just as another slug sang through the air and chipped concrete from the column. A puff of smoke erupted from the column.

He thought he knew the general direction of the gunfire, but he couldn't locate the shooter. It had to be a sniper. Brody glanced at Joule's motionless body on the ground. He didn't see how Joule could have survived. There wasn't much blood on Joule's temple. You didn't bleed when you were dead.

Brody crouched and scurried behind a silver Range Rover.

A distant shot rang out. Brody could barely hear it. The sniper must have been using a sound suppressor. The bullet shattered the Range Rover's rearview mirror.

Hunched over, sweating, Brody whipped behind a dark green Mustang.

A bullet sang over his head. Brody couldn't tell where the bullet landed.

Adrenaline coursing through his system, he backed and filled between motor vehicles till he reached the stairwell, rammed the crash bar on the stairwell's fire door with his elbow, and burst onto the landing. He barreled down the steps to the second floor, where he had parked his rental.

Weaving between cars he reached his rental, clambered into the driver's seat, and blew out of the parking garage, tires shrieking.

He knew asking Wo Fong any more questions about the experiment would be hazardous to his health.

Chapter 53

Alone in the chaos, sirens knifing through the night, he slept fitfully.

He kept dreaming of writhing snakes eating his entrails. Instead of entrails he had snakes coiled in his stomach. One snake kept trying to crawl up his throat out of his mouth, suffocating him. Jerked awake, jackknifing up, he looked down at his body in horror to see his arms had turned into fer-de-lance, as well as his legs that were slithering on the bed obscenely.

He screamed.

He gagged as a copperhead pit viper squirmed out of his mouth and craned around, flicking its forked orange-red tongue. Brody's face turned red and blue as he suffocated on the copperhead's body wedged in his throat. He had only seconds to live before he ceased breathing.

He screamed again.

Now he was really awake.

Before, he had dreamed he was awake and screaming. There were no snakes. His arms and legs were where they should be. He felt his mouth. He could breathe through it. No pit viper's head was protruding from it, hissing.

Brody was only able to sleep a few more hours.

He got up early, grabbed hotcakes, a sausage, and scrambled eggs at a McDonald's, and scarfed them down with orange juice at the crack of dawn. He saw a cop enter the restaurant. Brody averted his head, knocked back the rest of his orange juice.

He set out for LA on the 5.

With any luck he would arrive in LA at around noon, depending on rush-hour traffic and how many breaks he took from driving.

He kept glancing in his rental's rearview mirror. Whoever had tried to shoot him after they got Joule might be tailing him. Out of earshot while Joule was talking to Brody, the shooter had no way of knowing how much Joule had told him. For all the shooter knew, Brody might know everything Joule knew—in which case Brody's days were numbered.

Brody hoped it wasn't the government trying to waste him. They had too many resources to trace him for him to be able to escape their clutches. The shooter wasn't necessarily working for the government. He could have been a university scientist connected to the experiment who wanted to keep it under wraps. But how many scientists were sharpshooters? And how many went around whacking people? Maybe it was DDW LLC that had hired the sniper. Possible. And Joule had told him DDW was a shell company for the Department of Defense. Brody kept coming back to the government as his adversary.

Brody pulled off the freeway into a rest area.

He dug his cell phone out of his trouser pocket and called Evelyn.

"I have news," he said.

"You found Tyler?" she said, expectantly.

"I found out the kind of experiment he was involved in at Stanford."

"What kind of experiment?"

"They refused to tell me—"

"You just said you found out—"

"Let me finish. I talked to a whistle-blower."

"Yes?"

"He managed to tell me they implanted a microchip in Keogh's brain."

"Jesus. Did they make Tyler into their robot?"

"I don't know what their plan is."

"Is that why he has no memory? Because of the brain surgery?"

"Could be. It's supposed to make him smarter than everybody else, according to the flack at the Neurosciences Institute."

"We need to talk to Tyler to find out what they did to him."

"We can't even find him, let alone talk to him."

"That's why I was hoping *you* had found him."

"This is big. His life is in danger."

Brody heard a helicopter hovering above him, its rotors churning up a racket.

Did they have a chopper tailing him? he wondered.

He shook it off. He was letting his imagination get the better of him.

"What can we do to help him?" said Evelyn.

"We need him to fill in the gaps about this experiment he participated in. Hopefully, he knows enough to stay away from his house."

"You think—"

"I'm convinced the Mensa murderer wants him as his next victim."

"I was talking to Macready. He says there are no signs of break-ins at any of the Mensa murder sites. He says the victims all knew the killer."

"The killer must know Keogh. Tell Keogh to stay away from his house."

"I can't tell him anything if I can't find him. That's where you come in. You need to find him ASAP."

She terminated the call.

Brody got out of the rental, stretched his legs, and bought a chilled plastic liter bottle of water at the minimart. The helo continued to hover overhead. Brody didn't look up at it, keeping his head down, as he returned to his rental, bottle in hand.

Brody slid into the driver's seat, whipped out his cell, and called Val.

"Has Keogh made any attempt to contact you?" he said.

"No way."

"I found out scientists implanted a microchip in his brain at Stanford."

"Holy shit. Why for Christ's sake?"

"To make him smarter."

"Smarter? He's a dufus. He doesn't even know his own name anymore."

"Let me know if he tries to contact you. I have to talk to him."

"You got things upside down. *I'm* the one that has to talk to him. And *you're* the one that's supposed to find him for *me*."

"I'm working on it."

"I want you to get Tyler to give me that prenup. That's your assignment."

"The microchip may be interfering with his thoughts."

"That's no excuse. Get a move on it."

She hung up.

Brody fired the rental's engine, pulled out of the rest area, and onto the freeway ramp.

Its rotors whumping, the chopper was following, he decided uneasily.

A sickening thought struck him. Had the sniper set him up as the fall guy for Joule's murder? Were the cops at Stanford putting it around that *he* was the one that had killed Joule? If so, he was a murder suspect there as well as in LA. He would have to continue to lie low.

The chopper was rising, backing off, banking to starboard.

Maybe they weren't going to bust him, decided Brody, breathing easier, accelerating on the freeway. Not yet, anyway, his relief short-lived as he thought of the cops in LA who would be chafing at the bit to cuff him the minute they laid eyes on him.

Chapter 54

Val drove her cream cabriolet Porsche with its red nylon roof retracted to Keogh's house to resume her search for the prenup. She parked in the driveway, let herself in, and found her way to his office.

Ten feet from the office door she became alert and halted. She heard a noise coming from the office. It sounded like a filing cabinet was being opened or closed.

She crept to the doorway, curious to find out who was in the room.

She saw Hodges standing in front of a grey metal filing cabinet, flipping through manila folders lined inside the top drawer.

"So you're not Tyler, huh?" she said, acidly.

Startled, he slewed around to see who was talking.

"I'm Sam Hodges. But I got curious about this guy that's supposed to be my dead ringer. I thought I'd come to his place and take a look around. After all, nobody would throw me out, since I'm his spitting image, according to you guys."

"You expect me to believe your bullshit? How'd you get in here?"

"The back door was open."

"Because you always leave it open. Now how would you know that if you're not Tyler?"

"Me? Not me. I'm Sam Hodges."

"Don't you get tired of playing this game, pretending you're someone else?"

"I don't know what you're talking about."

"If you're not Tyler, I'm gonna call the cops. How's that grab you?"

"There's no need to do that. I'll leave."

"Just give me the prenup and we can get married."

"I'm not gonna marry a total stranger. And I don't have any prenup."

Val folded her arms across her chest. "We've been seeing each other for the last three years. How can I be a stranger?"

"I'm not Tyler whatever. I'm Sam Hodges. Got it?"

He slammed the filing cabinet's drawer shut.

"Is the prenup in that drawer?" said Val.

"Ask your future husband."

"I am."

"You are messed up. I don't know you from Adam."

"I know this much. Somebody's trying to kill you."

He stared at her. "Go on."

"The serial killer that killed your Mensa pals wants to do you."

"Why?"

"He's in some cult. Satan worshipers or voodoo followers. He's wasting all your buds."

"Then I'm glad I'm not this Keogh guy. I don't want some nutbag cult after me."

"Pretending you're someone else isn't gonna save you. The homicidal maniac will see right through you."

"Ah, you don't know anything."

"I know a con man when I see him. You're Tyler Keogh, engineer."

"I don't drive a train. I haven't even been on one since I was a kid."

"Not *that* kind of engineer. An aeronautical engineer."

"Don't tell me who I am. I'm Sam Hodges. I run my own private mailbox rental business. I don't want to brag, but I also play the stock market and I'm damn good at it."

"Oh, sure. Give it up, baby. I know all about you. You got a microchip implanted in your grey matter."

He stared at her nonplussed.

"That's right, I know," said Val. "I got a PI on your ass, Tyler."

Hodges burst out laughing.

"What's so funny?" she said, taken aback.

"A microchip in my brain? That's insane."

“Stanford scientists implanted the microchip and wiped your memory. They brainwashed you.”

Hodges shook his head. “Where do you come up with this stuff? Oh, sure. A mad scientist got ahold of me? *Ha ha*.”

Val changed her tone, looking at him with concern. “You really don’t know who you are, Tyler?”

“I really know who I am. Who you are is a mystery.”

“They made you crazy?” she said, her voice breaking. “Those creeps.” She approached him, her stilettos clacking on the floor. “Let me give you a hug. Then you’ll remember.”

She hugged him.

He didn’t respond, standing there, his face blank.

“Snap out of it,” she said. “Bring back the old Tyler I fell in love with.”

“I don’t know who you are,” he said, and broke away from her.

She watched him with befuddlement and dismay.

“They turned you into a monster,” she said, her eyes tearing.

She thought she caught sight of a trace of a smile on his lips, but it vanished as quickly as it had appeared. She must have imagined it. His blank face didn’t recognize her. Like he was one of the pod people. He was starting to scare the crap out of her.

“Are you finished?” he said.

She didn’t say anything. She felt crushed. She didn’t know what to do. She loved the guy, but they had messed him up. She couldn’t think straight. She couldn’t cope. She had to get out of here.

Chapter 55

Brody made it back to LA a little after two o'clock.

He met Evelyn at her condo's pool. She was lying on her back in an apricot bikini on a white vinyl chaise longue sunning herself, a pina colada with a lavender umbrella in the glass on a square white metal coffee table beside her.

Not many people around, he noticed. They could talk freely. He didn't see any cops. They would have no reason to be watching her.

He crossed the deck to her, his muscles still tense and kinked from the long ride in his rental down I-5, his sweat-damped trouser legs sticking to the backs of his legs. He looked around him, wondering if Joule's assassin had followed him here from Stanford. He had kept checking his rental's rearview mirror the entire trip and hadn't made a tail.

"What's wrong?" she said, watching him through her fashionable bug-eyed dark glasses with white plastic frames. "Are you being followed?"

"I was just checking," said Brody.

He pulled a deck chair over to her and straddled it. Leaning toward her he could smell her coconut-scented tanning lotion.

"Did you find out anything?" she said.

"They performed surgery on Keogh."

"Surgery? What kind of surgery?"

"Brain surgery."

She sat upright in alarm. "He never told me there was anything wrong with his brain."

"There wasn't."

"I don't understand."

"The flack at Stanford's Neurosciences Institute wouldn't tell me anything. Some guy called Wo Fong. A whistle-blower named Joule filled me in."

"If there was nothing wrong with Tyler's brain, why did they operate on it?"

“To make him more intelligent. He already had a high IQ. They boosted it to five times that level by implanting a microchip in his brain.”

“Is that why he has amnesia?” she said, appalled. “Because they diced his brain?”

“Looks that way.”

“Then the surgery was a failure,” she said, her shoulders slumping. “He’s now a vegetable.”

“Not according to Joule. He seemed to consider the surgery a success.”

“But Tyler can’t even remember who he is.”

“So he says.”

“Is there anything we can do about it?”

“Not with the government behind it.”

“Why would the government do brain surgery on Tyler?” she said, unable to get her head around it. “He didn’t work for the government.”

“It gets worse.”

“How could making Tyler a vegetable get worse?”

“They shot the whistle-blower who clued me in.”

Evelyn’s jaw dropped. “Oh no. There must be something we can do.”

“It might not be him. He says he’s not Keogh. It could be someone that looks like him.”

“It’s him.”

“Why would he have genuine ID that says otherwise?”

Bowing her head Evelyn scratched her scalp. “There’s a lot I don’t understand.”

“I’m in the same boat. I still can’t figure out who hired the hit man who tried to waste me at the construction site.”

Her hand shook as she grabbed her pina colada and raised it to her lips splashing some of it out. “Don’t remind me.”

“You’re lucky you weren’t there.”

Evelyn heaved a sigh. “Since Olivia is safe, I can tell you the truth. You’ll probably figure it out anyway. Maybe you already have.” She sucked in her breath. “I—I hired him.”

Brody drew away from her in astonishment. Anger gnawed at his insides.

"You hired the guy to blow me away?" he said, incredulous.

"My daughter was kidnaped. The kidnapers wanted you to stop looking for her, but you refused. What else could I do? I didn't want to do it, but Olivia's life was at stake. Can't you understand?"

There was a long silence between them.

"I understand," he said, standing up, "but I can't work for you any longer. I feel like killing you in retaliation. Christ, you tried to have me whacked."

"I did it to save Olivia's life," said Evelyn, her voice pleading.

She bowed her head, sobbing.

"Tell me why I shouldn't kill you," said Brody.

"I was forced to do it. My back was against the wall. You or Olivia had to die. I chose you."

He said nothing for a long time, letting her stew in her own juice.

"Don't worry," he said. "I'm not gonna whack you. I have every right to, but I don't operate like that. We're quits."

"I'm sorry. I had to do it. I had no choice."

Deep down, he had known it was her who had hired the mechanic. What were the chances she would get a flat tire and not show up at the construction site when the hit man tried to whack him out? Slim and none.

"I'll send you my bill," he said, his face stony.

Smoldering, he stalked off.

He ought to drop Val as a client, too, and walk away from the entire Keogh affair. But, like Evelyn and Val, Brody wanted to know what was going on. If the government was conducting unethical experiments that were harming the test subjects, the public had a right to know, he decided—especially if they were hiring hit men to take out whistle-blowers and anyone asking questions to uncover the truth.

"What can we do for Tyler?" she called after him.

Brody said nothing, kept walking.

He really ought to kill her. Hell, she might try to whack him again.

But he doubted it. Her daughter was safe. He had killed the kidnaper. Why should she try again?

Change in plans. He was working for Val now.

Chapter 56

Brody drove his rental to Val's luxurious, well-appointed condo in Brentwood.

He managed to find a parking space on the side of the street, arriving just as someone was pulling out.

He strode to the security gate at the high-rise condo, found Val's name on the directory, and buzzed her room. She buzzed him in. He took the elevator to her apartment.

Clad in a low-cut scarlet minidress that clung to her figure, she reeked of liquor as she let him into her living room.

"The government's behind Keogh's brain surgery," he said.

Unsteady on her feet, she closed the door behind him. She didn't act surprised.

"They rewired his brain," she said.

"What do you mean?"

"I met him at his house."

"You did?"

She sat down on a plush velvet recliner, almost falling onto it, and crossed her legs.

"I went to his place to look for the prenup and found him there," she said.

"Hodges?"

"He's not Hodges. He's Tyler. What would Hodges be doing in Tyler's house?"

"Did he claim he was Hodges?"

"Yeah. He says he's Hodges. That microchip you said they implanted in his brain wiped his mind. He doesn't know who he is."

"How do you know it's not an act? Maybe he's pretending to be Hodges."

She lifted a glass of tequila off the coffee table beside her and took a pull on it.

"I could tell if he was pretending," she said, slurring her speech. "It was like he had no idea who I was. It was . . . scary and . . . sickening at the same time. I wanted to throw up."

Brody thought about it. "That doesn't explain his driver's license in Hodges's name."

"He had someone forge it for him."

"He'd have to be a top professional to forge one of those. They're not easy to duplicate."

"So? He hired a top forger. He's got plenty of dough."

Brody paced around the room, mulling it over.

"Either that or the government provided him with the documents," he said. "That would explain why they passed as the real thing. In effect, they *are* the real thing because they're printed by the government."

"It's him, but he's not the Tyler I know and lost my heart to. He's some kind of unfeeling robot. He doesn't even like being hugged. What the hell did those mad scientists do to him?"

She started weeping.

Brody found a Kleenex box on a bureau and handed her a tissue.

She wiped her face.

"We need to figure this out," he said.

"There ought to be a law. How do these government guys get away with turning people into robots?"

"Is he still at his house?"

"When I left, he was there."

"What was he doing there? If he's pretending to be someone else, it's risky for him to go to his house. If the cops found out about it, they'd know he was faking."

"He was looking for something, I think."

"What do you want me to do now?"

"Turn him back into the real Tyler, the man I want to marry."

"Maybe a psychiatrist—"

"I don't want a shrink. I want Tyler back."

"His life is in danger. The Mensa serial killer is at large. If he finds out Hodges is Keogh . . ." Brody's voice trailed off. "I need to talk to Keogh to find out if he has any friends into voodoo or Nazi occultism. These are ritual murders."

Val stared out the picture window into the distance.

"Did he tell you where he lives as Sam Hodges?" he said.

"No," she said, her mind wandering. "What am I gonna do?"

"Do you know where he lives?"

"Oh, I saw his license at the police station. His address was a PO box in Rancho Palos Verdes."

"He must have money."

"He's very successful. Or he was. Now that his brains are scrambled, who knows?"

"He might be making even more money with his advanced intelligence."

"If this is what he's like when he's smarter, I preferred him when he was stupid. At least he was a human being back then. He had his faults, but at least he had feelings. What he is now is scary."

"What do you want me to do?"

"Turn him back to his normal self."

"A surgeon would have to remove the microchip from Keogh's brain."

"Find Tyler and bring him back to me so I can talk some sense into him." She made a moue. "I can try, anyway."

"If the cult killer doesn't get to him first."

"Don't let that happen," she said, her voice steady. "I'm not giving up on him. We can't let him run around like this, not knowing who he is. He doesn't know what he's doing. He might end up marrying one of his shack jobs."

"Or maybe he *does* know what he's doing. He could be lying about not knowing his real name."

"Why would he lie to me? He knows he can't fool me." She took a pull on her tequila and made a groaning sound. "They turned him into a zombie," she said, staring into the distance, unblinking.

"I don't think you can trust him."

"You can't trust anybody. That's the problem. Whenever I trust anyone, I get burned. Can't anybody tell the truth anymore?"

"You sound bitter."

"This isn't the first time I've been double-crossed. It's a dirty, lying world. Open your eyes."

Val knocked back her tequila, trying to drown her melancholy in booze.

"Do you think I'm a loser, Brody?"

"No."

"I think we're both losers. You and me," she said, her voice slurred. Eyeballing him she plucked at the top of her minidress, pulling it down, revealing more cleavage. "Maybe we're good for each other. Whaddaya think?"

Brody felt sorry for her. Maybe she really did love the guy, even though he was coming across as a prize shitheel. On the other hand, maybe she was bummed out because she was about to lose out on Keogh's dough since Hodges wasn't going to admit he was Keogh and marry her.

Brody headed to the door.

"I'm kidding," Val called after him in her booze-loud voice.

Brody booked.

Chapter 57

Brody drove to Keogh's house and picked up on a couple of squad cars cruising the neighborhood. He decided not to risk a visit to the house in hope of finding Keogh. The guy had probably bugged out by now.

Instead, Brody drove to Lou Arano's house in LA. Arano was at the top of his list of suspects in the Mensa murders. The murderer had to be stopped before he got to Keogh.

When Brody arrived at Arano's Spanish-styled white stucco bungalow in Culver City, Arano was dead.

He hadn't been dead long.

His blood leaked on the living room's hardwood floor hadn't fully coagulated. Sensing death a couple of blowflies swirled over the stiff, preparing to lay their eggs in it, where the emerging maggots would consume and disintegrate the deceased.

Brody had found the body after entering the bungalow through the unlocked front door.

Arano was lying on his back in a pool of his blood minus his arms. The killer had hacked Arano's arms off at the shoulders, flexed them at the elbow, and posed them near Arano's bloody torso, which had been gutted so Arano died slowly. Too slowly, it seemed. The killer had delivered a coup de grâce with a knife thrust to Arano's temple to hurry things along, leaving a bloody slit in the flesh.

Brody didn't see the knife nearby.

The killer must have had enough blood to use as ink by the time he knifed Arano, but he didn't finish his graffiti. Something or someone must have spooked him, causing him to cut short his ritual. He didn't get a chance to scribble Acid Is Groovy after scrawling Li Grande Zombi in Arano's blood on the wall, which was dripping with the stuff.

At the shoulder socket of each of the dismembered arms the killer had sketched on the floor with a black Magic Marker an erect rattlesnake tail.

Brody thought he saw a snake slithering through the spilled blood toward him. Closing his eyes he shook his head to clear it. When he opened his eyes, the snake was gone. Out of the corner of his eye he saw an electric green mamba whip out of the living room and disappear. It happened so quickly he doubted his eyes.

He scoped the living room. He didn't see any more snakes. A sofa and a leather recliner had been overturned as if Arano had put up quite a struggle before losing his life.

Arano had hated his fellow Mensa member Keogh, but Arano wasn't the serial killer.

Brody was running out of suspects. Mensa was running out of members.

Brody picked up on a black sun medallion two feet from Arano's head. The ritual killings were continuing. When would they ever stop? Brody wondered. Would every member on the board of directors have to die to end the killings? What did the victims have to do with the SS and voodoo?

Brody walked around the room casting around for clues, careful not to step in the blood and leave footprints. Beside the overturned sofa he found a knife that had been thrust into the hardwood floor, presumably the knife that had been used on Arano's temple. The bloody knife was pinning a photo of a man's face to the floor. Brody approached the photo to get a better look at it. Tiny drops of blood had splattered the man's face, but Brody recognized the man. It was Keogh.

The message was clear. Keogh was next on the killer's hit list.

Brody's mission to find Keogh had just become more urgent. Did the killer know Keogh was pretending to be Sam Hodges? Brody wondered.

Brody realized the knife wasn't an ordinary knife. It was a dagger with markings on its black handle. Just below the pommel nut were silver SS runes. Below them was a silver eagle with its wings spread and a swastika under its talons. The cross-guards were made of nickel.

There was writing on the dagger's blade covered with a thin coating of drying blood.

He hunkered down to make out the words in gothic font. Despite the blood, he could discern the German words: *Meine Ehre heisst Treue.*

He didn't know German so he couldn't translate the words. Something to do with the Nazi SS, since it was an SS dagger.

He stood up.

It dawned on him that Tess wasn't here. She had been at all the other Mensa murder scenes when he visited them. Why wasn't she at this one? Had he lost her tail? Or had she already been here and left before he had arrived? He had suspected she had followed him to most, if not all, of the crime scenes. All save Arano's.

Could Tess be the serial killer? he wondered. He doubted it. What would be her motive? Unless she was clinically insane. Or could someone have hired her to kill these people? Maybe she wasn't a PI like she claimed. Maybe she was a hired gun. She had said she was working for a client. Maybe she had lied about the PI part. If she was a paid assassin, who was she working for?

All Brody knew for sure was he was running out of suspects and Keogh was running out of time. Keogh's name was next on the kill list.

Brody started. He heard a noise in another part of the bungalow.

He drew his SIG and stole toward the direction of the sound, noticing daubs of blood smeared on the floor. The killer could be here, finishing up.

Brody edged toward the bedroom's open doorway and poked his head around the jamb, gun at the ready.

He didn't see anything.

Then his eyes locked on a venomous krait writhing on the long-napped olive carpet at the foot of the bed like it was winding through grass.

He holstered his pistol and retreated from the bedroom.

He was getting sick of seeing death close up.

The nature of his job revolted him at times.

He had to try to put his mind inside the mind of the killer to figure out what was motivating the guy—if you could figure out what was motivating a psycho. Psychos had their own version of reality, which didn't gibe with anybody else's.

What would drive a cult member to murder the members of the LA Mensa board of directors? Sacrifices for his sick religion? But why sacrifice Mensa members? Why select brainy types? Brody couldn't get his head around it.

The voodoo god Li Grande Zombi wanted intellectuals sacrificed to him. At least, that was what the cultist must have thought.

Brody was flummoxed. An acid-dropping voodoo/SS cult that worshiped a snake god? He had never heard of such a cult, but wacko cults were a dime a dozen in California, where the land of eternal sunshine bred them like man-eating Venus flytraps.

He didn't want to enter such a sick mind. He fought against it. Why did he ever pick a job like private detective? Dealing with psychos, serial killers, and mass murderers. Risking his life on the job. Whatever prompted him to seek such a lonely job? Why hadn't he joined the police force, where he would have had fellow cops to cover his six and pass the time of day with?

Maybe it was because he wanted to be his own boss. *Better to reign in hell, than to serve in heaven.* Well, he had got his wish. He should be happy. He was in hell.

Brody shrugged. Like father, like son, he guessed. It was in the blood. It wasn't the cultist who was cursing him, though the guy might have been casting spells on him with a load of voodoo mumbo-jumbo—talismans, gris-gris, snakes, mind-altering drugs, and whatnot. No, it wasn't the cultist cursing him. It was his own blood.

He had to stop thinking like this. It was bumming him out. Let somebody else do this miserable job.

Maybe it was the smell of blood, murder, and death in the air. He had to get out of this nightmare crypt.

Chapter 58

Brody stole out the back door, hoping to elude nosy neighbors.

He drove away in his rental, debating whether to tell the cops about Arano's murder. He felt his cell phone vibrate in his trouser pocket. He hung a right into a Home Depot parking lot and parked.

He was able to take the call before the persistent caller rang off.

"I'd like to speak to Scott Brody," said a woman's voice.

"Who is this?" said Brody, not recognizing the voice.

"I'm Judy Wasson. Is this Scott Brody?"

"Yeah."

Wasson, he thought. The name sounded familiar. The name of the first Mensa murder victim.

"I'd like to hire you to find my husband's murderer," she said.

Brody was curious what she had to say. Maybe she could help him with his investigation. However, he was already working for Val.

"How did you get my name?" he said.

"On the Internet."

Warning flags went up in his mind. Did she know the cops were looking for him as a suspect in her husband's murder? he wondered. Could she be working for the cops as a lure?

"Uh, I'm working for another client," he said.

"I need to know who did this to my husband. I'm not going to let him get away with it."

"Have you talked to the cops?"

"I don't have a good relationship with them."

"Do you know if anyone threatened your husband, or was in a fight with him?"

"Not that I know of."

"Did he belong to a cult?"

"Myles? No way. He didn't believe in that baloney."

"Did he take psychedelics like LSD?"

"No. He was a very rational man."

"Why would a cult want to kill him?"

"It makes no sense. They must be lunatics. Drugged up nutbags. I don't want to talk anymore on the phone. Let's discuss this in person."

Brody suspected a trap. Had Lt. Macready put her up to this? Cops could be waiting to sandbag him if he arranged a meet with Judy.

"I told you, I already have a client," he said.

"What's wrong with having two clients? You earn twice as much money that way."

"Conflict of interest. My current client is also involved in the Mensa murder case."

Silence.

"Believe me, I'd like to help you," said Brody. "I want to nail this serial killer. Your husband wasn't his only victim."

"I have a photo that might interest you."

"A photo of what?"

"Of my husband with other Mensa members."

"What's so special about it?"

"All of the murder victims are in this photo, along with Tyler Keogh and several other members."

It might be helpful, decided Brody. "I'd like to see it."

"Then we need to arrange a meet so I can show it to you."

"Where did you get this photo?"

"It was in our master bedroom."

"When was it taken?"

"There's no date on it."

Brody smelled a trap. He realized he was sticking his neck out, but he needed a decent lead.

"Where do you want to meet?" he said.

"Anywhere you want, as long as it's not too far away. I don't like driving long distances."

Brody wanted to make sure she wasn't being followed by the cops or anyone else.

He suggested they meet at Will Rogers State Beach. She agreed.

He terminated the call and accessed the Internet on his smartphone to translate the German phrase on the SS dagger's blade. *Meine Ehre heisst treue*. My honor is loyalty. It was the motto of the SS.

Chapter 59

Brody arrived at Palisades Park where he could watch Judy Wasson park from the top of the cutbank as she entered the beach parking lot that bordered the Coast Highway below. She had told him over the phone she was driving a black BMW.

From the bluffs, where he stood, he had a clear view of the Coast Highway and the beach. It was the middle of the afternoon, and traffic was beginning to pick up. Any time he saw a black BMW enter the beach parking lot he watched it to see who got out.

She had e-mailed him a photo of her so he would know what she looked like. Asian, in her midthirties, she wore her black hair in a perm. She had a flat nose, broad features, high cheekbones, and an epicanthic fold over her eyes. A mole on the right side of her chin distinguished her. He didn't think he would be able to discern the mole all the way from the bluffs, though. She had said she would wear a red blouse to help him ID her.

He watched a black BMW pull into the beach parking lot under the brilliant blue sky. He didn't see any squad cars tailing it.

A grey-haired man in his sixties emerged from the driver's seat.

Brody resumed watching the Coast Highway for cars entering the parking lot.

Ten minutes later, a black BMW sedan turned into the parking lot. Brody didn't see any black-and-whites behind it, nor did he see any unmarked cop cars, which were usually black nondescript cars with a powerful antenna mounted on their trunks.

A woman in a red blouse clambered out of the BMW's driver's seat.

Brody watched her for five minutes as she strolled toward the beach.

He didn't pick up on anyone following her.

He descended the wooden treads on the long dirt stairway cut into the scarp that zigzagged down to the Coast Highway. He crossed the pedestrian bridge that spanned the highway, angled across the parking lot, watching Judy fitfully, and, spotting no one suspicious near her, strolled up to her.

"I'm Brody," he told her.

She nodded at him.

They walked along the asphalt path that skirted the parking lot.

"I didn't see anyone following me," she said.

"I didn't either."

He couldn't tell if she knew the cops suspected him of murdering her husband. If she knew, she either wasn't letting on or she didn't believe he was the murderer. She showed no signs of being afraid of him.

A squalling seagull swooped over them and air-mailed a glop of guano onto Judy's do. She didn't react as if she knew she had been pelted. Maybe she hadn't felt it.

Brody canvassed the beach in search of surveillance. The beach wasn't crowded on a weekday. He didn't catch sight of anyone watching him and Judy. A Coast Guard cutter sliced through rolling waves parallel to the shoreline, leaving a curdled wake. A black-and-white helicopter whumped overhead bearing south.

A police helo, he decided, but it wasn't necessarily surveilling him. It could be conducting a routine patrol of the beach. It didn't hover over them. It kept flying south.

"Do you have the photo?" Brody asked, eying Judy, ignoring the turd in her hair.

He wouldn't be surprised if the gull returned and tried to land in her hair mistaking it for a nest.

Judy reached into her purse and withdrew a color photo, which she handed to him.

They halted on the asphalt, as Brody inspected the picture.

"The people in the picture are all on the Mensa board of directors," said Judy. "They were at a Mensa-sponsored picnic."

Including Keogh there were nine people either sitting at a redwood picnic table or standing nearby in front of a lake. On the right side of the photo was an arm. Whoever it belonged to couldn't be seen.

Brody recognized the five murder victims: Myles Wasson, Heloise Delacroix, Eugene Frantangello, Xochitl Cordova, and Lou Arano. He also recognized Lisa Chang. The two remaining picnickers he didn't know. He hoped Lisa Chang was still alive, but he hadn't contacted her lately.

"Who are these two?" asked Brody, pointing them out.

"That one's Gottfried Mann, and the other is Kawhi James."

"Do you know whose arm that belongs to off to the side?"

"No."

"Have you been in contact with Mann or James?"

"Why should I? We don't socialize. That was the only time I ever saw them."

Fiftysomething, Mann was well over six feet, pushing six five, Brody would say from the looks of him in relationship with the others in the picture. With salt-and-pepper cropped hair and blue flinty eyes, he wore wire-rim glasses. Standing at the end of the table, he had a pasty porcine face that evinced annoyance at being present.

In his late thirties, Kawhi James was a lanky African American with a shaved head. Staring at the photographer with large black eyes, he had flared nostrils, thick lips, and a narrow, dimpled chin bracketed by large ears.

"You've been a big help," said Brody. "Could I keep this photo?"

"As long as you give it back to me later." Her voice caught. "I don't have a lot of pictures of Myles."

"No problem."

"Does this mean you'll take my case?"

Brody pocketed the photo and shook his head. "I have another client."

She didn't like his answer.

"I'll tell you what," said Brody. "If I find anything important, I'll fill you in."

"Do I have your word?"

"You do."

"I need to know who the killer is," she said, her jaw set. "I'm not gonna rest till I find out."

"Neither am I. The piece of work needs to be taken off the streets."

"And fried."

They turned around and repaired to her BMW.

"By the way, you got gull guano on your head," he said.

"Oh, thank you *so* much," she said with a smile.

Maybe English was her second language, he decided.

Chapter 60

By the time Brody scaled the wooden planks that snaked up the cutbank and reached the top, he was gasping for breath. He wasn't out of shape, but it was a long climb and he had ascended rapidly.

He phoned the DMV from his rental parked inside a public parking garage.

After ten rings Brody was about to hang up when somebody answered. A live person. Brody was impressed.

"Hello," he said. "I've been in an accident. The person who crashed into me left the scene after showing me his driver's license. I need to contact him regarding body work on my car. Can you give me his address so I can contact him?"

"What is his name?" said a woman with a brittle voice.

"Sam Hodges."

There was a pause.

"We have a lot of Sam Hodges," she said. "Could you give me something more? Do you remember what city he lives in?"

"Let me think. Rancho Palos Verdes, I believe."

"Yeah, here he is. He has a PO Box."

"Do you have his residence's street address? It's urgent I talk to him."

"We don't normally give that information out."

"I need to talk to him in person."

"Why?"

Brody turned over answers in his mind. "He dropped one of his credit cards at the scene of the accident. I need to return it to him."

"You could send it to him in the mail."

"Things get lost in the mail all the time."

"Are you injured? Do you need an officer?"

"No."

"Was the other driver injured?"

"No."

She acquiesced to his request and read Hodges's address out loud.

Brody memorized it and hung up.

He punched out Lisa Chang's number. He wanted to make sure she was all right.

Nobody answered.

Not a good sign, he decided. But it didn't necessarily mean she was dead.

He found Kawhi James's number on the Internet and tried it.

No answer.

He located Gottfried Mann's number on the Internet and called him.

"Hello," answered a man's peremptory voice.

"Could I speak to Gottfried Mann?"

"State your name and purpose."

"Scott Brody. I'm a private detective. I have reason to believe your life is in danger."

"What the hell is this about?" said Mann, vexed and put out.

"Several of your Mensa colleagues on the board of directors have been murdered."

"That's preposterous. I have a good mind to report you to the police for threatening me."

"Not all of the murders have been reported by the police."

"Then how do *you* know about them?"

"I told you. I'm a PI."

"You should have your license revoked."

"You heard of Myles Wasson's murder, haven't you? It was broadcast on the news."

Mann did not answer right away. "I heard of it. I wasn't close to the guy. What's that got to do with me?"

"I'm trying to find out. Are you involved in any cults? Voodoo or SS cults?"

"What the hell are you talking about?"

"I have reason to believe a cult of hopheads obsessed with voodoo and the SS murdered Wasson and the others."

"Are you insane?"

"Look, this is on the level. You can't make this stuff up."

"Oh, I get it. I have a German name, so you think I belong to an SS cult. Is that it, you son of a bitch?"

"That's *not* it. I've asked the same question of the other members on the board."

"But they didn't have German names, so you figure I'm the killer," said Mann, his blood boiling.

"Do you know anything about the experiment performed on Tyler Keogh?"

"What experiment?"

"He was involved in a secret experimental operation at Stanford."

"What's that got to do with anything?"

"He went into hiding after he went under the knife. He's afraid the killer is hunting him."

"You're a lunatic. Secret experiments, cults, the SS, mass murders. You're the one that's a hophead."

"I know it sounds incredible, but do you know anyone involved in cults?"

"Wait a minute. What is your name again?"

"Scott Brody," said Brody, hoping he was making progress.

"You're the one the cops want for Wasson's murder. I knew I heard that name somewhere."

"Your life is at stake. Watch your back."

"Is that a death threat? Why, you . . ."

"*Meine Ehre heisst Treue*."

"Fuck you. I'm siccing the cops on you," bellowed Mann, and slammed his handset down.

Brody didn't know what to make of Mann's reaction. Did Mann recognize the motto of the SS? The guy could have been trying to scare him away with his bluster, meaning Mann could be the serial killer. Or he could have been genuinely agitated by Brody's questions, meaning they could have scared him into believing he was going to be murdered. Either way, Mann had vaulted to the top of Brody's list of suspects, which was dwindling by the minute what with the rest of the suspects dying.

Brody had to speak to Keogh.

Now that he knew Keogh's address, he would pay Keogh a visit and ply him with questions.

Keogh must know something about the murders, or he wouldn't be pretending to be someone else. He might even know the identity of the killer, which would further imperil his life.

Chapter 61

Brody looked up Sam Hodges's phone number on the Internet, but it must have been unlisted.

The only way he was going to talk to Keogh/Hodges was in the flesh. Which was the way Brody wanted it so he could search the guy's face to make sure he was coming clean when he claimed he was Hodges.

If his own sister and fiancée said it was him, it had to be him, as far as Brody was concerned. Brody would be able to tell how good a liar Keogh was when he claimed to be Hodges. It would be like the first question on a lie detector exam. Brody could gauge Hodges's subsequent answers from his facial tics when he lied.

Brody was about to slot his key in the ignition and fire his rental's engine when he felt his cell phone vibrating in his trouser pocket. He fished out the cell. He had an e-mail from Tess. He opened it.

Thought you should see this, said the e-mail. I paid Lisa Chang a visit.

Attached was a short video. Brody played it.

It showed Lisa Chang's head split in half with an ax, exposing half her brain. There was something sticking out of Chang's gaping mouth. It was a snake's tail, Brody realized. Beside the other half of Chang's skull that lay in a pool of blood on the floor was an ax. The camera panned to the wall, which displayed Li Grande Zombi and Acid Is Groovy written in blood.

How did the snake get in Chang's mouth? Did the killer stick it down her throat, and it burrowed into her intestines? wondered Brody with revulsion.

Serial killer victim number six.

Tess had paid Chang a visit and found her dead, decided Brody. Or had Tess murdered Chang? That didn't track. If Tess had killed Chang, why would she send him a video of Chang's corpse?

And yet Tess had been at almost every murder scene. He had witnessed her at them.

It was almost as if she had been following him to the sites, or as if she had expected him to arrive after she had got there. She also might have been hiding from him at the murders where he hadn't seen her when he had arrived. Or she could have arrived before him, wasted the victim, and booked before he got there.

Brody had questions for her. He called her.

"Is that snake in her mouth alive?" he said. "I can't tell from your video."

"What snake?" she said.

"The snake in Chang's mouth."

Tess paused as if eyeballing the corpse. "There is no snake in her mouth."

Brody checked the video she had e-mailed him.

"Can't you see it in her mouth?" he said.

"There's no snake in her mouth."

"Then what's in her mouth?"

"The haft of a knife."

Brody rubbed his forehead. He was sure he could see a snake sticking out of Chang's open mouth.

Was he losing it? he wondered. Was he seeing snakes everywhere he looked because he was thinking of the snake god Li Grande Zombi? The power of suggestion? Was his mind poisoned by the snake god? He didn't buy it. He may have been an epileptic, but he wasn't insane. *Epilepsy* didn't translate to *insanity*. Maybe he was overworked. These grisly murders were getting to him.

"It sure looks like a snake," he said.

"I don't think so."

Brody dropped the subject. "Why did you go to Chang's?"

"I had questions for her. I thought she could help me find the killer."

"You and the killer must think alike."

Pausing, Tess didn't know how to take his remark.

"I'm putting myself in the mind of the killer," she said. "To catch a killer you have to think like one."

"You're damn good at it."

"Are you trying to insinuate something?" she said, piqued.

He didn't want to get into it with her. "Not at all. I was about to do the same thing and pay a visit to Chang. Who do you plan to interrogate next?"

"I—uh. Why should I tell you? We're not working for the same client. Where are you?"

He wanted to try something. He decided to tell her.

"I'm on my way to Hodges's house in Rancho Palos Verdes," he said.

"Who did you say?"

"Sam Hodges."

He hung up.

Was he going to find her at Hodges's place? he wondered. How could she know where he lived? Or did she know more about these murders than she was letting on? Was she in fact the serial killer?

Chapter 62

Sitting in her car in front of Chang's pink Victorian-style house complete with a turret in Moorpark, Tess felt a migraine coming on. Maybe it was all the dead bodies piling up.

But she was used to death. She had seen death before. It wasn't as if her job sheltered her from life. If anything, it did the polar opposite.

And yet, so many stiffs. She counted six so far. And the killings would go on.

Her eyeballs throbbed in their sockets. She could feel razor blades slicing through them, discharging electrical synapses of pain through her mind. Explosions of pain in her head rocked her. She felt dizzy and thought she might pass out from the resonating blasts. A curtain of black specks slammed down on her vision then disappeared.

It was getting hot in the Valley. Sweating, she turned her car's AC on. The appliance's cacophony aggravated her migraine. She considered turning off the AC, but the heat was oppressive.

She plucked her cell phone from her purse. She decided she better place the call.

"He's coming to your house," she said.

"What?" he said. "I can't hear. There's too much noise. Where are you?"

"I'm in my car."

"I can't hear you. I'm not paying you for calls I can't hear."

Grudgingly, Tess turned off the AC.

"He's coming to your house," she repeated.

Pause.

"That's impossible," he said. "How does he know my address?"

"He didn't say."

A longer pause this time.

"Hello?" she said, thinking he had left the phone.

"Fine," he said, sounding merry. "Let him come. This should be fun. I was starting to get bored. There's nothing worse than boredom."

Tess didn't know where he was coming from. Well, it was *his* money. He was the one that had hired her. She was just doing her job.

"Is that all?" she said.

"Did you find Chang?"

"I found her corpse."

He hung up.

Tess turned the AC back on and popped another migraine pill into her mouth.

She had two people left to pay a visit—Gottfried Mann and Kawhi James.

She wished she could get rid of this blinding migraine before she drove to their houses. No worries. Brody was heading elsewhere. She didn't have to follow him this time because he was heading straight to her client, who could keep an eye on him without her help. Unless Brody had been lying to her about going to see Hodges, he wouldn't be at Mann's or James's.

She stiffened in the driver's seat. It was possible he had been lying. If he had suspected something was hinky, he might have lied to her over the phone. But what good did lying to her about a visit to Hodges do him?

The migraine pill was kicking in. She felt more relaxed.

She wondered how Brody had found out about Hodges and how much he knew.

Chapter 63

Brody drove his rental to Rancho Palos Verdes. He had to be on the lookout for cops. They didn't know what kind of car he was driving, but Macready had put out a BOLO on him as well as on his Mini. Brody drove carefully to the peninsula, not driving too fast or too slow.

He had a lot of questions for Hodges/Keogh. He wondered if the guy would give him any straight answers.

In his side-view mirror Brody picked up on a motorcycle cop closing in on him. The CHP cop pulled alongside him. Brody scrunched down in his seat, trying to look shorter. He couldn't tell if the cop was looking at him thanks to the black-tinted visor on the CHP helmet. Brody didn't look in the cop's direction.

The cop weaved in front of him.

Brody felt his heartbeat ratcheting up.

Maybe everything was OK, he decided. The cop hadn't switched on his flashing lights nor sounded his siren. On the other hand, why was the guy going so slow, forcing Brody to reduce speed? Had the cop recognized him? No way to tell. Brody couldn't see through the helmet visor.

Brody would just have to sweat for a while, waiting . . .

He didn't want to cool his heels in a jail cell on a bum murder rap. He wondered if his forehead was sweat-beaded. The cop would see it if it was.

The cop pulled into the right lane and shot away.

Brody let out a sigh of relief.

Feeling uncomfortable telescoping down, he straightened up to his full height and continued driving to the peninsula.

He reached it without incident and drove past the Point Vicente Lighthouse run by the Coast Guard in Rancho Palos Verdes. He drove on the bluffs along the coast with their majestic panoramic view of the Pacific Ocean. The lighthouse's white tower was over one hundred feet high built of reinforced concrete.

Brody followed the directions the GPS's female voice was giving to him to reach Hodges's house. Located in a posh neighborhood of palatial estates that basked in the beach's direct sunlight, Hodges's residence stood out for its brutalist architecture of earth-toned concrete with narrow windows that looked like crenels in a castle on each floor. The top floor was all glass, shaped like a rectangular flight control tower with a wider perimeter than the lower floors of the building.

An electronic steel gate blocked the entrance to the sweeping driveway. Next to the gate was a sign that said in large black block letters Trespassers Will Be Shot.

Brody pulled up to a speakerphone in front of the gate and pressed a red plastic button on it.

"Hello," crackled a voice in response. "Who is this?"

Brody decided to use his real name, though he harbored doubts about Hodges's willingness to talk to him.

"Scott Brody. I'm here to see Sam Hodges."

To Brody's surprise, the gate swung open, as if they were expecting him.

He drove his rental along the winding drive and parked behind a low-slung scarlet Ferrari 458 Spider with its distinctive silver horse rampant logo on the rear. He climbed out of his car, traversed the slate steps that led to the manse's front door, and rang the doorbell.

Another speakerphone, this one situated above the doorbell, crackled to life.

"Mr. Hodges is at the swimming pool," said the same male voice that had greeted him at the gate. "He will see you in the back."

Since the door didn't open, Brody figured he was supposed to walk to the backyard.

He followed the slate steps that led around the building to the back and spotted a kidney-shaped pool, whose water glistened turquoise in the cloudless sunlight.

Chapter 64

A fortyish guy in emerald green bathing trunks and an unbuttoned Day-Glo lime aloha shirt with images of palm fronds on it was lying on his back on a deck chair, his eyes protected by blue-tinted wraparound shades, soaking up rays, as three zaftig twentysomething women in thong bikinis pranced on their bare feet around the pool deck. A margarita with a wedge of lime on the sweaty glass's rim stood on a small white metal table beside him.

The sound system was blasting Janis Joplin's "Piece of My Heart" over loudspeakers.

Brody angled across the deck to Hodges.

Before he reached Hodges, an armed rent-a-cop intercepted him.

"We don't permit firearms on the premises, sir," said the beefy guy, just this side of thirty, his black suit tight for his musclebound frame. "Are you armed?"

Brody thought about lying, but decided not to cause a ruckus.

"Yeah," he said. "I have a license to carry."

"Hand over your gun, please," said the guard, extending his open hand.

"I said I have a license."

"Your license doesn't include these private premises, sir."

Brody shrugged, leaned down, rolled up his trouser leg, withdrew his SIG from its ankle rig, and handed it to the guard, who retreated with it and stood fifteen feet behind Hodges. Brody picked up on two armed bodyguards near the house's back door.

"I'm a private detective," said Brody, coming to a halt beside Hodges. "Do you mind if I ask you a few questions?"

Hodges sat up and removed his Maui Jims, revealing his satyr's face with washed-out blue eyes that looked like they had been to hell and back. His chiseled lips curled enigmatically.

Tyler Keogh in the flesh, decided Brody.

"What's this about?" said Keogh.

Brody glanced at the three women.

The blonde in a pink thong was close to six feet tall and had a tattoo of a pink rose on her right thigh. She was rubbing tanning oil on the back of a brunette who was a head shorter and clad in a salmon thong, while another brunette with a swarthy complexion sporting a lavender thong watched them, smiling, holding a salmon concoction in a martini glass sprouting a miniature aquamarine paper umbrella.

"She's from TJ, she's from Palm Springs, and she's from Camp Pendleton," said Keogh, pointing them each out and watching them with a grin.

"Camp Pendleton?"

"Some of those marine girls, wow, is all I can say. They'll knock your socks off. They work out a lot at the gym. See for yourself."

"Where did you meet them?"

"One of those sugar baby websites. Eat your heart out."

"Do they know you're getting married soon?"

"You're coming at me from outer space," said Keogh, losing his grin.

"Val Holiday, your fiancée, wouldn't be too happy to see your friends with you."

Why was Keogh messing around with these sugar babies when he had Val the Bod as his fiancée? wondered Brody. Then again she did have a prickly personality. Still . . .

"I don't know any Val Holiday," said Keogh.

Brody's eyes took in the brutalist mansion. "You look like you do pretty well for yourself."

"You could say that."

"Aeronautical engineering pays that well?"

"Who said I was an engineer?"

"I thought you were an engineer."

"I play the market. I'm ten times smarter than Warren Buffet, so, yeah, I make out like a bandit when I pick stocks."

"Your sister says you're an aeronautical engineer."

"What sister?"

"Evelyn."

Hodges/Keogh shifted on his seat. "Look, I don't know where you get your info. I don't have any sisters."

"Aren't you really Tyler Keogh the aeronautical engineer pretending to be someone else?"

"I'm really Sam Hodges, the market savant, not pretending to be anyone." Keogh wasn't grinning. "I don't have to pretend. I'm the real deal."

Brody couldn't see any tells on Keogh's face. Could the guy be telling the truth? Brody wondered. Keogh was coming across like Jay Gatsby, a self-made millionaire with a shady past. Keogh reeked of dirty money, as far as Brody was concerned. Keogh didn't act like an aeronautical engineer. Or was *act* the operative word? Was Keogh acting a role? If he was acting, he was damn good.

"You can level with me," said Brody. "Your sister sent me to find you."

"I *am* leveling with you. I *don't* have a sister. I have a hedge fund."

"I don't see the connection."

"There is no connection. There is no sister."

"I understand why you're pretending to be someone else."

"Why would I pretend to be someone else? I'm happy with who I am."

"You don't have to play this game with me. I know you were a test subject at Stanford, where you had brain surgery."

Keogh stared at him, said nothing, his face blank.

Then he burst out laughing.

"What in the world are you talking about?" he said, grinning.

"You're pretending to be someone else because of the serial killer who's offing members of Mensa's board of directors. You figure if you pretend to be someone else, he won't be able to hunt you down and whack you."

"It's funny you should mention that Mensa serial killer."

"Funny?"

"I'm a bit of a detective myself when it comes to serial killers. I like to find out their identities before the cops do."

"You don't say."

Keogh stood up. "Why don't you come inside with me? I have something to show you. I didn't know you came here to ask me about the serial killer."

"I came here because your sister wants to know if you're all right, and I'm offering protection for you because the killer is coming after you next."

"No, he's not."

"How can you be so sure?"

"Because he's already here."

Brody did a double take.

Keogh chuckled.

"This is no joking matter," said Brody. "The Mensa maniac is a drugged-out sadist who has killed six people so far, and you're next."

"Let me put your fears to rest. Come with me."

They made a beeline for the mansion's back door and entered through it into the kitchen, two bodyguards in tow. Two more bodyguards stood in the backyard near the pool.

If Hodges/Keogh wasn't worried about being the next victim of the serial killer, why did he have so many bodyguards? wondered Brody.

Brody followed Keogh, unsure what to expect. Why was Keogh lying about his true identity if he wasn't in fear for his life? Had Val been right when she had said the Stanford experiment had wiped his memory so he had no idea he was Keogh?

Chapter 65

Keogh and Brody crossed the kitchen, which had a fashionable island in it, and descended a flight of steps to the capacious, dank, dim-lit cellar.

Brody's hackles rose. He felt like Fortunato in Poe's "Cask of Amontillado" being led to his entombment by the maniac narrator.

"There's nothing to be afraid of," said Keogh in a less-than-reassuring voice. "Come over here."

Descending, Brody glanced over his shoulder. The two stone-faced bodyguards were bringing up the rear.

Brody was liking this less and less.

They reached the bottom of the creaky wooden steps.

"Where are you taking me?" said Brody.

"Don't worry. I'm gonna show you why you shouldn't be afraid anymore."

"Afraid of what?"

"The serial killer."

The air smelled musty, noticed Brody, wishing he had stayed outside at the pool.

"You're the one who should be afraid," he said. "You're on his hit list."

"Whatever gave you that idea?" said Keogh, halting.

"At the latest murder I saw your photo pinned to the floor with a bloody SS knife."

"It's immaterial."

"It means your life's in danger. You're his next target."

"No way."

Keogh resumed walking through the cellar.

"When are you gonna admit you're Keogh?" said Brody.

Keogh said nothing.

A leaky faucet dripped into a black metal farmhouse sink on Brody's right. He thought he could hear a rat scurrying in the corner, but he might have been imagining it. He didn't see a rat anywhere. He couldn't see anything very well in the twilit basement. A couple of grime-coated windows blocked any sunlight from entering the room.

"The knife stabbed *your* face in the picture," said Brody. "Get the message?"

Brody followed him to a heavy wooden door constructed of boardwalk planks, wishing he had his SIG.

"No problem," said Keogh.

"I know they implanted a microchip in your brain. That's why you can't remember who you are."

"I know who I am. You're the one that doesn't know who I am."

"You are Tyler Keogh, and a psycho is stalking you."

"I'm Sam Hodges, and I have something interesting locked behind that door for you to see."

Keogh withdrew a key from his trouser pocket, inserted it into the lock on the heavy door, and swung open the door to a small unlit room.

Brody peered into the room's darkness, straining his eyesight. "I can't see a thing."

Keogh flicked on the light switch near the doorjamb.

The sudden light blinded Brody, forcing him to squint.

Flabbergasted, he made out a tall man whose wrist was chained to a ringbolt in the wall. Standing, dressed in a black wool Nazi Waffen SS Totenkopf uniform and a peaked visor cap with an eagle, swastika, and skull and crossbones on it and silver braids above the visor, the man squinted back at Brody, his eyes becoming accustomed to the light.

"Let me out of here," he demanded, glaring at Keogh.

"Let me introduce you to the Mensa Maniac, as you dubbed him," Keogh told Brody. "Gottfried Mann."

"Don't listen to him," said Mann. "He dressed me in this ridiculous SS uniform and handcuffed me here. He's out of his mind."

"Shut up," said Keogh.

Lying on the concrete floor out of Mann's reach were SS knives of varying manufacturing dates and model designs, along with a glass-fronted terrarium that contained a black mamba, which was actually dark brown. The mamba raised its coffin-shaped head and opened its mouth displaying the black insides, from which it got its name, and hissed.

Keogh turned to Brody. “You see. I caught Mann before the cops. Using my advanced intellect I was able to determine his identity and capture him.”

“Have you told the cops, Sherlock?” said Brody.

“Not yet.”

“Do you have proof Mann is the killer?”

“Proof? What more proof do you need? Look how he’s dressed. And look at his collection of SS knives, one of which you found at his last murder.”

“Those aren’t my knives,” said Mann. “And this isn’t my uniform. Don’t listen to him.”

“And look at this,” Keogh told Brody, opening his hand and displaying a silver ring in his palm. “He had this SS *Totenkopfring* with his set of SS knives. Himmler gave these skull rings only to his best SS officers. The rings weren’t allowed to be bought or sold. He had 14,500 made, but demanded their return in 1944. Only 11,500 were returned. In 1945 he blast-sealed them in a hillside near Wewelsburg Castle. The rest of the rings were either lost on the battlefield or were never returned to Himmler by their recipients. They have become quite a rare collector’s item and cost many thousands of dollars.”

Brody inspected the ring. It featured a death’s head and various runes on the outside of the band. On the inside were engraved the recipient’s and Himmler’s names and the date of issue.

“Did you ever notice how much a ring looks like a snake?” said Keogh.

“No.”

“What about the ancient mystical symbol of the ouroboros—a snake eating its own tail? It’s shaped like a ring.”

“I never thought about it.”

“Do you dream about snakes?”

“No.”

Why would Keogh ask such a question? wondered Brody. How could Keogh know about Brody's snake nightmares? Keogh couldn't know, decided Brody. The guy was just guessing.

Keogh closed his hand and pocketed the skull ring.

"What are you trying to prove with all this Nazi SS info?" said Brody.

"I'm proving Mann was obsessed with the Nazi SS mystique. Otherwise, why would he collect all of this memorabilia, including the SS knife that killed Lou Arano."

"How does that explain the graffiti written in blood on the wall? Li Grande Zombi."

"Himmler and his SS were into the occult. Which explains the runes on their skull rings. Mann took it one step further. He worshiped the voodoo snake god Li Grande Zombi."

"What was his motive for the murders?" Brody asked Keogh.

"Jealousy. Mann didn't want any rivals as the smartest man in the world. He wanted the title all to himself. So he killed fellow Mensa member Myles Wasson."

"What about the other murders?"

"Again jealousy. He was jealous of the members of the board because they thought they were smarter than he was. He knew he was smarter than all of them put together. He got revenge by killing them. And . . ."

"And what?"

"And he found out he liked to kill. So he kept killing, and he'll keep killing till somebody stops him."

"These are *his* knives and *his* uniform," said Mann, trying to yank his arm free from the ringbolt. "And that skull ring is his, not mine. I'm not a murderer. I was afraid the killer was on his way to get me next when Hodges came to my house and kidnaped me."

"He's not Hodges," said Brody. "He's Tyler Keogh. Don't you recognize him?"

"Am I supposed to?"

"He's on the Mensa board of directors with you."

"I don't socialize with them."

"I have a photo of you at a picnic with him."

Mann shook his head in irritation. "I don't remember. It's possible I was there. I have other things on my mind. Stuff like that—picnics, social functions—I don't pay attention to."

Brody didn't know what to think. All he knew for sure was one of them was lying. He couldn't tell from their faces who the liar was. He didn't know if Keogh was lying about being Hodges or he actually believed he *was* Hodges. The government had done a number on his brain when they had implanted a microchip in it.

"*He* must be the killer," Mann told Brody. "That's why he has all this kinky Nazi stuff in his basement."

Keogh laughed. "What a liar. That's all his stuff. I found it in his house when I grabbed him and took him here."

"You need to tell the cops," said Brody. "You shouldn't have touched the evidence. Now your fingerprints are on it."

"What if I don't tell the cops?" Keogh paused two beats. "I'm thinking about starting a museum of serial killers in my basement. I'm gonna lock a serial killer in each room and create a museum devoted solely to them. People will come from millions of miles away to pay for the opportunity to see it," he said, gesticulating wildly with his hands.

"You see, he's mad," Mann told Brody. "What kind of twisted mind would dream up such a heinous scheme? Let me out of here."

"My advanced intellect is light years ahead of your petty Mensa IQ," Keogh told Mann. "You can't even recall a picnic you went to."

"Because I don't give a damn about picnics," said Mann.

"Do you admit you were at the picnic?" Brody asked Keogh.

"I wasn't at any picnic with this homicidal maniac," answered Keogh.

"What do picnics have to do with high IQs?" scoffed Mann. "Let me out of here."

"You are not a visionary like I am," said Keogh. "You are hobbled by your insufficient intellect."

"I have one of the highest IQs in the nation," said Mann. "That's how I got into Mensa."

"That's your problem. Mensa IQs are only a fraction of mine," said Keogh, enjoying himself.

"Your arrogance is insufferable. The arrogance of a maniac who has no concept of reality."

Keogh's mood underwent a sea change. He fumed. "Shut up, you ignorant bottom-feeder."

He strutted toward Mann and kicked him in the groin.

Groaning, Mann doubled over in pain.

Keogh stalked out of the room, flicking off the lights, ushering Brody with him, and slamming the door shut. He locked the door.

"False imprisonment is a crime," said Brody. "So is kidnaping. You're risking a jail sentence."

"He's a monster. Once you get a taste for human flesh, you never lose it. It's why they have to put down man-eating lions in the jungle. Do you want me to free him so he can resume his killing rampage?"

"Tell the cops."

"Are you sure you want me to do that?" said Keogh, cocking an eyebrow at Brody. "I'll have to tell them you're in on this with him."

"Me?" said Brody, flummoxed. "I never even met the man."

"According to the news reports, the cops think you're the Mensa killer. They'll think you're Mann's partner in crime. Remember the Hillside Stranglers? They were two maniacs working in tandem strangling women. Even psychos can have partners."

"The cops are wrong about me."

"Now that I think about it, how do you know so much about these murders—unless you *are* Mann's partner?"

"Because I'm investigating them. I'm a private investigator. That's my job."

"Get him," Keogh told his bodyguards, backing away from Brody.

The two bodyguards, who had been trailing them all along, advanced on Brody, whipping out pistols. Brody froze. The lead bodyguard with a mohawk seized Brody's arm. Brody pulled free. Mohawk tossed his gun to his left hand and threw a haymaker at Brody's jaw. Brody reeled backward from the impact of the blow and rubbed his aching jaw.

"If he resists, shoot him," said Keogh.

"Now I can file assault charges against you," said Brody, continuing to massage his jaw.

He didn't resist when Mohawk latched onto his arm again.

"Is that why you really came here?" said Keogh. "To free your partner Mann and make me your next murder victim? Of course. I didn't see it before. Now it's crystal clear. *Two* Mensa maniacs. You guys had everybody fooled. Everybody but me."

Chapter 66

Brody chided himself for not expecting a trap. It had been far too easy to get onto Keogh's property.

Brody still couldn't tell if Keogh knew he was Keogh, or his mind had been irreparably wiped by the Stanford experiment. Keogh might actually believe he was Hodges.

"Take his cell phone," said Keogh.

Mohawk patted Brody's trouser pockets until he located the cell. He plucked out the cell and tossed it to Keogh. Turning back to Brody, Mohawk jabbed him in the kidney. Wincing, Brody jerked away from Mohawk. Mohawk smiled.

The two bodyguards, reeking of onionlike body odor, frog-marched Brody into a room similar to Mann's. Without ceremony they shoved him inside. He staggered to the wall and wheeled around to face them, seething.

Keogh's figure replaced theirs in the doorway.

"You'll never get away with this," said Brody.

"Capturing a serial killer?" said Keogh.

"They'll throw you in the joint for false imprisonment and kidnaping. You'll never get out."

"What are you gibbering about? They'll give me a reward when they find out what I've done. I caught the Mensa murderers for them."

"You and I both know I'm not the Mensa murderer."

"I'll sell tickets on the black market for the public to see you and your cohort Mann here in captivity."

"What kind of a sick mind do you have? What did those government experimenters do to you?"

"Pleading insanity won't help your cause. I got you dead to rights, Mr. Serial Killer."

"You're the one who's lost your mind, you idiot. The serial killer's still out there. And he's gonna keep on killing. You're next on his list."

Laughing, Keogh slammed the door in Brody's face and locked it.

Brody rushed the door and pounded his fists against it in frustration.

"You really think I came here without telling anyone?" he cried, the tendons in his neck bulging. "The cops are on their way this minute."

Brody had to calm down and think.

Turning away from the door, he surveyed the small, windowless, musty room. In the corner was a motheaten mattress on a box spring. In the opposite corner was a miniature en suite bathroom with a porcelain sink and toilet but no bathtub. Near the bathroom doorjamb was a cheap wooden chair.

He wondered if Mann was really the serial killer. Mann had SS knives and a black mamba in his room, implicating him in the murders. And he was dressed in an SS Totenkopf uniform. He certainly looked guilty. And yet Mann had denied everything, claiming the knives and uniform weren't his. He could have been lying, decided Brody. Or maybe Keogh was framing the guy. With all his money Keogh could buy Nazi memorabilia on the Internet no matter how expensive.

But what about Tess? wondered Brody. He had thought she might be the killer. He had seen her at multiple crime scenes, but he had never seen Mann at any of them. Which didn't prove anything. Mann could still be the killer. Keogh could be telling the truth about that.

Brody's head ached. He was twisting his mind into a pretzel wrestling with his thoughts.

He sat down on the creaky chair. He had to figure a way out of here.

Brody was convinced Keogh knew he was coming to his manse. Keogh wasn't surprised at all to see him when he showed up at the front gate, even invited him inside. How did Keogh know? Nobody knew he was heading to Keogh's. He hadn't told anyone. Wait a minute. The DMV clerk who had given him Keogh's address could have figured out Brody was fixing to see

Keogh. But why would the clerk tip off Keogh? It didn't figure, decided Brody.

Brody thought about it. He had told Tess. Had she told Keogh? Why would she? How could she have got his phone number? Or had they met in person? Brody would be surprised to learn they knew each other.

Brody was convinced somebody had tipped Keogh off.

Brody heard the door opening.

Mohawk stood in the doorway, snarfing a pizza wedge. His cohort handed him something from behind. Mohawk flung it into the room and hurriedly shut the door.

Chapter 67

A Day-Glo green snake flew into the room, writhing through the air. Brody bolted to his feet. A green mamba, he decided with apprehension.

The snake landed on the floor with a thump.

Maybe there had been another snake in the terrarium with the black mamba that Brody hadn't seen.

His adrenaline jacked up, Brody watched the electric green mamba undulating on the floor. Mambas were known for their speed. If provoked, they would strike like lightning.

Feeling attacked as it had hit the floor, the green mamba opened its mouth and hissed.

Brody stood stock-still.

The snake was five-odd feet long. Settling in, it assessed its surroundings, flicking its tongue as if tasting the air. Brody did likewise without flicking his tongue.

He saw nowhere to hide. The bathroom didn't have a door. He couldn't hide in there. A green mamba's bite was deadly. He would have to kill the snake.

He supposed he could try to beat the mamba to death with the chair, but he would get only one chance to smash the mamba's head. If he missed, the mamba would retaliate quickly and bite him. Trying to land a direct hit on the mamba's head with a chair leg would be extremely difficult, considering the shape of the chair and how awkward it was to aim it, especially at such a tiny target as the mamba's head. Brody didn't like his chances.

Without a weapon Brody figured he had only one other way to kill the snake. With his bare hands.

And he had to kill it.

He didn't see them living together in peaceful coexistence in this small room. He would be living in constant fear as long as the mamba was alive in the room with him. Like living with a time bomb ticking off the minutes left in his life.

His heart in his mouth, Brody edged toward the mamba, careful not to make any noise.

The mamba was barely squirming.

Brody kept inching toward it, well aware that he was in its striking distance. He studied it and located its tail.

He took deep breaths and slowed his breathing, calming his exploding nerves, his face sweating. He hoped none of the sweat would drip onto the floor and alarm the snake.

Was he sure he wanted to go through with this? he wondered. If anything went even slightly amiss in his planned attack, he was dead. He saw no other options. He must carry out his assault.

Circumspectly, he reached toward the snake's tail a fraction of an inch at a time, his back stiff with tension. He told himself to relax. He leaned forward, his arm extended, his hand open, toward the tail. He would get only one chance to do this. He could afford no mistakes. He had to grab the serpent's tail. A couple more inches and he would be able to seize it.

He eyeballed the green mamba's head, making sure it wasn't turning toward him preparing to strike. He avoided making any sudden moves that would elicit an attack.

The mamba didn't seem interested in him. Or was it feigning indifference?

His hand was near enough to the mamba that he could grab the tail. He steadied his breathing, trying to calm himself.

What the hell was he doing?

The mamba could bite him any second. Was he nuts to try this? His heartbeat raced, deafening him with its thundering roar. Could the mamba hear his heart? Would the mamba react to the commotion ginned up by his heartbeat?

If he didn't make his move now, he would never make it.

He lunged forward, snagged the tail, jerked up the mamba, and snapped it like a whip before the mamba had a chance to bite him.

The mamba hung limp in his hand, its neck broken. Blood streamed out of its mouth onto the floor.

Satisfied it was dead, Brody dropped it at his feet and kicked it away, his heartbeat continuing to thump out of control. The mamba slid to a halt against the wall and lay like a coil of intestines.

Brody heaved a huge sigh of relief.

Chapter 68

Tess sat in her car in a Moorpark strip mall's parking lot recovering from her migraine and wondering what was going on with her client. She was wearing black-framed polarized black-tinted Jackie O shades to block the blinding sun that aggravated her headache. Her pills were working, alleviating her headache, allowing her to think straight.

Her AC droned in the background, preventing the relentless Valley sun from rendering her car a life-threatening furnace.

Her client Sam Hodges had hired her to keep track of Brody while Brody was investigating the serial killings and to find out what Brody knew about them. Which was why she had phoned Hodges and told him Brody was headed his way. She figured Hodges would want to know.

She wondered why Brody wanted to see Hodges. What did Hodges have to do with the serial killings? She didn't see any reason Brody would want to contact Hodges. She had never met Hodges. He had hired her over the phone. The only way she could contact him was by phone.

She needed Hodges's address. She wanted to meet him.

Ordinarily, she didn't accept clients she had never seen. However, he had offered her a lot of money, too much to turn down. Until now she hadn't minded that he wanted to remain in the shadows. Now she wanted to know what his involvement, if any, was in the murders.

With her smartphone she found the DMV's address and called them.

"Hello," she said. "This is Officer Gronkowski of the LAPD, badge 5746. I'm trying to find the address of Sam Hodges in Rancho Palos Verdes. Could you help me with that?"

It was illegal to impersonate a police officer, but in her job she had to stretch the rules. How would anybody find out it was her, anyway? She was making the call with a burner app on her phone that nobody could trace back to her.

"One moment," said the DMV clerk.

A couple of minutes later he came back on the phone and gave her Hodges's address.

"Thanks," she said, and terminated the call.

She would pay a visit to Hodges later.

First she had to check on Gottfried Mann, who wasn't answering his phone. She wanted to find out if he was alive. If he was, she wanted to warn him his life was in danger. She would have to do it person at his house.

She didn't have to follow Brody for the time being because Hodges would be able to keep track of Brody himself when Brody arrived at Hodges's place.

Tess fired her engine, put the car in gear, and drove out of the parking lot.

Chapter 69

Brody sat in his room mulling over jumping the next guy that opened his door, whether it was Keogh or one of his bodyguards.

The problem was, there probably would be more than one at the door. Brody could overpower one guy, but the others would overpower him or blow him away.

Brody didn't know what Keogh's game was. Why had the guy locked him up? Did Keogh seriously think he and Mann were the serial killers, or was Keogh just saying it as an excuse to keep him locked up? If so, what ultimately was the point of keeping him under lock and key? Did Keogh really mean it when he said he was making a museum of serial killers he was going to sell tickets to?

With a microchip implanted in his brain, Keogh's actions were unpredictable, decided Brody. Could the surgery have affected his personality? If Mann was telling the truth that the Nazi SS Totenkopf memorabilia wasn't his, then it must have been Keogh's, in which case Keogh could be the serial killer. Which would explain his lack of fear of being the next victim of the killer.

Could Mann be believed? wondered Brody. He found it plausible.

It was equally as plausible that Keogh could be believed. Except Keogh was a known liar. Every time he refused to admit he was Keogh, he was lying. But then again, the Stanford experiment could have wiped his mind and caused him to forget his real name. In which case he wasn't lying about his not being Keogh—he genuinely believed he *was* Hodges.

Brody heard a noise at the door. He stiffened in his seat.

He had to decide whether he had any chance of success of staging an ambush. He came to the conclusion he must try.

He bolted to his feet and prepared to charge the door. He had noticed earlier that the door swung outward.

When he saw the door opening, he sprang forward, slammed into it, and shoved it open, hoping either to knock over his captors and rush past them to freedom or to disarm one of them and hold them at gunpoint. He burst through the door, bowling over Mohawk, who had been opening it.

In the ensuing scuffle, Keogh trained a Beretta 92X Centurion pistol loaded with an extended magazine on Brody.

Brody tried to manhandle Mohawk between him and Keogh, using Mohawk as a shield. The powerful Mohawk jerked free of Brody's grasp and shoved Brody giving Keogh a clear shot at Brody.

"Get back in the room," said Keogh, motioning with his Beretta at Brody.

Brody chose discretion over valor and decided to retreat. He backed into the room.

"Hold your hands up," said Keogh.

Brody complied.

Puzzled at not seeing the snake, Keogh scoped the room. He picked up on the green mamba's crumpled body lying in a heap near the doorjamb.

"You killed Earl," he said, disappointed.

"Earl tried to kill me," said Brody.

"Earl wouldn't hurt a fly."

"I doubt that. He was a green mamba."

Brody lowered his hands.

"He was a venomoid," said Keogh.

Brody looked puzzled.

"Its venomous glands were surgically removed. I don't want you to die." Keogh paused. "Not yet, anyway. I have questions for you. And you're the star attraction of my museum. Sam's Museum of Horrors, I think I'll call it. Why did you have to kill Earl?"

"You wanted me to make friends with him?"

"You're suffering from ophidiophobia."

"I can't even pronounce it, let alone know what it means."

"Fear of snakes."

"Why do you even care?"

"I'm trying to show you you have psychiatric problems. These problems caused you to commit murder."

"You're the one with all the snakes. Like that's normal. Snakes were at the scenes of the murders. Wait a minute. Maybe you worship snakes. Is that it? How about Li Grande Zombi?"

"I don't know what you're jabbering about."

"I'm talking about the writing on the walls of the serial killings—as if you didn't know. I thought you had made an in-depth study of the crimes in order to find the killer's identity."

"What does graffiti on a wall have to do with me?"

"A lot—if you're the one that put it there."

Keogh chuckled. "Do you really believe that nonsense?"

"You have snakes in your house. The serial killer worships snakes, in particular Li Grande Zombi. Therefore, you're the serial killer. You don't have to be a genius to put two and two together. Do you practice voodoo and drop acid, too?"

"Your syllogism is spurious. Just because I own snakes doesn't mean I worship them. I don't in fact worship anything, certainly not a made-up snake god called Li Grande Zombi."

"Then you admit to knowing who Li Grande Zombi is. Most people don't know."

"Most people are idiots, including you. Haven't you been listening? I'm smarter than the smartest people in Mensa," said Keogh, tapping his temple. "Li Grande Zombi is worshiped in voodoo. Tosh like voodoo is for superstitious fools."

"Do you worship a black sun, too? You left talismans of black suns at your crimes."

"A black sun is a mythical source of knowledge. I repeat, *mythical*. In other words, false. Why worship a lie?"

"Do you have an alibi for what you were doing at the time of the murders?"

"I don't need an alibi. I haven't been charged with anything. Gottfried Mann is your partner in the killings." Keogh paused. "Now it's my turn to ask questions. Why are you so interested in this Keogh fellow?"

"My client thought Keogh had been kidnaped or killed. I was hired to find him. You."

"Then you blew your assignment. I'm not Keogh."

"My client thinks otherwise."

"Who *is* your client?"

"I'm not at liberty to say."

"I have an alternate explanation for your interest in Keogh. You wanted to find him to make him the next victim in your string of serial killings. Your client's hiring you to find Keogh was a serendipitous accident."

"I believe I've figured out why you committed the killings."

Keogh harrumphed. "That would be a miracle, since I'm not the killer."

"You were jealous of your Mensa acquaintances and afraid the government might want to perform the Stanford experiment on them, making them as smart as you, or smarter. You can't tolerate anybody being as smart as you. Your arrogance forbids it. Your arrogance also made you think you could get away with murder, even mass murder."

"You might sell that scenario to the movies, but not to the courts. The courts need something called evidence, and you have none."

Brody thought about it. "Your brain surgery at Stanford must have unleashed a violent impulse in you. You think you're better than everybody else and can do anything you want—even commit murder. Similar to Himmler's SS, you consider yourself above the law, untouchable, accountable to no one. I would go further. You enjoy the act of murder."

"You think you're smarter than I am, but when all is said and done, you got caught. You're the killer, and this is your prison cell," said Keogh, gesticulating to the cramped room.

"Being smarter than everyone doesn't make you morally superior."

Keogh chortled. "What's morality got to do with intelligence?"

"Nothing. Which is proven by your existence. A genius serial killer."

"I bend the world to my will. The world doesn't bend me."

"The world bends everybody. Some of us break. Some keep going."

"Spoken by a true loser."

"Your brain surgery turned you into a psycho. Maybe you were borderline nuts to begin with, and the surgery put you over."

"Get used to your accommodations. You're gonna be here the rest of your life."

"You can't keep me here."

"Don't you want to know the meaning of Li Grande Zombi?"

"Yeah, Keogh. Why did you scrawl it in blood after you committed murder?"

"I feel like I've been reborn when I kill, brought back to life like a zombie, so to speak."

"In other words, you worship yourself. You were sacrificing bodies to yourself, not to a god, when you killed."

"Who better to worship than myself? I feel like Prometheus unbound, full of unbridled energy. Beyond good and evil."

"Then you confess you're the killer."

"I confess I know the meaning of the serial killer's graffiti. I confess I've penetrated the steel curtain that shrouds the inner workings of his psychotic brain."

"That's good enough for me. You did the killings, and you trapped yourself in your own lies."

"Blaming me for your murders won't make it so." Keogh commenced rubbing his hands together in eager anticipation, his eyes glowing. "I need to start selling tickets on the dark web to my museum of psychopaths. People will pony up big bucks to view you and your cohort serial killer Mann."

"You should be selling tickets to view you. What about Acid Is Groovy? Why did you write it?"

"A red herring left by the perp, in other words, you," said Keogh, pointing at Brody.

"Blaming me for your crimes is growing old."

"What crimes? I've committed no crimes."

"What about those two hit men you sent to whack me and my father in the desert?"

"I thought you were getting too close to finding me, so I enlisted their services. You're lucky to be alive. I changed my mind after they flopped. I decided you were making my life interesting. If there's anything I hate, it's boredom. I let you live, so why are you complaining?"

"Vincent Joule didn't live. A sniper's bullet cut him down at Stanford thanks to you."

"I don't know any Vincent Joule. Stanford, huh? Must be the government's dirty work. The government doesn't get mad. It gets even."

"You can tell it to the judge after I get through naming names."

"None of your false accusations are going beyond this room. I will surgically remove your tongue before you go on exhibit in my museum of serial killers."

"You really think you can get away with this?"

"For dinner we'll be serving MREs," said Keogh, unperturbed. He glanced down at the lifeless coil of green snake at his feet. "I ought to make you eat Earl. In the animal kingdom, animals eat what they kill. You're no better than an animal."

Departing, he locked the door behind him.

Brody stormed to the door and, grimacing, launched a barrage of kicks at it, trying to force it open. To no avail. It was a sturdy door.

His foot throbbing with pain, he limped back to the rickety chair.

Chapter 70

Tess drove to Mann's house in Moorpark, pulled into his driveway, and parked behind a white late-model Volvo. She strode along the pebble pathway to the front door and rang the doorbell on the lemon-painted stucco Mission Revival bungalow.

Nobody answered.

She didn't think he was home.

She stood beside a blue agave in front of his arched picture window that had a sepia marquee over it, careful to avoid getting pricked by the succulent's thorns. A grillwork of black metal bars protected the window. She peered inside the living room, which had a parquet floor and a ceiling fashioned of exposed varnished beams.

The well-appointed living room was empty save for its furniture. Nobody home.

She wouldn't mind living in this house. On her salary it was out of the question. She would never even be able to make the down payment.

Now what? she wondered, backing away from the window. Another empty house belonging to a Mensa member. With another dead body in it?

She retreated to her Mustang, fished her cell from her purse, climbed into the driver's seat, and placed a call.

"I can't find Gottfried Mann," she said. "His house is deserted."

"Why are you looking for him?" said Hodges.

"He's on the serial killer's hit list."

"I doubt it."

"What do you want me to do next?"

His answer surprised her.

"Nothing," he said. "Your job is done."

"Did Brody arrive at your place?"

"No."

"No? He told me he was going there," she said with concern. "He should be there by now."

"He must have changed his mind."

"Don't you want me to continue following him and reporting to you where he is?"

"I don't need your services anymore."

"Why not? I don't understand."

"I'm not paying you to understand."

"What about the serial killer?"

"Your job was to keep track of Brody and keep me posted. That's all. Your job is done."

"What has changed—"

Hodges hung up.

Tess could not make heads or tails of it. She punched out Brody's number. Brody didn't pick up.

Maybe he was driving and couldn't answer his cell, she decided. He should have been at Hodges's by now.

A black Chevy Suburban with tinted windows pulled into the driveway behind her, blocking her. It looked like the one the feds had driven when they pulled her over and hassled her about Brody on the Coast Highway.

She felt her headache coming back. She could do without feebs.

When the Suburban's driver's-side door opened, it confirmed her suspicions.

Sporting dark business suits Drago and Mirisch piled out.

"What the fuck are you doing?" said Drago, standing next to her Mustang's driver's-side door and leaning toward her, his hands on the window frame's steel sill, his mirrored shades flaring in the sun.

Mirisch stared at her, grim-faced.

"What are you talking about?" said Tess.

"You told Brody we're onto him and spooked him so he's hiding from us," said Drago.

"I never did," she lied, knowing she was committing a felony, her heartbeat accelerating.

"Then how come he's lying low?"

"How should I know?"

"Don't you understand English? We told you to warn him to stay away from the serial killings."

"I haven't been able to find him."

"I have a good mind to run you in for obstructing a federal agent in the line of duty."

"I'm not obstructing you."

"You told Brody to hightail it because we're looking for him. That's aiding and abetting a criminal."

"I didn't tell him about you."

"Then why's he gone to ground?"

"Why ask me? I have nothing to do with him."

Drago adjusted his shades, sneering. "We know you're both investigating the Mensa serial killings."

"We're working separately. We have different clients."

"I don't want to argue about this. Where is he?"

She didn't know. He should have been at Hodges's, but Hodges said no.

"I dunno," she said.

"Stop jerking my chain," said Drago, clenching the windowsill, his knuckles turning white.

"I can't tell you what I don't know."

"Tell him to back off and drop the case, or we'll yank his PI license. And we'll yank yours, too, if you don't play ball."

"We're just doing our jobs. There's no law against that."

"You're sticking your noses where the government doesn't want them. Enough said."

"But why? Why don't you want us to investigate the serial killings?"

"That's official business. Eyes only. And warn Brody off, or we'll bust him."

Drago released the sill and exchanged glances with Mirisch. They swaggered back to their Suburban.

Maybe Brody could explain to her what was going on, decided Tess, watching the feds in her driver's-side mirror.

The Suburban backed out of the driveway.

Tess phoned Brody. It went straight to voicemail. Tess left a message.

"We need to talk," she said. "The feds are on my case about you. Call me back ASAP."

Chapter 71

A trapdoor was opening in the ceiling, spilling green mambas onto Brody as he lay supine on the beat-up mattress in his cell. Green mambas squirmed all over him.

He froze. He dared not move. Any kind of movement on his part might instigate the mambas to turn on him and sink their fangs into his flesh.

Scores of them were slithering over him. They were all over his face, suffocating him with their slimy green scales pressed against his nostrils and mouth.

How was he supposed to breathe?

He coughed.

A green mamba stuck its head out of his mouth. Brody was choking to death on the mamba. How did it get down his throat? Did it squirm down his throat while he was sleeping? He coughed, struggling desperately to breathe, as the mamba filled his throat.

His face turned red. He felt like his head would burst if he didn't get any oxygen in his lungs.

He screamed and jackknifed up in bed, flinging the mambas off of him, blinking his eyes rapidly as if to clear his vision. Eyes bulging, gasping for breath, he scoped out his room.

He didn't see any mambas, save for the dead one lying near the door. He craned his neck up and checked out the ceiling. He didn't see an open trapdoor with green mambas writhing out. His mouth was empty. No mamba protruded from it. He could breathe fine. He took a gulp of air.

He had been dreaming.

He heard knocking on one of his walls. He started.

"Are you all right?" said a muffled voice through the wall.

Brody bolted out of bed and pelted to the wall.

"Hello?" he said, pressing his ear against the wall.

"I heard you scream."

"Just a nightmare. Is that you, Mann?"

"Yes. Why did he lock you up?"

"He says I'm your partner in the serial murders."

"I didn't do those. He dressed me in this stupid SS uniform and planted all that Nazi memorabilia on me. And that black mamba in my room. He put it there."

"Why would he frame you?"

"To cast suspicion away from himself. He's the serial killer."

"How can you be sure?"

"He has to be. It explains why he needs a fall guy to take the rap for him."

Brody nodded yes. "It also explains why he's keeping me prisoner. To deep-six me because he knows I know he's really Tyler Keogh. He must figure I know he's the serial killer."

"What are we gonna do?"

"He must have dreamed up a Nazi dope addict cult member who worships snakes as the murder suspect to cast suspicion away from him." An idea took shape in Brody's mind. "And Evelyn's daughter Olivia."

"What?"

"He must have had his niece Olivia kidnaped using her as leverage to coerce Evelyn into firing me and keeping me from finding and unmasking him."

"Run that by me again," said Mann, befuddled.

"He's a sociopath. His own relatives mean nothing to him."

"All he cares about is his snakes."

"We need to get out of here before he decides to kill us."

"I'm open to ideas."

"We need to find a way to signal for help."

"I thought I heard you say somebody was going to come looking for you if you disappear."

A bluff, decided Brody, which Keogh didn't fall for.

"We can't count on anyone saving us," said Brody. "I believe Keogh's being protected by the government."

"What? What the hell are you talking about? Why would they protect a serial killer?"

“The whistle-blower Vincent Joule who told me about the experiment on Keogh was killed to shut him up. The assassin must have been a government hit man.”

“Jesus. If the government’s protecting him, we’re doomed.”

“I’ve been thinking about this. It explains why his phony Hodges’s identification documents are so realistic—the government printed them for him.”

“They wanted him to kill the Mensa board of directors?” said Mann in disbelief.

“I doubt it. They didn’t know they had created a homicidal maniac with their brain surgery. But now . . .”

“Now what?”

“They have to continue to protect him so the public doesn’t find out they created a Frankenstein monster.”

“Which means, they’re gonna kill us to shut us up. If Hodges doesn’t kill us, the government will. We’re screwed six ways from Sunday.”

“I don’t know if they’d go that far,” said Brody, unconvincingly.

How could he sound convincing when he couldn’t even convince himself? he wondered.

“Which branch of the government are we talking about?” said Mann.

“The Department of Defense.”

Mann groaned. “We’re dead meat.”

“The US marshals must be in on it, too, because they’re in charge of the witness protection program that prints up phony identities and provides people with alternate lives.”

“I may use one of these Nazi SS daggers on myself.”

Brody pricked up his ears. “Can you reach them?”

Mann fetched an audible sigh. “No. I’m chained to the wall. I was dreaming out loud.”

“The US marshals are in the Justice Department, as is the FBI. The feds could be in on this, too.”

“Will you shut up? Aren’t things bad enough already without having the FBI after us?”

"The only way the government can effectively cover up this monster they've created is by silencing everybody who knows about it. That includes you and me."

"*Silence* meaning, *kill*?" said Mann, his voice feeble.

"It *would* be the most effective way."

"Hodges gave me a Nazi SS uniform. Why didn't he give me a cyanide capsule hidden in a false tooth like the one Goering had so he could escape being hanged at Nuremberg?"

If the Nazi memorabilia wasn't Mann's as he claimed, how did Mann know where Goering had hidden cyanide at the Nuremberg trials? wondered Brody. On the other hand, you didn't have to be an expert on Nazism to know Goering had poisoned himself with cyanide.

"We're not beat yet," said Brody. "We'll think of a way out."

He wished he believed it.

Chapter 72

Tess drove her Mustang to Rancho Palos Verdes and located Hodges's brutalist manse. She parked out of sight of his front gate to ponder her next move without being seen by his security guards.

She dug her cell phone out of her purse and called Brody.

The call went straight to voicemail.

She terminated the call. She couldn't understand why he wasn't answering.

Had Brody arrived here yet? she wondered. If so, why wasn't he picking up? Had something happened to him? Namely, had Hodges done something to him? And why did she care? Why didn't she just cut and run and forget about Hodges and Brody? After all, Hodges had fired her.

She surveyed Hodges's property. She got the feeling something was wrong. She couldn't put her finger on it. Call it a warning from a sixth sense.

She made up her mind and drove to Hodges's locked front gate. She read the sign: Trespassers Will Be Shot. She spoke into the speakerphone mounted near the gate.

"Who is it?" crackled a voice through the speaker.

"This is Tess Hardwick to see Sam Hodges."

"About what?"

"To collect my paycheck."

Silence while the guard consulted with someone.

The gate swung open. Tess drove up the drive, parked behind a rental car, and cut the Mustang's engine. She could tell the Camry sedan was rented thanks to the plastic frame around the license plate which advertised the rental company's name. Hodges had a visitor. Maybe it was Brody. Maybe he had finally arrived.

She tried calling Brody one more time.

Voicemail.

Why wasn't he picking up if he was here? she wondered.

Alarms were going off in her mind.

She called Lieutenant Macready at LAPD headquarters and got a receptionist who put her through to Macready.

"Macready here."

"This is Tess Hardwick. I've found Brody at Sam Hodges's place in Rancho Palos Verdes."

"Wait for us. We're on our way."

"Something's hinky here. I'm going in."

"Stay where you are and wait. He's a mass murderer," said Macready.

Tess hung up.

She admitted she could be headstrong at times. Like now. Macready had given her good advice. To hell with it.

Remaining in her car, she withdrew her Glock from her purse and ejected the magazine to make sure it was full. Satisfied, she slammed the magazine back into the Glock's butt, racked the slide, chambered a round, and replaced the Glock in her purse.

On the qui vive, she climbed out of her Mustang, casting around for Hodges.

She could smell the pleasing aroma of the freshly mown front lawn. She didn't see anyone. She made a beeline for the manse's front door. She rang the doorbell.

Out of the corner of her eye she saw a beefy security guard with his pistol drawn cutting across the lawn toward her, cut blades of grass sticking to the tops of his jogging shoes staining them green. Attached to the pistol's muzzle was a sound suppressor. He trained the pistol on her.

Adrenaline shooting through her, she whipped her Glock out of her purse and fired at him. He returned fire, grazing her arm with his bullet, and crumpled on the lawn, her Glock's bullet lodged in one of his lungs. Lying on his back on the grass he coughed up red blood, his chest making sucking sounds.

He was drowning in his own blood, she knew, and would be dead soon.

Senses sharpened from her rush of adrenaline, she decided not to enter through the front door, expecting an ambush inside the house. Instead, she circled around the lawn to the backyard, gun in hand. Surely, everyone in the house had heard her piece's report.

She wondered how many security guards Hodges employed. She would find out soon enough. She could see the water in a turquoise-painted pool shimmering in the sunlight in the backyard.

A shot rang out.

She belted across the lawn for cover and hit the dirt hiding behind a stand of agaves. They wouldn't stop any bullets, but at least the shooter couldn't see her. From her prone position she scoped out the area.

She spotted a bald security guard in jeans and a black blazer with a pistol in his hand standing behind a barbecue at poolside. He was staring in her direction aiming at her. She hugged the ground and fired back at him. He ducked behind the grill.

He exchanged fire with her.

Bullets slammed into the agaves in front of her chewing them apart.

She wouldn't last long here, decided Tess. Her heartbeat a rapid-fire staccato, bathed in sweat, she tried to figure out her next move.

Chapter 73

In his cell Brody came to attention as he heard gunshots outside. He knew something was up.

He started pounding on the door with the bottom of his fists.

"I'm sick," he cried. "I'm sick. The mamba bit me before it died. Help me."

He stopped hammering the door, listening to hear if anyone was coming. He didn't hear anybody.

"I'm poisoned." He coughed his guts out. "I'm poisoned. I need a doctor."

He pounded on the door again.

"Shut up," somebody yelled.

"That snake bit me," said Brody, coughing.

He heard movement at the door. He backed away to mount a forceful charge, keeping his eyes on the door.

The door cracked.

He barreled toward it, rammed his shoulder into it, and knocked the guard backward.

Pouncing on the guy, driving him to the floor, Brody tried to wrest the pistol out of the guard's hand. The guy grabbed Brody by the throat with his free hand. Brody tried to swipe the guy's hand away. No soap. Brody felt his throat burning under the guy's viselike grasp.

Brody fought harder to rip the piece from the guard's mitt. The guy wouldn't let go.

Struggling to breathe Brody kneed the guy in the groin, the guy trying to crush Brody's Adam's apple. The guy groaned. Brody wrested the gun from the guy's grasp, tore his reddened throat free, and jumped off the guy.

"You said you were sick," said the guy, his face ashen, looking like he was going to puke, squirming on his back, his groin killing him, nausea spreading through him.

"I'm sick of being your prisoner."

Gun in hand, Brody kicked him in the head, knocking him senseless.

Brody examined the piece. It was a SIG P226.

Where were the other guards? he wondered.

As if in answer to his question, Brody heard the stairway creaking. He looked at the stairway. Descending the steps Mohawk caught sight of him and whipped out his pistol, his eyes wild. Brody fired at him.

Wounded in the leg, Mohawk gasped and scurried back up the steps out of sight.

Brody heard a noise on the other side of the cellar. He cut his eyes toward the sound. A tubby guard in a neon orange and blue madras shirt and khaki cargo shorts fired at him, missing. Brody fired back.

Tubby moaned, his ear blown off, bright arterial blood spurting down his shoulder. Tubby waddled for cover behind a grey metal filing cabinet that stood against the wall.

With a severed major artery a person would bleed out in minutes, Brody knew. But the artery in the ear was small, and the blood loss wouldn't kill Tubby for quite a while. Tubby wasn't going to die from his wound, not for a long time anyway. Brody let loose another shot at Tubby. The slug drilled a hole into the filing cabinet, peeling back a crown of jagged teeth in the thin metal.

Tubby returned fire.

Brody was standing in the open. Tubby's bullet whistled over his head, missing him by less than an inch. Brody sought cover.

He ducked back into his cell.

The guard he had kicked in the head lay on his back unconscious.

Brody thought he heard the whumping of a helo overhead. Reflexively, he looked upward seeing nothing but a ceiling. He could feel the room vibrating. He glanced at the stairway, saw Mohawk's foot descending, and fired at it. Mohawk yelped and retreated up the steps.

Bullets flew in Brody's direction from Tubby. Brody backed away from his room's doorway, sidestepping Tubby's line of fire.

Brody heard Tubby open the door to Mann's room.

Brody heard Mann scream for help, followed by three sharp pops.

Mann's screaming stopped.

Keogh's museum of serial killers wasn't going to happen, decided Brody—unless Keogh planned on stuffing their corpses.

Brody craned his head around the doorjamb casting around for security guards. Tubby let loose a bullet at him. Brody ducked back into his room. Under the bullet's impact the jamb splintered neck-high. Trapped, decided Brody. Mohawk would descend the steps any minute and reinforce Tubby if Brody didn't keep firing at Mohawk to keep him at bay.

What would happen when he ran out of bullets? Brody wondered in distress.

The chopper's whumping sounded louder. The chopper was continuing its descent. Brody's room shook as if hit by an earthquake.

He wished he knew what was happening outside. He had to know before he made his next move.

Chapter 74

Tess looked up at the sky from behind the stand of agaves, shielding her eyes from the dazzling sun with her hand.

An LAPD Bell 206 Jet Ranger was hovering over Hodges's yard.

Two SWAT officers clad in black body armor were standing in the hatchway with automatic weapons trained on the backyard. One of them brandished a Heckler & Koch HK416, the other an HK MP5.

The short thickset thirtysomething guy with the MP5 raised a loudhailer to his mouth and addressed the estate's security guards, who were gazing up at the helo. His younger, slimmer partner with wide black eyes and cropped black hair kept his eyes peeled and his HK416 at the ready.

"This is the LAPD," said the thickset guy. "Throw down your weapons."

A twentyish guard sporting a Vandyke opened fire on the hovering aircraft.

"Let's take him out, Gino," said the thickset SWAT cop, brandishing his MP5.

"My pleasure, Kroger."

The two SWAT officers opened fire on Vandyke, who ran for cover. A hail of machine-gun slugs cut him down. Staggering, he crumpled, dropping his pistol, burying his face in the grass.

The guard standing near the barbecue commenced firing at the helo.

The SWAT team pelted the grill with bullets filling it with lead.

Tess picked up on Kroger selecting her for a target. She tossed away her Glock and waved her empty hands at the helo.

"I'm the one that called you guys," she hollered at them, doubtful they could hear her over the thundering din of the rotors.

The chopper continued its descent, guided by the pilot intending to land on the concrete pool deck. Its rotors whipped the pool, churning and rippling the water, raising a racket.

The guard beside the barbecue cut and ran.

A tattooed guard in jeans and a navy polo, his biceps bulging his shirtsleeves, armed with an AR-15 appeared in the kitchen doorway and peppered the helo with bullets. Gino fired a burst at him with his HK416, as the helo landed. Bullets stitched the guard's chest cutting a bloody swath. The guard's knees buckled, even as he continued firing his AR-15 into the ground.

The helo's rotors whirled lazily to a halt, rocking and dipping. Tess could hear police sirens on black-and-whites approaching the estate at speed.

Kroger and Gino deplaned onto the pool deck, guns at the ready.

A guard opened fire on them with an AR-15 from a half-open window in the kitchen.

The two SWAT officers laid down a barrage of fire at the window, blowing it into shivers of glass. Somebody screamed in agony in the kitchen.

Kroger used the loudhailer again.

"This is the LAPD. Thrown down your arms and surrender."

A shot was fired from the kitchen in response.

Kroger and Gino fired bursts into the kitchen and took cover behind the barbecue. The pilot clambered out of the helo's cockpit with a Benelli M4 Super 90 12-gauge shotgun and fired two blasts into the kitchen door, blowing gaping holes in the wood. Shotgun in hand, hunching over, he bobbed to Kroger and Gino behind the barbecue.

"The kitchen door's gonna give," he said.

Chapter 75

Through the doorway to his room Brody studied the guard he had rendered unconscious lying on the floor seven feet away. He wondered if the guy had a cell phone in his trouser pocket. He decided to find out.

He craned his head through the doorway and searched for Tubby, which drew Tubby's fire. Two bullets sang toward Brody, who pulled his head back into his room. He had been able to make out where Tubby was hiding.

Brody stuck the SIG P226 around the doorjamb and fired in the general direction of Tubby, forcing Tubby to pull back and seek cover.

Brody bolted to the blacked-out guard and patted down the guy's trouser pockets. Brody squeezed off two more rounds at Tubby when he spotted Tubby peeking around the filing cabinet trying to draw a bead on him. Brody located a cell phone in the guard's left trouser pocket, withdrew the phone, and hightailed it back to his room, drawing fire from Tubby, who splintered Brody's doorjamb with two bullets.

Brody tried to operate the cell phone.

It was password protected.

He cursed in frustration.

He studied the phone and saw it worked with a fingerprint ID. He would have to return to the guard for a thumb print.

He fired two shots around the doorjamb in Tubby's direction and peeled out to the guard. He put down the SIG, snagged the guard's thumb, and pressed the print against the phone ID button. Nothing doing. He prepared to try the other thumb. Tubby fired at him. The slug tore into Brody's left hand. Brody jerked back at the projectile's impact. He scoffed up the SIG and fired back at Tubby. Tubby withdrew from sight, howling as the bullet ripped across his scalp, drawing a stream of blood.

His pulse pounding like mad, Brody put down the SIG and tried the laid-out guard's other thumb against the phone's fingerprint reader, fighting the pain he felt in his wounded hand.

Bingo. The phone opened.

Brody snagged the SIG and whipped back into the room, his bullet-punctured hand leaking blood.

Cursing loudly, a sheet of blood smearing his face and blinding him, Tubby fired errant shots at Brody. Brody disappeared into his room.

Brody called Tess, wincing from the pain in his wounded hand.

"Hello," said Tess.

"This is Brody. I need your help."

"Where are you? Why don't you answer your phone?"

"I'm in Keogh's cellar. He's keeping me prisoner. Where are you?"

"I'm here in Hodges's backyard."

"There are at least two armed guards down here—one in the basement with me, the other at the head of the stairs. There may even be more with him on the first floor that I can't see."

"There's a SWAT team here. I'll relay your message."

The chopper he had heard, decided Brody.

"Wait a second," he said. "Don't hang up."

"We're getting ready to charge the kitchen. We've taken out all the guards that were outside. Only . . . ones in . . . building remain," she said, her voice dying out.

He could barely hear her.

"Listen to me," he said. "Keogh is the serial killer. Take him alive."

"What? I can't hear . . . Keogh what?"

Brody glanced at the cell phone's battery icon. It was red. The phone was dead. Fit to be tied, he flung it across the room.

Chapter 76

Standing with the SWAT team, Tess started when she heard an explosion behind her. She wheeled around and, from her vantage point in the backyard, picked up on a pillar of smoke rising in the area of the front gate as a gust of wind blew it into view.

"Macready's here," said the SWAT team pilot, remarking the direction of her gaze. "They blew the front gate."

As if on cue, sirens shrilled down the driveway to the house. Cruiser tires shrieked to a halt.

Kroger's walkie-talkie crackled to life.

"This is Lieutenant Macready. Over."

"Kroger here. Over."

"I'm going in the front door, while you go in the back. Do you copy?"

"Just give the word, Lieutenant. Over."

"Are you meeting any resistance?"

"Roger that. We're taking fire from security guards."

"How many? Over."

"Three stiffs in the backyard. I don't know how many guards are alive in the house."

Tess grabbed Kroger's wrist. "Let me talk to him."

"Who's that?" said Macready.

"A woman we found here. She was exchanging fire with the guards."

"I have to talk to him," she told Kroger.

"She wants to talk to you, Lieutenant."

"Put her on."

Kroger handed the walkie-talkie to Tess.

"This is Tess Hardwick, Lieutenant."

"I told you to wait for us. Why the hell did you engage?"

"I thought Brody needed help."

"Brody? Brody's the serial killer. Over."

"No, he's not. He called me and told me he's being held prisoner in Hodges's cellar. Don't shoot him by mistake."

"Look here, lady. Don't tell me what to do. I'm here to arrest Brody for the Mensa murders. Why are these security guards firing on us? Over."

"I have no idea. They started it. They fired on me after they let me in through the gate. Then they opened fire on your helo when it descended to land. Over."

"Firing on us makes no sense. Over."

"They're Hodges's men. He must've put them up to it. Over."

"Put Kroger back on. Over."

Kroger snatched the walkie-talkie from Tess before she had a chance to protest.

"Kroger here. Over."

"Where's Hodges?" said Macready.

"I haven't seen him. He must be inside the house. Over."

"I want him alive. I want to know what the hell is going on. If he told them to fire on us, he's facing attempted murder in the first. Did you take any casualties? Over."

"Gino got winged. He'll live."

"You don't sound too happy about it," said Gino, who had overheard Kroger.

Kroger snickered at him.

"Who was that?" said Macready. "I couldn't hear."

"Nobody," said Kroger. "Over."

Gino looked like he wanted to shiv Kroger.

"Roger," said Macready.

"What's our next move?" said Kroger. "Over."

"On my mark we storm the house. We're going in hard. Get in our way and get dead. Nobody fires on a cop without paying for it. Do you read me?"

"Loud and clear. Over and out."

Guns at the ready, the SWAT team prepared to charge the kitchen door.

Gun in hand, Tess felt her heartbeat accelerating. "I'm coming with you."

"No, you're not," said Kroger.

"Three," came Macready's voice over the walkie-talkie. "Two. One. Go."

The SWAT team sprinted toward the kitchen door, opening up with their automatic weapons, blasting the windows to bits and shredding the door with bullets.

Nobody fired back. They were either all dead, or they had retreated into another room in the house.

Belting behind the SWAT team, Tess heard gunfire erupting from the front of the house.

The SWAT team burst into the kitchen raking it with bullets. Two corpses lay on the floor, bloodying the white ceramic floor tiles.

Tess heard Macready and his men storm into the living room. Gun at the ready, she followed Kroger, Gino, and the pilot making for the living room via the kitchen. They joined forces with Macready in the living room, where they encountered no resistance.

"Where are they?" said Macready, sweeping his pistol across the living room.

"Brody's in the cellar," said Tess.

"Throw down your weapons and surrender," said Macready in a thundering voice, bellowing into the bowels of the house.

Silence ensued.

Everybody in the living room listened for a response from the rest of the house.

A Beretta 92X Centurion pistol loaded with an extended magazine flew into the living room and skidded along the hardwood floor.

"I surrender," came a voice.

Tess looked toward the direction of the voice that emanated from a hallway.

"Enter the living room where we can see you," said Macready, aiming his Glock toward the hall. "You got ten hair-trigger guns with ten itchy trigger fingers aimed in your direction. Walk slow with your hands open above your head."

Chapter 77

Keogh padded into the room, hands raised, unarmed.

"This has all been a big misunderstanding," he said.

"Stop where you are, Hodges, Keogh, or whatever your name is," said Macready. "Why did you fire on the SWAT team?"

"My security personnel got scared. They thought I was under attack by terrorists."

"That's not gonna fly. My men identified themselves in the helo."

"They told me they couldn't hear above the din of the rotor wash."

"You really think the judge is gonna buy that?"

"I never gave them the order to fire."

"They fired on me," said Tess.

"They thought you were an intruder," said Keogh. "Can I put my hands down?" he asked Macready.

"How could they think I was an intruder?" said Tess. "They were the ones that opened the front gate for me to enter."

"Ask them," said Keogh, starting to lower his hands.

"When I say so," Macready told Keogh, gesturing with his Glock for Keogh to keep his hands raised.

"Check my gun. It hasn't been fired. I shot no one. Why are you arresting me?"

"Your security personnel fired on police officers. It's called attempted murder."

"I never gave them the order to shoot."

"Why are you carrying a gun?"

"Because you attacked my house opening fire on us. I was prepared to defend myself. I thought you were terrorists."

Macready shook his head no. "We identified ourselves, and you know it."

"I couldn't hear anything what with all the gunfire."

"I'm not buying it."

"I thought terrorists were impersonating police officers. I have a lot of enemies, Lieutenant, because I have a lot of money."

"When one story doesn't work, you dream up another. Huh?"

"What's that supposed to mean?"

"You're gonna need a lot of money to afford a dream team of lawyers."

Keogh smiled, looking relaxed. "You have no idea what you're getting yourself into, Lieutenant. I suggest you rethink your position."

"I'm not rethinking anything."

"I caught the Mensa serial killers."

"Did you say *killers*?"

"There are two of them. Scott Brody and Gottfried Mann."

"I know about Brody. He had help?"

"They're both locked up in my cellar. You should thank me."

"I'm not gonna thank you for trying to cap my men," said Macready, his face flushing. "The DA will thank you with a nice long prison sentence where you can make new friends in the shower."

Keogh chortled. "I'll never see the inside of a jail cell. You can't comprehend what you're getting into. Your best option is to release me and forget about all of this."

"I don't like your smug face," said Macready, stalking toward Keogh, clenching his teeth.

"Lieutenant, shouldn't we free Brody," said Tess.

"The reason I'm gonna free him is to bust him for the Mensa murders," said Macready, facing Tess.

"That's the only smart move you've made so far," said Keogh, with a lopsided smile.

"Shut up, and lead us to the cellar, wise ass." Macready turned to a uniform. "I don't trust this guy. Cuff him."

"The blood was draining from my arms," said Keogh, lowering his arms with relief.

The uniform cuffed Keogh's hands behind his back.

"You're violating my rights as a free citizen," said Keogh.

"Walk," said Macready.

Chapter 78

In front of the cellar door, looking miserable, Mohawk stood with a bleeding leg. His gun lay on the floor beside his foot.

"Is that a SWAT team slug in your leg?" Macready asked Mohawk.

"No, sir."

"It better not be."

"Brody did it."

"Brody? Where is that SOB?"

"Downstairs. He's got a piece."

"Cuff him," said Macready.

Another uniform cuffed Mohawk.

"Lead the way down," Macready told Mohawk.

"He'll shoot me," said Mohawk, breaking into a sweat.

"Better you than me."

"This is murder."

Macready yelled into the cellar. "Brody, this is Lieutenant Macready. We're coming down. Throw down your weapon and surrender."

"There's an armed guard down here, Lieutenant," said Brody.

"Everybody in the basement, throw down your weapons," Macready hollered down the staircase.

"I surrender," said Tubby. "I got no beef with Five-O. There's a serial killer down here."

Tess heard two iron objects strike the basement floor.

"Let's go," said Macready. "You first."

Grudgingly, Mohawk limped down the wooden stairs.

"Get a move on it," said Macready.

"My leg took a bullet," said Mohawk, wincing, hobbling, favoring his right leg.

"I'll give it company if you don't get the lead out."

Mohawk grimaced and continued descending, reaching the middle of the staircase.

"I'm not armed," he yelled into the cellar to avoid taking fire from Brody.

He set foot on the landing and surveyed the dim-lit cellar.

Unarmed, Tubby was standing near a filing cabinet, his mutilated ear bleeding down his neck.

"I'm bleeding to death," he said. "The serial killer shot me. Get me to a hospital."

His wounded hand wrapped in his blood-soaked handkerchief, Brody exited his room when he saw Macready standing on the steps above Mohawk.

Macready trained his Glock on Brody. Brody raised his hands above his head.

"What happened to your hand?" said Macready.

"They tried to kill me," said Brody. "I defended myself. They shot Gottfried Mann. Look in his cell," said Brody, nodding in the direction of Mann's cell.

"Keep your hands up where I can see them," said Macready.

Brody complied.

"He's the one that tried to kill *me*," said Tubby. "He's also the one that shot his partner in crime Mann. Together they did the serial killings."

"He's selling you a bill of goods, Lieutenant," said Brody. "The bullets in Mann's body will match Tubby's gun."

"Knock it off," said Macready.

Keogh stepped onto the cellar floor after Macready.

"Brody is lying," said Keogh. "He's very clever. The reason we couldn't figure out who the serial killer is is because there are two of them working together. Brody and Gottfried Mann almost got away with the perfect murders."

Gun in hand, Macready cast around Mann's cell and found Mann's cuffed bullet-riddled corpse lying on his stomach on the floor.

"You shot him while he was handcuffed," said Macready. "What's the point?"

"Killing means nothing to Brody," said Tubby.

"*He* shot Mann," said Brody. "Ballistic tests will bear me out."

"What's with that getup he's wearing?" said Macready.

"It's a Nazi SS Totenkopf uniform," said Keogh.

"I don't see a gun in his hand or on the floor," said Macready, tipping over the body with his foot to see if there was a gun beneath Mann.

There wasn't.

"He shot the poor guy in cold blood," said Brody. "It was an execution."

"Brody shot him to keep him from talking," said Keogh. "He figured Mann would spill the beans about their working together as serial killers."

"Brody?" said Macready, wanting to know Brody's side of the story, exiting Mann's room.

"Keogh is the serial killer," said Brody. "He'll say anything to save his neck."

"Motive?"

"He underwent an experimental operation at Stanford. They implanted a microchip in his brain. The side effects were homicidal impulses."

Macready jacked his eyebrows.

"Is this true?" Macready asked Keogh.

"It's laughable," said Keogh, grinning. "I never had any brain surgery. My name's Sam Hodges, not Tyler Keogh. Brody will say anything to save his skin."

"How do you know Keogh's first name is Tyler?" said Brody.

"You told me when you accused me of being Keogh."

Brody couldn't recall if he had used Keogh's first name in Keogh's presence. He was under the strong impression he hadn't.

"He's trying to gaslight me, Lieutenant," said Brody. "He's been trying to do it all along to get me off his scent. He used snakes, psychedelics, voodoo, the Nazi SS, whatever."

"Speaking of the Nazi SS, did you see all those SS knives in Mann's cell, Lieutenant?" said Keogh.

Macready peered into the room, taking in the knives that lay on the floor. "What about them?"

"They're Mann's. I found them in his house. He used a knife just like those on at least one of his victims. And look at the SS Totenkopf uniform he's wearing. He believed he was a member of the SS. The Totenkopf was the 3rd SS Panzer Division. Its insignia was a death's head. It became known as the Death's Head Division and was infamous for its brutality. They committed the Le Paradis massacre."

"Never heard of it."

"They gathered together the ninety-nine British soldiers who had surrendered after defending a farmhouse in Le Paradis, France, lined them up against a wall, and machine-gunned them. Only two survived. Death's Head Commander SS Haupsturmführer Fritz Knöchlein was tried for war crimes and executed in 1949."

"How do you know so frigging much about the SS?"

"I'm well read, Lieutenant," Keogh said, smiling. "Is that a crime these days?"

"That microchip implanted in your brain doesn't hurt any," said Brody.

"Are you still harping on that fairy tale?" said Keogh, laughing. "Are you jealous of my massive brain power? Maybe if you cracked a book, you might learn a thing or two."

"I wish Mann was still alive so we could question him," Macready said, more to himself than to anyone else.

"They executed him to prevent him from declaring his innocence to you," said Brody. "He told me Keogh planted that SS memorabilia on him and made him wear that uniform."

"Suppose I accept your theory that Hodges—Keogh, whatever—is the serial killer. What is his motive?"

"Jealousy of the other Mensa members on the board of directors. He considered himself smarter than everyone else. However, he felt threatened by their high IQs. He was probably worried the government would operate on them, too, and make them even smarter than him. And . . ."

"And what?"

"And he likes killing. He found out about his lust for blood during his first kill. His blood lust is a side effect of his brain surgery. Killing once wasn't enough for him. He had to go on killing. Thanks to his operation, murder acted like a drug on him, addicting him."

"What is your name?" said Macready, pointing at Tubby.

"Oscar."

"You're under arrest for murdering Mann."

"You can't believe Brody. He'll say anything to save his skin," said Oscar, hot around the collar.

"I'm busting the two of you. Ballistics will clear this up in no time."

"All right, all right, I'll tell you the truth," said Oscar, wiping blood and sweat off his neck.

"Get talking."

"Hodges ordered me to shoot Mann. I was following *his* orders."

"OK, Hodges. That's another charge against you."

"He's lying through his teeth," said Keogh. "I didn't order him to shoot anyone."

"You double-crossing snake," spluttered Oscar.

Oscar dove for his gun on the floor, latched onto its grip, and aimed at Keogh from a prone position on the concrete.

Tess fired her pistol three times at Oscar. Bullets plowed into his throat and back. Blood jetted from his carotid artery, spewing onto Keogh. Oscar's neon madras shirt turned bloodred. His gun hand fell limp.

"Nice shot," said Keogh, wiping Oscar's arterial blood off his face with distaste. "You saved my life."

"I thought he was aiming at me," said Tess.

Macready's cell phone chimed. He took the call and listened.

Chapter 79

Macready terminated the call. He turned to Keogh.

"You're under arrest for the murder of Lou Arano."

"Never heard of him," said Keogh.

"That kind of defense won't get you off the hook. A lot of serial killers don't know their victims. They kill randomly."

"What was that phone call about, Lieutenant?" said Brody.

"Forensics found Keogh's fingerprints on the SS knife used in the Arano killing."

"I thought there was no record of Keogh's fingerprints in your database."

Macready pulled a face. "I misspoke. They found Hodges's prints on the knife. We took Hodges's prints when he was down at the station and entered them into the database. The fingerprints found on the knife matched Hodges's."

"And Hodges is Keogh."

"According to you. I have no proof Hodges is actually Keogh. I do have proof that Hodges killed Lou Arano. Whether this guy is Hodges or Keogh makes no difference to me. He's being charged with murder."

Keogh laughed. "Is this a joke?"

"What's so funny?" said Macready, flushing with anger. "You're going on trial for murder. Wait till they convict you. Then we'll see who's laughing."

"You're gonna have egg all over your face when this is over," said Keogh, chuckling.

"Are you on drugs? Is that it? Is your brain fried from acid? Don't you understand the gravity of the charges against you?"

"You're the one that's gonna be on drugs after you get humiliated at the police station for busting me."

Macready shook his head in bafflement.

"Maybe he's gonna enter an insanity plea," said Brody. "That's why he sounds like he's having the time of his life while you charge him with murder in the first."

Grim-faced, Macready nodded. "Could be. He's trying out the insanity plan on us to see if it flies."

Feeling faint from loss of blood, white-faced, Mohawk collapsed on the floor with a heavy thud.

"Where's the damn ambulance?" said Macready.

Keogh guffawed. "You're gonna be sorry you ever messed with me, Lieutenant."

Taken aback, Macready glowered at Keogh, who continued laughing his head off.

"We got you dead to rights, funny face," said Macready. "Laugh all you want. See where it gets you. You want a one-way ticket to the funny farm? Maybe you'll get your wish and spend the rest of your life there. Who cares?"

Keogh laughed. "They got a straitjacket waiting for you at the station, Lieutenant, ready to strap on when they order you to release me."

Brody figured Keogh was overdoing it if he was seeking an insanity plea. Enough with the laughing, Brody decided. No matter how high Keogh's IQ was, the guy wasn't going to walk scot-free after he had left his fingerprints on a murder weapon. Maybe the guy was laughing because he realized how hopeless his situation was. The goonish, creepy laugh of a wino on the street wallowing in his own vomit.

"Crazy as a loon," muttered Macready.

"Where did you put my cell phone?" Brody asked Keogh. "I need to make a call to my client."

"It's in the kitchen, which was shot up by the SWAT team," said Keogh.

Brody heard an approaching ambulance's keen in the distance.

"Is anybody alive in the kitchen?" Macready asked the SWAT team.

"No," said Kroger. "A couple of stiffs lying on the floor. They fired on us."

"Will you get these handcuffs off of me, Lieutenant?" said Brody. "Keogh's the serial killer. You got his prints on Arano's murder weapon. What more do you need? I had nothing to do with it. Why are you holding me?"

Macready dragged his feet, not in any hurry to release Brody.

"Maybe you were in on it with Hodges," said Macready. "How about it, Hodges, or whatever your name is?"

"I had nothing to do with the serial killings," said Keogh. "How many times do I have to tell you?"

"You can't believe a word he says, Lieutenant," said Brody.

Macready shrugged, reluctant to release Brody.

"Do you promise not to make a run for it?" Macready asked Brody.

"I'm not going anywhere," answered Brody. "I want this mess cleared up with Keogh behind bars. I'll be happy to give you any info I have."

Macready mulled it over.

"Take off his cuffs," he told one of his men at length. "But you're coming downtown with me, Brody. You're part of this investigation."

A uniform unlocked Brody's cuffs.

"Fine," said Brody, massaging his freed wrists, noticing his wounded hand was starting to bleed again through the handkerchief he had swaddled around it. "I need an EMT, too."

"What are you doing here anyway?" said Macready.

"Keogh locked me in that room and told me he was gonna create a museum of serial killers in his basement. He was gonna charge customers to come and ogle me and Mann."

"That's the most ludicrous thing I've ever heard," said Keogh. "Do you expect anyone to believe that nonsense?"

"You're the wacko that dreamed it up. You ought to know."

Keogh laughed, shaking his head in disbelief.

"I can't believe you're letting this serial killer go," he told Macready.

"He's not going anywhere," said Macready. "He's coming with us. *His* fingerprints aren't on the knife that killed Lou Arano. It's time for you to lawyer up, Hodges, if you got any sense."

Keogh scoffed. “I don’t need a lawyer. You got no case.”

“Suit yourself. I need to Mirandize you. You have the right to remain silent—”

“I don’t need to remain silent. I got nothing to hide.”

Macready cleared his throat loudly and continued Mirandizing Keogh.

Chapter 80

Brody retrieved his phone that was lying on the blood-splattered Formica countertop in the kitchen.

"Don't call the media," Macready told him, watching him, eyes hard.

"I'm calling my client," said Brody, sidestepping a puddle of blood on the floor tiles. "Could I have some privacy?"

"Make a run for it and my men have orders to shoot to kill."

Macready waved his hand dismissively and stalked out of the kitchen into the living room.

"I'm giving you five minutes," he said over his shoulder, holding up five fingers.

Brody sneered at Macready's back.

He called Val on his cell.

"Brody here," he said. "The cops busted Keogh for whacking Lou Arano."

"What?" said Val in shock. "What are you talking about?"

"Keogh is the serial killer."

"That's insane. The serial killer is gonna kill *him*. Tyler wouldn't hurt a fly. He's a vegan, you know."

"So was Charles Manson."

"Tyler isn't a Charles Manson psycho. Believe me."

"Maybe that was true before the Stanford experiment. Not anymore. The government turned him into a homicidal maniac."

"Why would they do such a thing?" said Val, incredulous.

"I doubt they did it on purpose. Apparently, they were trying to increase his intelligence by implanting a microchip in his brain. The surgery had unexpected side effects."

"Ohmigod. I don't believe this is happening. Where is he?"

"We're going to the police station downtown."

"I'll get him a lawyer and be right there."

"He doesn't want a lawyer. He claims he doesn't need one."

"What? Has he lost his marbles?"

"Frankly, it sounds like he has."

Chapter 81

The SWAT team piled into their Bell Jet Ranger and lifted off from Keogh's backyard.

Macready and his convoy of black-and-whites transported Keogh and Brody downtown to the police station.

At the station the cruisers disgorged their passengers, who climbed the concrete steps and entered the building.

"I'm gonna love listening to you explain your way out of this," Brody told Keogh in the hallway.

Keogh smirked. "I'm not gonna have to do any talking. This is over before it even begins." He turned to Macready. "I want to make my phone call now."

"You finally realized the gravity of your predicament, huh? Time to lawyer up."

"I'm not calling my lawyer. There's no need."

Macready led Keogh to the watch commander's desk.

"Then who are you calling?" said Macready.

Without missing a beat Keogh said, "The FBI."

Macready gave him a look. "This isn't a federal case."

"Oh, but it is. Could you unlock my handcuffs?"

"These are all local murders. They're under our purview."

"Can I make my call?"

"Go ahead," said Macready. "For all the good it'll do you."

Macready unlocked Keogh's cuffs.

"Don't try anything," said Macready.

"I have no reason to," said Keogh, looking relaxed.

He withdrew his cell phone from his trouser pocket and placed a call.

"Federal Bureau of Investigation," came the reply.

"This is Sam Hodges. I'm under arrest for murder at the LAPD station in downtown LA."

Keogh terminated the call.

Macready shook his head in disapproval. "It's your dime. You wanna waste it, that's your decision. No more calls for you."

Macready clapped the cuffs back on Keogh.

"The cuffs are pointless," said Keogh. "They'll be off in minutes."

"Time to book you and then we'll throw you in the tank. I got news for you. Nobody smiles in the tank."

They trooped to another room where a police clerk would take Keogh's personal information and fingerprints and confiscate his private possessions.

Before Keogh and his police escort reached the booking room, two men in black business suits and navy blue neckties swaggered toward them from the other end of the hallway and blocked their path. Two uniformed US marshals stood behind the suits.

"That was fast," said Keogh, grinning.

Brody smelled Lysol as if the cleaning crew had recently scrubbed the linoleum floor.

The lead suit, middle-aged with a receding hairline, big feet, and a bulbous nose, flipped his FBI badge out of his jacket's breast pocket and displayed it to Macready.

"Special Agent in Charge Henry Duclos of the FBI," said the suit.

"We don't need your help to book a murder suspect," said Macready, glancing at Duclos's badge to vet it.

"The suspect is in our custody now," said Duclos, removing a folded legal document from his jacket's breast pocket.

"Says who?"

Duclos handed Macready the document, which Macready unfolded with a sneer and commenced to read.

"Says the attorney general of the United States," said Duclos. "Sam Hodges is now in our custody."

"This is a local matter. You have no jurisdiction here."

"That document signed by the attorney general of the United States makes it our jurisdiction. Hodges is now in the custody of the US marshals."

The two marshals moved toward Keogh.

"Hold on a second," said Macready, apoplectic, spittle flying out of his mouth. "We didn't even get a chance to book him yet."

“No need,” said Duclos. “We’ll take care of everything. It’s out of your hands.”

“The man’s a serial killer,” said Brody.

“His fingerprints are on the murder weapon, for Christ’s sake,” said Macready.

“Are you sure about that?” said Duclos.

“Unless forensics is lying to me.”

“Why don’t you double-check with them?”

“I’ll make you eat your words,” said Macready, digging out his cell phone and calling the forensics office.

“Bring me the set of fingerprints you found on the knife that killed Lou Arano on the double,” he said into his cell.

“Gimme a minute, Lieutenant,” said the forensics technician.

“Make it snappy.”

A few minutes later the technician returned to his phone.

“Uh . . . uh . . . Lieutenant—”

“You sound like a halfwit. Uh . . . uh . . . ,” said Macready, mimicking him. “Spit it out, man.”

The technician cleared his throat.

“Those prints have gone missing,” he said, his voice thin.

Macready couldn’t believe his ears.

“Missing? What’s missing?” he said, beside himself.

“They’ve been misplaced. We can’t find them anywhere.”

“Well, get them for Christ’s sake.”

“We don’t know what happened to them.”

“What the hell does that mean?”

“They vanished.”

Macready stood nonplussed.

Then he exploded.

“The chief is gonna hear about this,” said Macready, white-faced. “Heads are gonna roll. Fuck. Get the murder weapon and dust it for prints again.”

“Uh—”

“Don’t give me *uh*. Get the knife and dust it again.”

The technician sucked in his breath. “We can’t find it.”

Macready slapped his forehead. “Jesus fucking Christ.”

Macready terminated the call. He glowered at Duclos.

"How could you possibly know those prints had disappeared?" said Macready.

"I just asked you to double-check," said Duclos, his expression stony. "I never said they had disappeared."

"And the knife. You didn't know it had disappeared, huh?" said Macready with withering sarcasm.

"Nope."

"Do you got a mole in my office?" said Macready, squinting suspiciously at Duclos. "And maybe he did a little dirty work for you in my forensics office destroying and stealing evidence. Which is against the law, I might add."

"Be careful what you say, Lieutenant. You're talking to a special agent in the Federal Bureau of Investigation."

"Well, you're talking to a lieutenant in the Los Angeles Police Department, the premier police department in the country."

"You're the one making slanderous charges, not me."

"Keogh's still the serial killer," chimed in Brody. "Just because his prints have been misplaced doesn't clear him."

"We'll determine that." Duclos turned to Macready. "And this man's name is Sam Hodges, not Keogh. Unlock his cuffs."

"I don't care what the hell his name is. Hodges, Keogh. He murdered Lou Arano."

"Just unlock his cuffs, and you can avoid any further embarrassment," said Duclos, calmly.

Shaking his head, smoldering, Macready removed Keogh's handcuffs.

The two marshals took a smiling Keogh into custody without cuffing him.

"What did I tell you?" Keogh said to Macready, gloating. "I'm not gonna spend five minutes behind bars. You got bupkes against me."

"Are you kidding?" said Macready. "We're gonna find the killer's knife and the photos of the prints on it that are supposedly 'missing,'"—he made air quotes—"and the feds are gonna throw you in their ADX supermax at Florence, Colorado. You can say hello to your next-door neighbor the drug cartel kingpin El Chapo. Neither of you will ever see the light of day again."

"Toodle-oo," said Keogh, grinning at Macready and waving good-bye with his fingers.

Chapter 82

Keogh climbed into the backseat of the black Chevy Suburban parked on the street in front of the police station.

Through the tinted window he could see Brody standing and glaring at him from the top of the steps in front of the station's lobby.

Keogh wanted Brody to see his grinning face through the tinted glass so he powered down the window and flashed a toothy grin at him. Brody's baleful expression didn't change. Keogh powered up the window, his face vanishing behind the black-tinted window.

He looked at the fed in the driver's seat and the one riding shotgun. They were both wearing black business suits and black-tinted sunglasses, their expressions wooden. The driver had a pocked face and neck thanks to a ravaging case of acne when he was a teen. His partner's face had a receding chin and could only be described as bland.

Keogh didn't recognize either of them. He had been expecting Drago and Mirisch.

"Where are Drago and Mirisch?" said Keogh.

"Their day off," said the driver.

"Oh. OK. Drive me home."

"To Rancho Palos Verdes?"

"That's where I live. Sam Hodges, at your service."

"Right, Mr. Hodges."

"Is there a problem?" said Keogh, noticing they had not started the SUV yet.

"No problem."

"Where is Duclos?"

"He won't be coming with us."

"I wanted to thank him for his prompt service."

The driver fired the Suburban's engine, shifted into drive, and pulled into traffic.

"Could you turn on the AC?" said Keogh.

"Yes, sir."

The AC hummed to life.

Keogh thought it odd that Drago and Mirisch weren't here. They were his usual chauffeurs whenever the feds came calling for him, which wasn't often. He couldn't think of a time when the FBI hadn't used those two to drive him.

Other than that, he felt good. Hell, he felt great. He was going home, free as a bird. Of course, the cops had shot up his house. But he figured the County of LA would foot the bill for the repair work, considering it was their cops that had exceeded their authority when they had done the trashing.

And there would be no trial, he knew. No charges against him for whacking out Lou Arano, or anyone else, for that matter. The murder weapon would never be recovered by police. He was certain the bureau had seen to that. Any and all other incriminating evidence would never be found. If found, it would disappear.

WITSEC had its perks, Keogh knew. The government didn't want him put on trial for anything, especially not murder. A trial would open a can of worms they couldn't afford to have opened. The existence of a government-funded experiment that implanted a microchip in his brain at Stanford would come to light, and the government would be forced to answer a lot of disconcerting questions they didn't want asked.

He couldn't get over the looks on Macready's and Brody's faces when they found out he would walk. Their visages would be forever engraved on his memory.

Life was good, he decided. So much better than before he had begun killing people when he had felt bored to tears. He had to keep his massive brain entertained or the resulting boredom would crush him with the black dog.

And life was even better now with his knowledge that he was invincible, that nobody could touch him with a government aegis protecting him. The feds were his ace in the hole. He could do whatever he wanted and get away with it. They would come to his aid every time.

He sat back in his seat and relaxed, comfortable in the AC-cooled air, falling asleep during the journey on the 110 south to his house.

He woke up as the Suburban drove onto the street that led to his driveway.

The driveway gate, of course, wasn't operational. The cops had seen to its obliteration by blowing it apart with C-4 plastic explosive when they had trespassed onto his property.

The two feds dropped him off on his driveway, reversed, and drove away.

Free as a bird, he sucked in a breath of a fresh coastal breeze and contemplated the pure azure sky. Was there anything better than freedom? he wondered, invigorated.

As he made his way toward the path to his front door, he saw an Asian woman wearing oversized sunglasses with white plastic frames approaching him. She had a mole on the right side of her chin. She must have been waiting for him near the front door, concealed by a big berry manzanita, when the Suburban had driven up the drive.

"Can I help you?" he said.

She withdrew a Ruger LCP II pistol from her purse and fired three .380 ACP bullets into his head at point-blank range. She didn't have to be a particularly good shot to strike him with all three bullets fired at such a close distance.

"That's for my husband Myles," said Judy Wasson, as Keogh lay sprawled at her feet, an expression of astonishment frozen on his bullet-shattered, blood-soaked face.

Not that it mattered to him, but one of the bullets had struck and disintegrated the microchip implanted in his brain.

Chapter 83

Brody parked his Mini in front of Evelyn Martin's condo, killed the engine, glommed onto a gift-wrapped present from the passenger seat, and got out of his car, his wounded left hand swathed in a clean bandage.

It was a nice day. A rare brace of clouds scudded overhead. He could feel and smell the thick briny sea breeze sweeping in from the ocean nuzzling his cheek.

He carried the small package, the size of a box for a pair of sunglasses, to the lobby's security door and buzzed her condo number on the speakerphone.

"Who is it?" said Evelyn.

"Brody."

She buzzed him into the lobby.

He took the elevator to her floor and found her room.

He should kill Evelyn for putting a contract out on him, which had all but cost him his life. But in her shoes, maybe he would have done the same thing. If he had a kid and the kid was abducted and threatened with death, wouldn't he have done anything the kidnapers wanted to save the kid's life—even if it meant killing a PI?

He decided he wasn't going to press charges against her for contracting a hit man to whack him. He had enough bad news for her.

He rapped on her door.

Evelyn peered through the door's peephole and, satisfied it was him, opened the door, albeit grudgingly, aware that he knew she had hired a hit man to whack him.

When she set eyes on him in the corridor, she felt guilty and became nervous, as if she didn't know how to act around him anymore. Biting her lower lip she fidgeted with her hair.

He got down to brass tacks.

"Your brother is dead," he said.

She widened her eyes with confusion and surprise.

"After he was released from the police station, federal agents found his body near his house," he said. "They say he committed suicide by shooting himself in the head."

"That makes no sense. He had just beat a murder charge. Why would he take his own life?"

"I'm telling you what they told me. They took his corpse into custody and aren't letting the LAPD anywhere near it. Macready is furious, of course. But there's nothing he can do."

"I'm his nearest relative. I should get custody of his body."

"I know what they'll say. They'll say it wasn't Keogh who killed himself. It was Sam Hodges, who didn't have a sister. So you have no right to exhume him, since you're not a relative."

"Why would they do that?"

"They have their reasons."

She looked at him with bewilderment.

"They do what they want," he said. "That's the government for you."

"I ought to sue them for what they did to Tyler."

"Good luck suing the government. They'll claim Hodges's death is a national security issue, and you have no right to sue, anyway, since you're not Hodges's relative. No court will touch it."

"Tyler wasn't himself anymore," she said, eyes morose. "They used him as a guinea pig and turned him into—I don't know what."

"I have a present for your daughter," said Brody, displaying it in his hand.

"Oh, how sweet. Come in."

Brody entered the living room.

"Olivia, come here, sweetie," called out Evelyn.

Olivia scuttled into the room in a frilly pink dress, her face ruddy.

"There's someone here to see you," said Evelyn.

Brody felt awkward. He squirmed in discomfort like he was wearing a suit that was a size too small. He wasn't used to being around little kids. He wasn't used to being nice.

"Hello," said Olivia, recognizing him as the man who had rescued her and greeting him with a smile.

He wasn't used to having people be nice to him, either—unless they wanted something from him, like money.

"Hi. I brought something for you." He handed her the gift.

Olivia opened it hungrily, tossing the wrapping paper on the carpet.

Her face beamed when she saw what was inside.

"You found Eeyore's tail," she said, withdrawing the tail from the box and discarding the box.

She pressed the tail against her cheek, smiling.

Brody smiled, too.

He figured it was a better present than killing her mother.

ABOUT THE AUTHOR

Award-winning author Bryan Cassiday writes thrillers and horror fiction. His previous Scott Brody crime thrillers are *Bolt* and *Murder LLC*. He wrote the post-apocalyptic horror thriller *Horde*, which is the sixth book in his *Zombie Apocalypse: The Chad Halverson Series*. *Horde* won the 2021 American Fiction Award for Best Horror Novel. He lives in Southern California.

www.ingramcontent.com/pod-product-compliance
Lightning Source LLC
Chambersburg PA
CBHW070832250626
47159CB00003B/747

9781737628217